Just Don't Fall

Just Don't Fall

EMMA ST. CLAIR

To all of the readers I've loved before...

I still love you. You're the best.
Thanks for allowing me to live the dream.

And I believe if we work together, we might one day be able to make fetch happen.

CONTENT WARNINGS

This is a light and funny romcom, but I want to help readers feel safe! Here are some topics that are touched on in the book:

- Parents being neglectful & parental abandonment (past)
- Controlling/overbearing parents
- A hockey player you WILL fall for
- A heroine who has never been kissed
- An attack cat

Spoiler alert: No one dies. There is no sex in this book. You will get a happy ending with no cheating and minimal angst.

CHAPTER 1

Parker

"I SIGNED a contract to play hockey. Not dance."

Oh, boy. Who's going to be the one to tell Logan Barnes he technically *did* sign a contract requiring dancing?

Not it!

Someone else can be the harbinger of bad news. I'll keep hiding like a coward in the back of the Summit's main conference room. I hunch down in my chair behind the rest of the Appies staff and the owner, Larry Jenson.

I chose this seat along the wall intentionally, hoping to stay out of Logan's view while also giving myself a discreet line of sight to admire him. I'm not ready for him to see me. *Yet.* But I'm more than happy to watch the man I haven't talked to in ten years. While I covertly stare, I'm silently preparing to deal with Logan as a professional.

Not as his ex-best friend's little sister who harbored a

massive crush Logan hopefully never knew about. Yeah ... let's leave *that* past in the past. We'll pretend my crush is still in the past too.

When Logan's statement is met with an awkward pause rather than an answer, his jaw flexes. It's truly a sight to behold in person. Every bit as alluring as it is in the black and white commercials where he's selling ... body wash? Some kind of specialty watch? I wasn't paying attention to the product. Just the man selling whatever it was.

All I know is that jaw muscle (among other things) makes Logan Barnes a *lot* of money.

His handsome features will NOT, however, get him out of the part of his contract specifically stipulating that he *will* be dancing. Like the rest of the team, Logan will be required to take part in videos for TikTok and other social media.

Did he not read the contract? Or did his agent not give him a heads up?

Glancing at Jeremy, I think his name is, I'd bet money he left this detail out when talking to Logan. He's got the face of a man I wouldn't trust to keep a succulent alive. Much less my career.

My jaw practically fell through the floor when I heard Logan was kicked down from the NHL and signed to the Appies, Harvest Hollow's minor league hockey team. We might be one of the best in the AHL, especially for being a fairly new affiliate. But we're known first for our viral TikToks and second for hockey. Most of our players have huge social media presences and leverage them for more sponsorships and better contracts. Many are called up to the NHL.

Logan, on the other hand, was sent down to us after he spent half a season out with a knee injury, followed by a fight with a fan in the grocery store. Add this to the rumors that

Logan has never been a team player, and this move is something of a last shot to save his career. Especially considering other teams could have picked him up during this move ... but didn't.

If Logan wants to get called back up to his old team or another team in the league, he's going to have to really prove something. And not just on the ice.

The Appies are stoked to have him. But the feeling ... does not appear to be mutual. Especially considering his surprise at what his contract here requires.

Throats clear but still, no one speaks. It's like everyone is silently drawing straws to see who's going to tell Logan the bad news. I'll take my invisibility as long as it lasts, thank you very much!

Because at some point, I will be face to face with Logan. And as the social media manager arranging the dancing videos in question, I'm about to be the person who Logan despises most.

Awesome.

The tension in the room swells to the point of being almost painful until Grant, the team lawyer and the epitome of serious lawyer stereotypes, taps the contract on the table. "Actually, one of the stipulations of playing for the Appies is that, in addition to your typical hockey duties, you will have certain entertainment requirements. You'll find it in section eight, clause three."

I lean slightly to the left, where I can see Logan's mouth. It's turned up in a sneer. For a man in the spotlight because of his job, Logan is almost a ghost. He's never had social media. He rarely does interviews, and when he does, he gives one-word answers about his job and says nothing personal. Even his sponsorships and endorsements seem to be hand-picked to exclude talking.

The man is a vault. Not so different from who he was back then. I think my brother and I were the only people Logan talked to outside of hockey.

"I'm not an entertainer," Logan says, shoving the contract away. "I'm an athlete."

Coach Davis fields this one. He is VERY invested in placating the best player our team has ever landed. "The Appies still put the sport first, Logan. We're a solid team. Everything else is just …"

He fights for a word, and I know him well enough to know he's trying to find one that's positive. Because, like Logan, Coach Davis is all about hockey and was slow to support the social media aspect. It's shocking he likes *me* so much, considering I'm the one who's always interrupting the serious hockey stuff to teach the guys the latest trending dances.

"The rest is just another part of the job," Coach says. The assistant coaches nod like bobbleheads.

"The main thing is hockey." Our team manager, Malik, leans toward Logan. "And when it comes to training and winning games, we don't mess around."

"Perhaps we should let our social media manager field some of these questions," Larry suggests. "Where's Parker?"

It takes me a full second—way too long—to realize my cloak of invisibility has been lifted. More like forcibly yanked off my body.

Thanks, Larry. I appreciate the way you found a fleet of double decker buses and threw me underneath them.

As though we're all in a movie, heads dramatically swivel toward me. The two men in suits whom I've been hiding behind roll their chairs out of the way, affording Logan a direct view of me, hunched over my tablet in an uncomfortable chair along the wall.

4

I suck in a breath as I wait for recognition to dawn in Logan's eyes. When I imagined this moment—which I did countless times once I found out Logan was coming—I pictured Logan blinking in surprise when he saw me. Maybe he'd look me over with appreciation in his gaze.

I mean, sure—I can't compare to the models and actresses and other women I've seen pictured with Logan over the years. Not even close. But I'm decent looking. *Definitely* better than the last time he saw me with frizzy hair and braces.

But Logan's hard expression remains as his green gaze lands on me. I can't tell if he genuinely doesn't recognize me or if he's just refusing to acknowledge our past personal connection in this professional setting.

Either way, it totally sucks to be me right now. There is zero softening of his dangerously hard jaw or his flinty glare. I tell myself not to be crushed by his lack of acknowledgement. I mean, Logan ghosted me and my brother, formerly his best friend, ten years ago. What did I really expect now?

Still. The idea that Logan doesn't remember me hits like a physical blow.

Coach Davis clears his throat. "Parker?"

Annnnd … I let the moment stretch WAY too long while lost in my thoughts. Everyone is waiting for me to speak. Waiting and staring. I give the beads on my fidget ring a spin and draw in a steadying breath.

"Right. Hi, Logan." I pair this awful greeting with a stupid little wave.

Kill me now!

"So, as it's been mentioned, your contract does have expectations that might be pretty different than what you were used to with your last team. Many minor league sports have found a happy marriage between athleticism and entertainment."

I've been trying to make the term *athlentertainment* catch on. But like the word *fetch*, it's never gonna happen.

"What does this mean?" Logan asks in what would best be described as a growl. Too bad it's an angry one, not a sexy one. Actually, no—it's definitely both. "I'd like specifics."

"He does well with specifics," Jeremy adds, like parroting what Logan says is having his back. I ignore the slimy agent instead of lobbing my tablet at his head and telling him to serve his client's interests better.

"Specifics I can do." Swiping my tablet screen, I bring up the aforementioned section of the contract. It's silly how my heart is racing and sweat is prickling at my hairline.

I begin reading. "There will be no less than fifteen theatrical appearances per season, distributed across social channels as well as repurposed for—"

"English," Logan says. Then, as though realizing how rude he sounds, he clears his throat and adds, "Please."

I set the tablet on my knees and meet his eyes head on. "We post at least one short-form video a day on TikTok, cross-posted to Instagram, with the content being combined and repurposed for YouTube later."

Logan only raises his dark brows slowly. I can almost hear him repeating *English*. I clear my throat, realizing that while I might not be talking in legalese, I'm using social media-speak. Already, I've lost the attention of half the room.

Not Logan. He is laser-focused on me. I'm torn between withering and blooming under his attention.

"We film a mix of content. Interviews. Clips from games, practice, the locker room. And yes—sometimes dancing or lip syncing to trending songs. But it's not *just* dancing." I offer

6

him a friendly smile. "Don't worry. Even our guys who have three left feet off the ice have adapted."

A few people chuckle.

They can laugh all they want. Thanks to our social media presence, all of our games are sold out, along with every suite and VIP box. There are whole Facebook groups dedicated to ticket swaps and exchanges. My strategy was inspired by the Savannah Bananas baseball team and their Fans First philosophy—but tweaked to work for an official AHL team.

Despite my contributions, Larry still acts like he has no idea who I am half the time. My direct boss, Brad, who heads up Communications, keeps having to remind the team owner who I am. Unfortunately, it's impossible for me to forget Larry and his walrus mustache served up with a side of light misogyny.

"We also do as much as possible on skates, and I make sure everyone is comfortable. I'll do the same for you, just like any other player."

Only … Logan's *not* any other player. And I don't mean because he's coming from an NHL team in Raleigh. He's not like any other player to *me*.

No one else chimes in, probably because now, Logan's ire is directed toward me. They're more than happy to let me take one for the team.

Thanks, guys. Really feeling the love.

I offer Logan my best smile—a real feat of strength considering the way my legs are shaking. "It won't take up too much time. I film throughout the week then usually once or twice a month, we batch some bigger content."

"Batch?" Logan asks.

"Filming several videos at once to post over time. Not

every player will be involved in the longer portions. I keep a schedule and make sure it's spread out pretty evenly."

There are a few guys who love the spotlight, and so long as their egos don't become too monstrous, I let them have it. This also keeps the guys who want to do less happy.

I'm not sure how it will work with Logan, who is still looking at me as though I've just set fire to his favorite sneakers. On the plus side, the glaring sure is making my crush curl up into a ball in the corner.

Maybe to kill it, all I needed was a little Logan animosity.

Unlike the thousands—millions?—of women who also have crushes on Logan Barnes, mine isn't because he's a hot hockey player. It's not because of his rarely seen crooked grin or the sexy scar running from the corner of his lip down to his chin, or his perfectly disheveled dark hair and piercing green eyes. Not even his broad shoulders, sexy six-pack, or his famously firm backside that's the face—or would that be butt?—of a big corporate sponsor.

Not that I'm *against* any of those assets. They just aren't my particular crush's origin story.

No—my crush on hockey's beautiful bad boy began on a typical Tuesday night fifteen years ago when he shared a half-eaten chocolate chip cookie with me and told my brother to stop being a jerk.

I was ten.

Logan was fourteen.

I guess you could say it was crush at first cookie.

Coach Davis jumps in, relieving me from Logan's glare. "The Appies are glad to have you, Logan. I know you'll bring good things to the team. We can hammer out these other details later."

That famous muscle ticks again in Logan's jaw, and I think he's going to argue or maybe insist again that he's not going to dance no matter what his contract says, but he says nothing.

Good boy. The first stage of acceptance is shutting up.

And just like that, the meeting is over. Finally.

I scurry out of the room, moving down the hall toward the elevator with my wounded pride in hand and my proverbial tail tucked between my legs. Not only did Logan not seem to remember me—*ouch*—but I can tell he's going to make my job harder than it has to be.

Short of having some kind of wardrobe malfunction or having someone read out loud my teenage diary confessing my love for Logan, I'm not sure how I could have enjoyed the meeting any less.

To distract myself from obsessing, I check my calendar and to-do list for this week as I step into the elevator. Today is marked as a research, planning, and video editing day for me. The first preseason game is a few weeks away, which means we need to ramp up the actual hockey-playing videos. I'll schedule time to attend practices and get some footage.

The elevator doors start to close when a big hand appears, forcing them back open.

And then Logan Barnes steps into the elevator.

My lungs deflate. My heart slows to a stop. And my eyes are probably about to pop out of my skull like some kind of cartoon.

Logan steps way too close to me as the doors slide shut behind him. I hold my breath, knowing my weakness for any and all male-scented products. Cologne. Deodorant. Aftershave. I'm a sucker for them all. Logan's scent is unidentifiable, but spicy and masculine and definitely yummy.

It was one thing to see his handsome face across the conference room. It's another thing to see—and smell— Logan up close.

9

Crossing his arms over his chest, Logan stays in my space, those green eyes piercing through me. I suck in a breath, waiting.

Is he this mad about having to do social media?

But as I watch, the hardness in his expression gives way to warmth and amusement. And something else I can't quite pinpoint. When he smiles, all my malfunctioning organs rev up into hyperdrive. I drop my tablet and don't even give it a glance.

"Well, well, well," Logan says. "If it isn't little Peter Parker, all grown up."

CHAPTER 2

Logan

I'm NOT sure Parker realizes she's backing away from me. Not like there's anywhere to go. And that's exactly why I cornered her on this elevator.

In a complex teeming with people, I needed a moment alone with her.

Parker. My former best friend's little sister. My ... friend? No, at four years younger than me, she wasn't quite a friend back then. More like a borrowed pesky little sister. Only, she never got on my nerves like she did Brandon's.

And there's nothing sisterly about how I feel now, standing this close to her.

I can't pinpoint exactly *what* I'm feeling. My emotions have been jumbled since I recognized Parker sitting in that conference room. Mostly, I was stunned that the gorgeous woman who somehow hid through most of the meeting was *Parker*. I think I hid my shock well.

So well, in fact, she looked hurt, probably thinking I didn't recognize or remember her.

As though I could forget. It did take a few seconds, but only because I hadn't expected Parker to be in the conference room.

Back in the day, she had the singular ability to make me smile, something I rarely had reason to do. She was always overflowing with energy and big ideas, like some kind of fiery woodland sprite fueled by straight espresso.

Speaking of fiery ...

I'm not prepared when she shoves me, both palms pressed flat against my chest. I stumble back and then grasp her wrists, walking forward until her back is against the wall.

"Don't call me that, *Wolverine*," she says.

"Don't call you little? Or don't call you Peter Parker?"

Her old nickname for me—taken from *X-Men*'s Logan, aka Wolverine—inspired mine for her. Though I usually shortened it to Pete.

Stupid, maybe. But it traces back to middle school. That's when I started playing hockey with Brandon and spent most afternoons at his place. Parker was in elementary school then. It's amazing how four years' age difference when you're in school is massive. It's nothing now.

"I'm not little," she says.

I eye her, trying to be respectful but still taking in her fitted black slacks and turquoise shirt. Professional. But even appropriate work attire can't hide how attractive she is. Parker is nothing short of stunning, and I'm still trying to wrap my head around the shift from my best friend's adorably dorky little sister to ... *this*.

Nope—she's definitely not *little*.

I'm staring. And I really need to stop.

Though I'm the one who trapped her here, I'm not sure what to say now. I'm like a house cat who finally caught a mouse and doesn't know what to do with it. Still, I don't release her wrists.

"I didn't think you recognized me," she says, her voice a little breathless.

"I could never forget you, Pete." The words come out a lot huskier than I mean them to, a lot more serious too. I quickly add, "But I didn't recognize you. Not at first. I wasn't expecting you *here*."

"Surprise?"

I chuckle, and then, realizing exactly how close we're standing and how I probably shouldn't keep holding her wrists, I step back. Not too far. Just one step.

"It's been a minute," she says, bending to pick up her tablet.

I should have done that for her, but I forgot the tablet was even there.

"That it has." I pause. "You work for the Appies," I say, stealing the title of Captain Ridiculously Obvious.

She smirks, regaining some of her composure. But I don't miss the way she clutches her tablet tightly to her chest like a shield. "And you play for them."

For now. I don't say this. No need to start my first day with talk of leaving.

She tilts her head. "Would you have been any nicer if you recognized me right away?"

"Unlikely."

She laughs then, which was my goal, and I catch a glimpse of the girl I remember. If Parker wasn't laughing, she was smiling. Always. She was a compact ball of sunshine

13

who drove away the constant storm cloud I lived under. For a while.

I don't realize I'm going to push the stop button until I do.

The elevator jerks and shudders to a halt, making us both stumble forward. I catch Parker by the shoulders and she bumps into me with a soft *oof*.

"What are you doing?" she asks, her voice breathy.

She smells like cinnamon and cookies and something familiar that hits me hard. The word that comes to mind is home. She smells like *home*.

It shocks me.

Honestly, nowhere ever *felt* like home, so it shouldn't have a scent. But it does, and it's somehow attached to Parker.

"Logan?" she says. "What are you doing?"

"I ..."

I don't know. Honestly. I don't.

And being this close to Parker, seeing her big brown eyes blinking up at me, feeling her muscles tense under my grip is only making it harder to locate words. My reaction to her should feel wrong when I think about who Parker was to me —Brandon's little sister. Was she even in high school when I left Harvest Hollow at eighteen?

Before I can scrape up some kind of answer or why things feel completely different now, Parker wiggles out of my grasp and pushes the button to start the elevator again. I watch as she regains control, feature by feature like she's following a checklist or something.

Loosen grip on tablet: check.

Shake out neck and shoulders: check.

Take a deep breath in through the nose, out through the mouth: check.

Reset expression to professional: triple check.

It's kind of impressive, really. And disappointing. Because I happen to like the less professional version of Parker I just saw—the one with her head thrown back while laughing or breathlessly staring up at me with her big doe eyes.

The elevator doors slide open a moment later.

"Walk with me," Professional Parker says, waving for me to follow her without so much as glancing back. "We have things to discuss."

My stomach falls. I can guess what things she means. Like why I left without saying goodbye to the two people closest to me in the world—her and Brandon.

When I heard that Raleigh was putting me on loan, I never would have expected to be sent to my hometown. The place I left at eighteen for good—so I thought. The second I got word I was coming back to Harvest Hollow, I thought of Brandon and Parker. I knew at some point, I might run into them. Without being on social media and having no connections to where I grew up, I honestly had no clue if either of them still lived here.

But if they did ... I knew I might have to answer for my stupid teenage actions. To explain or attempt an apology.

I just didn't expect it ... today.

"I guess you're only fast on the ice," Parker calls back, shooting me a look over her shoulder.

I *am* lagging behind, lost in thought. Parker is a good twenty feet ahead of me. I jog to catch up, then put an arm around her shoulders to slow her speed. She ducks out of my hold and picks up the pace.

"Have you traded in your figure skates for speed walking shoes?" I ask.

"Maybe you're just slow, Barnes."

I'd forgotten how Parker always called me by my last

name whenever she gave me grief. Wolverine for fun. Barnes when she was pointing out mistakes after one of Brandon's and my games. It makes me grin now.

I slide my hands into my pockets as I follow her through a doorway. Parker's office is hardly bigger than a closet with no window and outdated ... everything. It also looks like a sticky-note store exploded.

No motivational posters or framed pictures here—just every available wall surface covered in the small, colorful squares.

"Whoa."

Parker grins as she drops into a cheap office chair that makes a horror-movie-esque sound. I'm a little surprised it holds her based on the severity of the groan.

"There's an order to my madness, I swear."

"I believe it."

And I do. The walls might be covered in sticky notes (some of her desk too), but they're clearly organized. Maybe with a ruler. From the quick glance I give the closest set of fluorescent pink notes, even Parker's loopy script is neat. Figures.

"Didn't you used to have two planners for every year?"

She beams. "I did."

I can tell there's something she isn't saying. "You still do, don't you?"

"Yep. Only now it's one physical, one digital." Setting her tablet on the desk, she wiggles her mouse to wake up the bulky desktop computer. The motor whirring sounds like a helicopter taking off. I'm getting the sense from Parker's noisy chair, old computer, and windowless office that the Appies's budget does not lean heavily into office space. At least not for Parker. Larry was more than happy to show off his luxurious office and Malik, the manager, had one almost as big.

"How old is that computer?"

She sighs, scanning her phone. "Let's just say they've discovered newer fossils. Sit."

I glance at the chair across from her desk. It's a lot nicer than the wobbly office chair she's in that protests loudly every time she so much as exhales. I sit, drumming my fingers on my leg, waiting for the inevitable questions dissecting our past.

Instead, Parker says, "Let's talk about your schedule."

I blink a few times, then shake my head. "Did you just trick me into having a meeting?"

Leaning forward, she puts her elbows on the desk and steeples her hands under her chin. "That wasn't my intent. But you followed me so nicely, like a little baby lamb." She grins.

I huff out a laugh. "Right to the slaughter, huh?"

Parker tilts her head, still smiling. "This doesn't have to be painful."

"That's where we're going to disagree."

Everything about this is painful. Getting kicked down to an AHL league team after almost ten years playing pro. (And yes, technically the Appies are still pro—it's just not the same.) Moving back to Harvest Hollow. The idea that *dancing* is somehow baked into my contract.

"Logan." Parker saying my name snaps me back to attention. Or maybe it's the seriousness in her tone. "It's going to be fine. You're in good hands here. Trust me."

But trust isn't a commodity I have in spades. And even if I could trust Parker, it doesn't make this idea any more appealing.

The real reason I'm against the idea of being forced into

social media isn't about who's behind the camera. Hockey is my profession. My job. If I've earned a reputation for not being a team player, it's less because I'm egotistical and more because I'm focused on being the best of the best. Hockey is serious business to me—even if I also happen to enjoy it.

Dancing in videos for TikTok is ridiculous. The opposite of professional.

I find myself imagining my father's reaction. Not that he'll ever see these videos. He certainly doesn't follow my career. But if he *did*, it would confirm all the things he said when I called to tell him I first got drafted right out of high school.

I was naive to hope getting drafted so young would impress the man who left before I was a year old. It was the second and the last time I talked to him in my life.

"I hope you have a real job lined up," he told me in lieu of congratulations. "Playing sports is just that—*play*. One day, probably sooner than you think, you'll want to get serious and settle down. Make sure you've got your real life career set in place."

I hung up the phone, some deep part of me crushed more than I'll ever admit out loud. It's not uncommon for pro athletes to have families and friends crawling out of the woodwork begging for money, cars, houses. It totally sucks to be seen as nothing but a paycheck or nothing beyond the sport. It's how my mom is. She doesn't care how I'm doing; she just wants money deposited every month to her bank down in Florida.

But between my two parents though, it's worse to have a father who didn't dignify my career or accomplishments enough to even *ask* for a handout.

No matter how much I wish it didn't bother me, every time I lace up my skates, I'm aware that some part of me is skating for approval I'll never get. Most of the time, I don't think about either of my parents. But being back in Harvest Hollow forced them to the front of my mind. And filming stupid videos like this only drives my father's point home.

And with all the negative press I've had lately, I really don't see how taking part in stupid videos will help. They'll just make me look more foolish. Not that I care about my reputation—unless it impacts my ability to play. All I care about is showing up and doing my job to the best of my ability.

"Yo, Boss."

I'm saved from my dark thoughts when a big man fills the doorway. His eyes go from Parker to me, and he grins. He's got a dark beard, darker eyes, and a shaved head. Probably one of my teammates.

I realize now I should have looked at the roster before arriving. But I was too stuck in my head to even think about it. Now I'll just look like some egomaniac who thinks he's a big shot.

"Van," Parker says, leaning back in her chair, which makes a loud pop. I wait for it to break, but it holds. For now. "Aren't you supposed to be with the trainer right now?"

"Just stopped by to say hi," he says, and I don't like the way he's smiling at Parker.

More like—he just stopped by to flirt.

Parker wiggles her fingers in a cutesy wave. "Well, then, *hi*. While you're here, this is your newest teammate, Logan Barnes."

I stand, shaking his hand as we size each other up. He seems like a friendly guy, and I'd appreciate it more if he didn't keep smiling at Parker like that.

Since when am I the possessive type? Especially with someone I'm not even dating?

19

But the tension in my shoulders doesn't ease until Van is gone after "welcoming" me. Okay, what he actually said is that he's looking forward to tearing me up on the ice, but it's the same thing.

Parker leans forward again, looking like she's about to launch into whatever she planned to tell me when she lured me in here, but another guy shows up.

"Boss," he says, knocking on the door frame.

He doesn't smile—doesn't look capable, actually. I find myself shaking his hand too hard as Parker introduces him as Nathan. He's giving me the same kind of once-over I'm giving him. One full of assessment and maybe suspicion.

"Knock it off, you two," Parker says, and Nathan steps back, giving me another look before turning to Parker.

"Lunch later?" Nathan asks, retying his long brown locks into a ponytail.

"Can't today," she says, frowning at the computer.

Does Parker routinely have lunch with the guys on the team? Or just this one? I find both ideas bother me. Almost as much as Van smiling at her did.

Nathan grumbles out some kind of response and disappears, only to be replaced by another one of my soon-to-be teammates. This one is all smiles, his lanky body full of too much energy.

Is there, like, a line of guys in the hall outside Parker's door?

"I'm Eli," the guy says, smiling so big it looks like it hurts. "So good to meet you, man. I can't believe you're here."

That makes two of us.

"See you later, Boss?" he asks Parker.

She glances at her phone. "At four."

"Cool." Eli looks at me again, still smiling. "Cool. Cool. Cool."

As soon as he's gone, I fix my eyes on Parker. "Did you have something you wanted to meet about? Because—"

I don't get to finish because one after another, what must be the whole team—or practically the whole team—pops in, one by one. Alec—the captain who somehow looks like a Disney prince come to life. Based on the way he struts, he might actually think he *is* a Disney prince. It makes me unreasonably happy when Parker rolls her eyes at him the second his back is turned.

Then it's Tucker and Dumbo—two defenders who come in together, making Parker's small office feel even more cramped. I don't bother to ask their real names. And a bunch more whose names I've forgotten.

Every guy calls Parker *Boss*. All of them look at her in a way I don't like. Not that they looked at her disrespectfully. The opposite actually—it's clear they hold Parker in high regard.

Which should ease my tension. Instead, it bugs me that these guys I don't know and don't trust have a familiarity with Parker that used to be mine.

Totally unfair. But feelings aren't always fair.

After what must be twenty minutes of this, I'm ready to slam the door in the face of the next guy who tries to set foot inside. Thankfully, I don't try it, because the last guy practically has to stand at an angle to fit in the doorway.

Giving me a quick glance, he hands a paper across the desk to Parker. "I brought you that list, Boss," he says. To me, he nods and says, "Hey, man."

I nod back, but Parker beams as her eyes scan the paper. "Thank you! This is awesome, Felix."

"See ya." He's gone before Parker can introduce us. At

21

this point, I've heard so many names, I'm likely to forget anyway.

But I am curious about the paper Parker's still eyeing. "What's that?" I ask.

She folds it once, then tucks it into her purse. "A list of book recommendations. Felix is our goaltender and resident bibliophile."

"Does everyone around here call you Boss?" I ask.

What I don't ask: *Are all the guys in love with you?*

Maybe *love* is the wrong word. But for most, there's definitely more than respect. Almost every one of them—maybe Felix aside—seems like they'd jump at the chance to be with Parker.

"Most of the players do. Not because I'm in charge of anyone. It's because I'm bossy. Soon, you'll be just another one of the guys, calling me Boss too."

I have no desire to be just another one of the guys, and not just because my time here should be brief. This team is a stepping stone. A brief interlude. A placeholder until I get called back up to the NHL. Hopefully.

But that's not the only reason I don't want Parker to see me as just one of the guys. *It's because of our history,* I tell myself. I was just as protective of her as Brandon was back in the day. I'm sure it's just more of that protectiveness making me feel so thrown off by other guys showing her attention.

"Why don't I talk you through how we'll welcome you on social media?" Parker says. "It won't be so bad. You'll see."

Doubtful. There's no way she could package this in a way that makes it not *so* bad. Unless she's going to let me get away with not speaking and barely showing my face. Chances of that are nonexistent.

"I'll ease you in with a player profile," Parker says,

clicking her mouse until a printer whirs to life, sounding almost as loud as her computer.

When Parker leans back to grab the single sheet from the printer, I tense, ready to leap across the desk and catch her if the chair gives way. I'm mildly disappointed I don't get the chance to swoop in and save her.

I'm no white knight, I chastise myself. *Probably best not to pretend I am one.*

Righting herself in the chair, Parker slides a piece of paper my way. I glance down to see what looks like a form.

"As soon as you fill it out, I'll make a plan for a video interview. I already have some ideas. I'm lucky to have known you way back when. Even if a lot has changed."

She sounds sad when she says that. I wonder if she missed me as much as I missed her when we fell out of touch —more precisely, when I ghosted everyone from my past. Guilt is an emotion I don't allow myself to feel most of the time. It's wasted energy. And yet, seeing Parker, I'm filled with fresh guilt and a heavy dose of regret over my stupid barely-an-adult decisions.

"And before you even think about *not* filling out the profile, it won't get you out of filming," Parker says, and I'm slightly unsettled she knew where my mind went. "It will just mean I can't tailor what we do to what you're comfortable with."

"So, you're saying I'll be even more miserable if I don't fill this out."

She beams at me. "I'm glad we understand each other, Logan." The smile disappears, and she pins me with a no-nonsense look. "I'll expect it on my desk by the end of the week."

I'm already starting to see why the guys all call her Boss.

Jerking my chin toward the door, I ask, "Is that normal?

Do guys just drop in here to see you constantly?"

Parker blinks at me. Then a slow smile steals over her face. "You don't know?"

I frown. "Know what?"

"They all came here to see *you*, Barnes."

"Oh." That's unexpected. And now I feel like a jerk for not being more friendly.

Still, I'd bet Parker has no idea how they all see *her*. Because it was obvious to me that most of the men who walked through the door would take any scrap she threw their way. Maybe they were here to meet me. But for many of them, that's not the only reason.

Either way, I'm not here to make friends. Not that I usually do anyway. But especially not here. The goal is to get in, prove my worth so my team wants me back, and get out. The end.

"You have no idea how excited the team is to have you. Word of advice before you go?"

I guess that's my cue to be dismissed, so I pick up the player profile and nod. "Sure."

"At least *pretend* you're excited to be here too."

I don't respond because I'm not excited and not pretending to be. I'm resigned for now. Bitter at the turn my career has taken. Eager to get back to Raleigh. Or anywhere else. Just not … here.

Only now I feel the slightest tug of regret thinking about leaving in a matter of months. Even this little bit of Parker has lightened my mood, just the way she always did.

Pausing in the doorway, I consider offering the apology I owe but wasn't asked for. The words are trying to form coherent sentences when Parker speaks.

"Oh, and Logan?" She grins at me. "Have fun at practice."

Now *that* I can do.

CHAPTER 3

Parker

"I THOUGHT I might find you up here," a deep, lightly accented voice says.

I'm so startled I almost drop my phone over the railing and onto the ice below. What's the drop—fifty feet? Eighty? Despite my heavy-duty case, if the fall didn't shatter the screen, the first player who skated over it would finish the job.

Clutching the phone to my chest, I swivel to glare at the only person who would dare sneak up on me. Especially up here on the metal catwalk above the rink. Most people don't even know how to get here.

"Javi, you can't *do* that," I tell our facilities manager.

He only chuckles, running a hand through his more salt than pepper hair. "Figured you'd expect it by now."

I should, considering the man is like a Houdini of the Summit, appearing and disappearing at will.

"How's it going down there?" he asks, peering over the side at morning practice.

"It's going. You know—same old."

I glance down, unable to help the way my eyes immediately zero in on Logan just as he takes a shot that Felix blocks. I can't hear words from way up here, but based on body language, a couple of the guys skate by and make cracks to Logan.

I smile. *Welcome to the Appies, Wolverine.* Getting razzed—which is probably way too innocent a term for the kinds of foul insults these guys hurl at each other—is just a part of being included on a team. They're giving Logan a hockey-style welcome. In no time, he'll be fully assimilated. And insulted. Same thing.

Unless ... Logan refuses to really *be* part of the team, keeping them all at a distance. My brother confessed a few years ago that he wasn't all that surprised when Logan ghosted him.

"I'm not sure I ever *knew* him. Like, we hung out. It was comfortable," Brandon once told me. "It's not like we didn't *talk*. But Logan never went deep, and sometimes he would disappear."

I frown as Logan shoves Nathan, who is inarguably the last guy you want to shove. It takes Tucker and Dumbo and Coach to separate the two of them. Not the best showing. I stop filming and delete the video I was taking.

Javi makes a disapproving sound, and I can't blame him.

"Come on, Logan," I mutter, willing him with the force of my mind to be better.

I know he's probably changed in the years since I've seen him, but I still know him. I do. Our talk in my office made me certain of this. He's still Logan. Good guy wrapped up in a rough—but pretty—package. Maybe now a little gruffer and world-weary, but the moment he called me Peter Parker, I knew he is still the guy I fell for all those years ago.

The hot, sweet one I looked up to and adored. The one whose name I doodled in notebooks. The one who always made me feel like I mattered.

No, Parker! Bad. Must not fall for the hot hockey player who already left you high and dry once! This particular crush is not about to rise from the dead.

Though I fear it's already too late. The crush has risen. More like ... it never died and just sat quietly like a troll under the bridge, biding its time. Within moments of him stepping close in the elevator, I was already a goner. Now, my best hope is to manage it. Keep that troll in check until Logan gets called back up and try not to spend too much time with him.

But even if being around Logan is bad for my own pathetic heart, I do want to see him bond with the rest of the Appies.

This team is full of great guys. Flawed and human and, well, *hockey players*—with the foul mouths and the women and the egos—but still great.

There's Van—way too into the ladies, who are into him right back. Watching his behavior off the ice makes me want to bathe in hand sanitizer. Nathan is a total grouch with a teensy, tiny bit of an anger problem. One that might be helped if Larry would listen to me about requiring weekly or even monthly therapy sessions for the guys. The whole team would benefit, even if Nathan is the one who needs it most. From what I've seen, Logan would be a close second.

Felix would spend his time alone with a book just as

easily as he'd have the whole team over. I'm still trying to decide if our goaltender is an introvert or extrovert.

"Things are just the same old?" Javi says. *"Really?"*

"Yep. Why wouldn't it be?"

"Logan Barnes."

I ignore the way hearing his name makes my heart skip, and instead adjust my phone to move into landscape mode. I haven't gotten much footage for YouTube lately. TikTok is our main focus, especially with the younger demographic, but we have several hundred thousand followers on YouTube, which I need to keep fed with new, longer form content in addition to the shorts.

Yep. Let's focus on content creation and not Javi's baiting.

I'm not even sure how Javi could *possibly* know what a big deal Logan's arrival is for me personally. No one but Brandon and my best friend, Mia, who have both known me forever, should be aware.

But just like Javi's magical ability to portal himself around the complex, the man seems privy to *everything*. Including my stupid heart and its back-from-the-dead or never-actually-died crush.

"He looks good," Javi says, leaning against the rail.

Yeah, he does. My internal teenager rears its immature head.

"He'll be a good addition to the roster," my mature, professional self responds, ending the video only to flip my phone vertically and start another. We usually overlay trending sounds or purchased music over the videos so my conversation with Javi won't matter in the background.

"If he can keep that temper in check and be a team player."

"He will." I say this with the utmost conviction, masking

my fear that Logan will *not*, in fact, keep his temper in check or be a team player.

Javi snorts but doesn't say anything else as he watches the guys, massaging his bad hand. From what he's told me, it got skated over in a game when he was a teenager. Severed nerves and bone damage mean chronic pain—and the end of hockey for him.

His parents, whom Javi says hoped he'd play soccer like a good Mexican boy (their words), still support his sport of choice. Even if Javi's not playing. They have season passes to the Appies, showing up to every game decked out in black and gray and turquoise, yelling insults that Javi assures me are far worse than what I hear in English. And believe me, you hear some *things* shouted at a hockey game.

I wonder how often Javi thinks about what could have been.

When I look down at the ice, it reminds me of my figure skating days with a cloyingly sharp bittersweetness. Not that figure skating was *my* dream. It wasn't. I wanted to play hockey like Brandon.

My father, being the master puppeteer he is, refused to pay for me to play hockey. Even more, he wouldn't sign any parental consent forms when I told him I'd just use my babysitting money to cover the cost. Brandon even offered to help chip in.

My mom, bless her sweet soul, is always on Team Dad and wouldn't cave when I begged her to sign the forms. Even though I suspect she silently disagreed with Dad about this.

So, it was either figure skating or no skating.

There were things I ended up loving. Mostly the sensation of flying across the ice and launching my body into the air. It's truly magical to leap and then to land—when I landed correctly. There were plenty of times I didn't, and the flying preceded a painful fall.

But the moments of pure freedom and perfect landings ended all too quickly. The pressure was immense. Being watched and judged for the tiniest of technical mistakes. Not to mention all the unwanted attention on my body, my outfits, even my expressions. When you're going through puberty while wearing skintight sparkles under a spotlight, it's impossible not to feel self-conscious.

For the first time in years, I wonder if I could land some of my old jumps. My muscle memory still retains the knowledge of how to do a lutz, but I question my current ability to land it without ending up eating ice.

"You okay?" Javi asks, his eyes still on the action below.

Before I can answer with something trite and probably a lie, Van checks Logan. They crash into the plexiglass with the kind of sound that makes my blood hum.

"Ooooh," Javi and I say in unison. Then we both laugh.

But only because this time, Logan doesn't react badly. The two seem to be laughing as they skate away.

There you go, Logan! More of that, please. Happy hitting. Not angry hitting.

"Did you get that one?" Javi asks.

I smile at my phone screen. "Of course."

"You don't miss much."

"Neither do you." I raise a brow and give him a look.

His smile is slow. "Let me know when you want to talk about the rookie."

I snort at Javi calling Logan a rookie. "I won't."

I frown as my phone screen shows an incoming call. My dad. Ugh. I've been avoiding his calls for days now.

"And on that note," Javi says, eyeing my phone with the tiniest wrinkle in his nose. "See you around, Ms. Parker."

Javi has always insisted on the Ms. but never uses my last name. Probably because of how dismissive and rude my dad was the one time he and Javi happened to cross paths. My father, Don Douglas, tech giant and real estate mogul, would never give the time of day to a man with a job like Javi's .

Thinking about that has me answering the phone in an irritated, "To what do I owe the honor of this phone call?"

There's a pause. Then a sigh. "Hello, Parker. This is your father."

I barely refrain from making a comment that will earn me a longer lecture. Only the sight of Logan, slapping the puck into the net past Felix has me smiling instead of snapping.

"What do you need, Dad?"

"Can't I simply call my daughter to check in?"

"Of course you can. But you don't. You get your updates from Mom and only call when you need something. So, what do you need?"

"Parker," he says in a warning tone that still makes me want to cower. Even if now, I don't.

My father isn't a cruel man. Just overbearing and demanding, running our household like a business, doling out commands and expecting our immediate compliance.

Mom mostly doesn't mind going along with him. So long as he doesn't stop her from heading up dozens of committees focused on charity work. She's smart and kind—but her loyalty and blinding love toward my father is her fatal flaw.

I'm proud of what she does—mainly getting wealthy people to write big checks to worthy causes—even if she's disappointed, I don't want to do the same. Or work for Dad like Brandon does. Mom doesn't guilt trip me or get passive aggressive—it's not her style. But I just know she'd love for me to be more connected with our family, the business, or with charitable work.

31

My brother toes the party line most of the time, though he holds no illusions and even less respect for our father. If Brandon wants to take over EverTech one day—which he definitely does—he has to play my father's game. Thankfully, he is not as much like our father in terms of personality, even if he shares Dad's sharp intellect and business acumen.

And me? I'm the black sheep who went to a liberal arts college, majored in communication, and gave up living with my parents' financial favors and support in order to take a job I love while existing on a diet of ramen.

Zero regrets.

"I wanted you to know I found you a date for the gala," Dad says, like he's telling me he had the tires rotated on my car. Or as though I *asked* him to find me a date.

To be clear—I did NOT ask for that. And my mechanic friend, Hazel, rotated my tires just last month. So, I'm all good there too.

"I told you already—I don't need you to find me a date for your *gala*," I say.

Our dad is hosting his own birthday party in a few days. But because it's my dad, this isn't just any birthday party. It's a GALA. Though, considering my mom is at the helm of the planning, it *will* be more of a gala than a normal birthday party. Mom found a way to tie it to a charity, which will mean silent auctions and a fundraising speech from someone who will praise my father for using his name for a good cause.

Dad has already made it very clear my attendance and my acquiescence playing the doting daughter is vitally important. So important, in fact, that he's been angling to pick out a date for me.

And I've been putting him off, vaguely hinting about having a date already—even though I absolutely have no date and no prospects. I'm hoping one might magically appear in time to save me from whomever my dad is picking out.

Since college, I've made every effort to wiggle out from underneath my dad's thumb. No way am I willingly crawling back under by letting him dictate my life—especially not my *dating* life. More than once, Dad has told me he wants me to "find a nice man" (read: a rich dude with something to bring to the table) and "settle down" (aka: stop playing at my "silly" job) and pop out a bunch of Douglas nepo babies.

GROSS!

The Douglas nepo baby and giving up my career part, anyway. As for getting married and starting a family, I definitely want that. On my *own* terms. With a man I choose.

"You remember Aaron Wagner?" Dad goes on, like I didn't respond at all.

"Sure. Friend of your friends. Smug smile and even smugger attitude. Hard to forget the dinner with him and his parents. Even if I'd like to."

"*Parker James.*"

"Using my middle name doesn't make me comply," I say, my attention dragged down to the ice where the guys are practicing a new play with Logan. Even though they're all geared up to the point of being almost unrecognizable from up here, I could pick out his broad build and his skating stride in a room with a hundred hockey players.

"I gave Aaron your number. The one he had must have been wrong. He said it went to some business."

It sure did: Franco's Birthday Clowns. Because after the dinner with my parents and the Wagners, that's the number I gave him.

It's what Aaron deserves. Clowns.

The Wagners are important to my dad, but I forget why and frankly, I don't care. The way Aaron kept incessantly hitting on me while staring at my chest—which, if I'm being totally honest, isn't all that much to write home about—tempted me to poke him in the eye with one of the breadsticks.

The only reason I refrained was because the breadsticks were fantastic. Aaron Wagner isn't even worth a good breadstick to the eye.

"Like I said, Dad, I don't need you to set me up with someone." Especially not Aaron.

"It's already done," he says.

"No," I say. "It really isn't." And then, I start down a stupid and dangerous path—one paved with lies. "I have a date."

There's a pause where Dad takes in my words. Regrouping, probably. Planning his countermeasures.

"Who are you bringing?" he demands.

"It doesn't matter who," I say, trying to scramble for some idea of who I can name. More than that, who I could actually *bring*. Because I cannot tell my father I have a date and then show up alone. "I'm not going with Aaron. Or any other son of some important business partner."

I'm distracted by movement on the ice. Eli has spotted me up here and is waving with his puppy-like enthusiasm. Van stops beside him and blows me a kiss. I wave back, grinning. Such goofballs.

When Logan looks up, skating the periphery of the rink, my stomach does a little shimmy. Even from afar, his attention affects me.

Dad's voice jerks me back into the unpleasant conversation I'm currently having. "How do I know you haven't made up some fictional date just to get out of going with Aaron?"

My father is a smart man. The track record of his business

34

is a testament to his acumen. But it's scary—almost Javi-level scary—how quickly Dad figured out my game.

"Of course I didn't make someone up," I lie, my gaze pulled again to Logan. He's stopped by the goal, his head tilted back, regarding me. He doesn't wave, but the little head nod I get is somehow better.

Because it's *him*. And when it comes to Logan, even the smallest scrap of attention has always felt like a five-course meal prepared by a Michelin-starred chef.

"Then give me a name," my father demands. "Your mother needs it for the guest list."

And my mouth, clearly faster at processing and more concerned with sticking it to Dad than with the consequences, says a name it really, really shouldn't.

"I'm bringing Logan Barnes."

CHAPTER 4

Parker

MY STUPID PARKING space might be overpriced, but the ten-minute walk from the lot to my apartment calms me down. Every time. Though today, admittedly, the charming vibe of the historic downtown isn't working its usual magic. At least, not on me. The handfuls of tourists strolling the streets seem to be enjoying it just fine.

Probably because they don't have Logan Barnes on the brain.

Tucked out of the way in the Appalachian Mountains between Asheville and Knoxville, Harvest Hollow has become quite the vacation destination. Especially in fall.

Even now, when it's early September and the leaves have barely started to hint at changing colors, there's just something in the air. I swear, it's like I can practically hear a chant: *Fall! Fall! Fall!* The air feels crisp, smells like smoke and pumpkin spice lattes, and the whole town seems to vibrate with the anticipation of cooler temperatures and some of the best fall foliage in the country.

Literally. We were voted Number Two Most Gorgeous Fall Town last year, only being beaten by someplace in Vermont. I've never been that far north, but if anyone could beat our fall leaves, even I can concede to the birthplace of maple syrup.

But I think the citizens of Harvest Hollow took the number two spot as a personal affront and challenge. The Beautification Committee is out for blood. Fall decor started going up in August this year, sneaking in the same way Christmas decor now appears in big box stores in October next to Halloween skeletons and Thanksgiving turkeys.

The first thing to go up on Maple Street were ribbons on the black lamp posts. Warm, buttery yellow (NOT mustard), cheerful orange, and cranberry red ribbons with giant bows. Oh, and apples—real and fake—placed anywhere at all possible, as a nod to our favorite local crop. One store has a whole row of apples dangling from the awning by ribbons. Real apples, apparently, based on the bite I see taken out of one.

This week, someone added twinkly lights—not to be confused with Christmas lights, which are red and green and go up the day after Thanksgiving. These are the soft white lights with the tiny bulbs, and they set the mood, making the whole street feel cozy as night falls. It's getting darker earlier now, the sun dipping below the mountains and casting long shadows on our valley in late afternoon.

I take a deep inhale, wishing there were some way to bottle this whole fall vibe up. I'd make a killing selling it online, marketing it as a fall elixir powerful enough to *almost* make you forget your old crush.

Okay, fine—the town magic is totally working on me.

I pop into the General Store a few blocks from my apartment. Since I worked right through lunch, my stomach is collapsing in on itself from hunger. And unless a fairy godmother showed up in my apartment while I was at work, there's nothing there to eat.

The General Store lives up to its name with a pharmacy in back and a random assortment of goods from T-shirts to greeting cards to the very basic food staples you might need in the zombie apocalypse: canned soups, saltine crackers, and pasta. Perfect for nights like tonight, when I'd rather pop in here than go to the actual grocery store.

The bell jangles as I walk inside, and Mel barely looks up from her *Archie* comic.

"Did you run out of ramen again, Parker?" Mel calls from behind the counter.

Her long, white hair is twisted into a gorgeous braid crown. I swear, every time I see the woman, she's got some new amazing hairstyle. Meanwhile I've got two looks: down in messy waves or up in a messy ponytail. If I'm feeling extra saucy (read: lazy), maybe a messy bun.

"Not so loud!" I tease, grabbing a three-pack of ramen. "Can't have you ruining my reputation."

Mel only chuckles. "What reputation?"

"Ouch, Mel. Ouch."

But … she's not wrong. Other than my job working for the Appies and the fact that my dad runs EverTech, I don't make waves. I'm too boring to have a reputation. And that's just fine with me!

"Even so, I'd prefer the whole town not know that I still exist on a college kid food staple."

"It's our secret." Mel makes a motion zipping her lips.

I don't really care who knows, to be honest. I have no shame. Though I can only imagine what my parents would say if they knew I buy food that's three packs for a dollar when I could be eating chef-prepared meals at home with them.

And all I'd have to do is move back home and work for Dad's company.

No thanks! I'll take my beef ramen along with my independence, thank you very much.

My phone buzzes with a call as Mel rings up my purchases of ramen, a loaf of bread, and a family-size pack of Twizzlers. My brother's face and name flashes across the screen. He and I talk several times a week, but him calling today is highly suspicious.

It could be because Brandon heard Logan started today. Or, it could be because Logan started today *and* Dad told Brandon I'm bringing Logan to the gala.

My brother will—to put it mildly—*not* approve. And I haven't figured out how to untangle or explain away my bold-faced lie. Yet.

Until then, I really, really don't want to talk to Brandon. Not on the phone. Not in person. Not in a box or with socks or any other rhyming or non-rhyming places. But if my brother could be summed up in one word, it would be persistent. The man could wear down a diamond, crushing it back into coal.

He immediately calls back when I don't answer. I groan and gird up my metaphoric loins.

Mouthing *Sorry!* to Mel, I pass her my debit card and answer Brandon's call.

"How was his first day?" Brandon demands before I'm even done saying hello. "Heard he was standoffish."

I breathe out a very real sigh of relief. This line of questioning means he doesn't know about my Logan lie. Brandon definitely would have led with that.

And of *course* Brandon would know Logan started today and how things went. He has someone on the team who serves as his eyes and ears. Aka: a spy and a snitch.

And when I find out who …

"Calm down, fanboy," I tell him.

"I am *not* a fanboy," Brandon scoffs.

There may be bad blood between my brother and his former best friend, but I happen to know Brandon follows Logan's career almost as obsessively as I do. And one day, I'll use this knowledge against Brandon. But I'm biding my time.

"Today was fine. Just like any other day," I say breezily.

It wasn't. And I know Brandon knows it wouldn't be. Not for the Appies. And certainly not for me.

"So, is it true—his big NHL ego can't fit inside the Summit?" Brandon sounds judgy. It's an older brother characteristic I'm quite familiar with.

Mel hands back my debit card and my bag of groceries. "He waded through a metric ton of paperwork and a bunch of meetings in the morning. I'm sure he just had an administrative hangover. He'll be fine tomorrow."

"And how was today for *you?*" Brandon asks, dialing the judgment up by a few thousand notches.

I pause. Because I have to answer this particular question with the utmost care and diplomacy. Like writing a peace treaty between two warring nations.

On my way out, I wave to Mel, who's already returned to the age-old Betty and Veronica love triangle. I'm Team Betty, for the record.

"Park?" Brandon says as I step outside. "How was it?"

I stop and lean up against the brick building. "Today was fine for me. A normal workday."

"Same old, same old, huh? Logan's just another player to you?" His tone is dripping with derision.

"Yep. Exactly."

"Oh, Parker. If only I believed you."

I wish Brandon were here so I could whack him with my bag of groceries. But that would squish the loaf of bread I bought.

"I don't particularly care if you believe me, Brandon. Now, do you have any pertinent things to discuss?"

"Like Dad's gala?"

I start to sweat under my jacket. We're walking awfully close to the landmine that is my big lie. "Can we talk about something more pleasant, please? Like inflation?"

Brandon chuckles. "Still in denial about the gala, huh?"

"What gala?"

Brandon laughs. "You know he doesn't believe you can find a date on your own, right?"

Normally, this would start a verbal lashing back and forth. But right now, I'm just grateful. Because now I'm certain Brandon doesn't know about my lie.

"Is it so hard to believe?" I ask lightly.

"Not because you're not awesome, Park."

"Aw, thank you! That was almost a compliment."

"It's because you never date."

What is it with my family and my dating life today? I SWEAR.

"I date."

"What's the name of the last guy you went on a date with?" Brandon demands.

"Jere ... brian." I clear my throat. "Jerebrian."

"Sounds like a winner."

"It's not his fault his parents chose a terrible name." Or that he doesn't exist and I made him up just now.

"So, are you bringing *Jerebrian* to the gala?"

"No. It didn't work out."

41

"Why not?" Brandon asks, and I just *know* he knows that Jerebrian isn't real and is waiting for me to admit it.

I'd prefer to double down instead. "Jerebrian, as it turns out, lives with his parents. And has no job. And also Mr. Eds didn't like him."

Brandon snorts. "Your cat hates everyone. Including you."

He's not wrong. My rescue cat spends most of his time skulking under my furniture and trying to swipe at my ankles when I walk by.

"Jerebrian also has a gambling problem. And gout."

I don't quite remember what gout is, but it suddenly popped into my mind. Wasn't it the thing Benjamin Franklin had from drinking too much Printer's Punch? I had no idea this random piece of trivia from my seventh grade history class was still floating around in my brain.

"Whatever," I say. "I'd rather not talk about Jerebrian anymore. He's definitely not an option."

"So, Jerebrian is out. Why don't you ask one of the guys on the team?"

"Hard pass. You know I don't date players."

Though not official Appies policy, it's always been my personal rule not to date any of the guys. It could just get complicated. And I really, really like my job.

"Just so long as you remember that applies to Logan."

Oh, boy. I don't like the direction we're heading now. I say nothing, not wanting to give anything away.

"You can't deny you're still carrying an Olympic-sized torch for him."

I want to argue but I'm *really* sweating now. "Bitterness isn't a good look on you, bro."

"And betrayal isn't a good look for anyone. Remember that, sis."

Like I could forget how badly Logan's sudden departure from Harvest Hollow hurt.

The difference between me and Brandon is—I forgave Logan. (Even if I'd still like an explanation for why he totally ghosted us.) I didn't let my anger sour into something ugly.

But trying to tell my older brother anything is like trying to teach a cement block to fetch and roll over. Not happening.

"Whatever else you do, just don't fall for him," Brandon says. "Again."

"I won't."

And it's true. But only because I can't fall for Logan *again* when my crush has somehow managed to continue uninterrupted for what amounts to half my life.

Man—it sure sounds sad when I put it like that.

"Sure, you won't," Brandon says.

"Byeeee, Brandon." I hang up.

Any relaxation stemming from the fall vibe has effectively been snuffed out by my meddling-but-means-well brother.

The aroma of coffee and cinnamon drifts out of Cataloochee Mountain Coffee as I pass. The scent is enough to make my mouth water, but if I have caffeine after ten in the morning, I don't sleep. Still, I can't resist stopping by most mornings a week on the way to work. Few mortals could. Especially when Heather makes the best chai latte I've had in my life.

It's dusk as I reach my building, my favorite time of day, especially in fall. The combination of the streetlamps and the twinkly lights bathes everything in a warm romantic glow. Well. It would be romantic if I weren't alone. And if my brother hadn't managed to cram multiple sore subjects into one conversation.

Speaking of romantic …

43

My chest constricts a little at the sight of a couple strolling hand in hand a few blocks away. They pause at Book Smart, the adorable bookstore where I'd happily spend my entire paycheck if I could. When the man holds the door open for the woman, stealing a kiss as she passes, I want to shout, "He's a keeper!" but I hold back.

Despite what I told Brandon, there have been no Jerebrians in a long time. My dating life has tumbleweeds the size of buildings blowing through it. I tell myself it's because I'm focused on work. Which is true. I'm busy. And, fine—I might have slight workaholic tendencies. But that's not why my proverbial dance card stays empty.

File that under: it's complicated. And I'm picky.

I turn down the small alley where the walkup to my apartment is, setting my bag down. I need both hands to manage the outer door, which has a nasty habit of sticking.

Maybe it's the cooler temperatures, but today, the door isn't just sticking, it's *stuck*. I shimmy the handle, then give the door a good kick.

"Come on, door. Be a good door."

I try cajoling first, using baby talk like I'm trying to convince a puppy to obey. But a wiggly puppy would be more responsive. The door gives me nothing.

I switch tactics, ramming my hip into it. "You have one job!" I scold. "And it's to open! Do your job, door!"

"What'd that door do to you?" a deep voice calls.

I freeze as Logan appears beside me. This cannot be my new reality, where he just appears at will in my life. I don't have the constitution for it.

"Oh, hi." I step back, tucking my hair behind my ears. "Where'd you come from?"

I'm perfectly normal. Not a woman talking to an inanimate object while attacking it with my full body weight.

He glances back toward the street. "Just reacquainting myself with the town. It's changed a lot."

"Yep."

I seem to have lost my conversational abilities. Whatever command and poise I had in my office earlier—even while fighting back all the Logan-inspired butterflies—it's gone. No command. Zero poise. I'm suddenly very aware of things like my hands and feet and the angle of my head and wondering what expression my face is making right now.

I'm also *very* aware of the huge lie hanging between us. The one where I said Logan was my date. I chew on the inside of my cheek and shift my weight from one foot to the other.

But Logan seems on edge too. He puts his hands in his pockets. Then takes them out and runs a hand through his dark hair.

Is he ... nervous? Around *me?!?*

Clearing his throat, he nods toward the door. "Need help with that?"

Right. The stupid door. I grab the handle, jiggling as I try ramming my hip into it again.

"It's just tricky," I say through a grunt. "It takes the right combination of wiggling the handle and brute force."

"Or maybe it just needs the right touch." Logan is suddenly right behind me, his big hand covering mine on the doorknob and his chest pressed against my back.

Right touch, indeed.

He presses his other hand flat against the door.

"It won't work," I tell him, flustered as awareness prickles along my hairline at his nearness and the heat of his body behind me. "You have to know just how to—"

With no warning, the door flies open.

The momentum sends us both flying right into the tiny

vestibule. Logan and I land in a tangle of limbs at the bottom of the steep staircase.

I don't register the pain at first. Just the delicious weight of Logan's body on mine. He somehow managed to slide a hand underneath my head before it hit the floor.

Hockey reflexes, man. Not a thing to be trifled with!

Logan's breath flutters over my cheek, and I feel the light scratch of his stubble on my jaw.

Dear door, I was wrong to reprimand and criticize you. You have given me this beautiful gift, and I shall forever be grateful.

"Are you okay, Parker?" Logan sounds worried, but also like he's as breathless and affected by this as I am.

Affected by the fall, probably. Not by the way our bodies fit together so well. Whereas that is ALL I can think about.

Better enjoy it! This will be the only time ever.

"I'm fine?" I say, far more question than statement.

"Are you sure?"

"No?"

He chuckles, which sends a delicious shiver through me. Because I *feel* the rumble of the laughter as his chest vibrates against mine.

He starts to shift, and I want to whine as his weight lifts off me. "I have to be crushing you," he says.

"I'm good," I say. *Really* good. To cover up JUST in case he can hear my thoughts and know that I never, *ever* want him to move, I add, "You're feeling a little light there, Barnes. Maybe we need to increase your caloric intake. Get the trainer to help pack some more muscle on you."

"I guess you'd know better than anyone." I can hear the smile in his voice.

"I would?"

"You're currently feeling up my abs."

I'm *WHAT?*

46

While I've been focused on things like Logan's hand cupping the back of my head and his stubble on my cheek, somehow I missed the very pertinent fact that my hand snuck its way underneath his shirt like a little thief.

And my hand is not passively resting on but *actively stroking* his six pack. Or is it eight? Definitely an eight-pack.

I jerk my hand away and immediately try to wiggle out from under Logan. "I am so sorry! It must be … an involuntary reaction."

He shifts his weight, allowing me to scoot away and sit up, my back against the stairs. I keep my head down, hiding behind my hair. Because I cannot face the man whose abs I just groped like some kind of ab-groping weirdo.

"Your hand involuntarily performs abdominal exams?" Logan asks, barely keeping the laughter out of his voice.

"Yep."

"So, you've done this to every guy on the team?"

Exasperated, I blow out a breath and finally hazard a glance his way. He's sitting up too now, watching me with a teasing glint in his green eyes.

"Just another part of my job," I say, trying my best to feign some semblance of calm.

"You mean a *perk* of the job?"

"Nope. Definitely not a perk. You have no idea how taxing it is," I say, rolling my eyes. "So many six packs, so little time."

He laughs, and my whole torso hums with a kind of deep, deep pleasure I rarely feel. Because Logan doesn't laugh much. Or he *didn't*. I can only think of a few times I've heard this sound. It's so rich and full that I want to grab my phone and record it so I can listen again and again.

I study him, wondering if maybe he *has* changed. Maybe he laughs all the time now. Maybe the rumors about him being intense and serious and having a quick temper were all exaggerations.

But then I remember how he was in the conference room earlier. Hard. Angry. Dismissive. That seemed like a different man from the relaxed, teasing, laughing version in front of me. And the one who trapped me in the elevator and joked in my office.

"What?" he asks.

I shake my head. "I'm just trying to decide how you've changed. *If* you've changed."

"And? What's the verdict?"

"Unsure. I'll let you know."

Logan tilts his head, and I will my cheeks not to blush under his gaze.

"Well, you haven't changed," he says after a moment. "Still the same Parker I remember."

And ... *there's* the inevitable disappointment as reality punches me right in the windpipe. Logan thinks I haven't changed. He last saw me a little over ten years ago. When I was fifteen. Practically a baby.

I *have* changed. I've changed a lot.

But if Logan still sees me as the same awkward kid he knew, as Brandon's dorky little sister, then ... I don't even know what to do with that.

I *do* know it means I cannot hold out any hope of my feelings being returned. Obviously.

"Can we forget this moment ever happened?" I ask.

Logan doesn't answer. But he does get to his feet, offering me a hand. "Come on, Parker. Clearly, I need to help you up to your apartment. If you fall through doors so easily, no telling what will happen if you try to make it up the stairs alone."

I've lost my shoe, and I just felt up Logan's abs without

consent. Not to mention the fact that I lied to my dad about Logan being my date.

I'm the hottest of hot messes. Ghost pepper level hot. Landfill level mess.

The same mess I've always been, I think miserably. *That's what Logan sees when he looks at me. A mess.*

"I don't need help," I say, grabbing my keys for the upstairs door. "You can go back to your homecoming tour of town. But thank you!"

"Okay."

Guilt spears me at the look on Logan's face. All lightness fled at my dismissal, and he immediately starts to close off again, reverting to the distant version of him in the conference room.

"Logan."

He stops at the sound of my voice, his hand on the knob. It takes a moment for him to swing his gaze my way.

"Stay."

His brow furrows slightly, and my cheeks warm. I want to kick myself. The man probably gets a similar proposition at least once a week, but for way more than what I'm offering.

I shake the bag of groceries. "For dinner."

Still, he hesitates. It shouldn't be a big decision, but I can see how torn he is. As nervous as I am, wanting to smooth away his uncertainty pushes me forward.

"Remember my inability to so much as bake cookies without starting a fire?"

At this, Logan's features soften ever so slightly. He chuckles. "I remember."

"Well, come on then. I can't be left unattended. I might burn down the building."

I start up the stairs, heart thumping. Hoping Logan follows, just as nervous that he will. Me—alone with Logan in my apartment? The thought practically has my hands shaking.

But I remind myself of how lost he just looked, how rejected. Worth it to invite him. Even if he doesn't stay.

When his heavy footsteps start up the stairs right behind me, I find myself biting back a grin.

CHAPTER 5

Logan

"ALMOST DONE," Parker says, wiping her face with her forearm and grinning over at me. "Are you sure you want to eat something I cooked?"

"I trust you, Pete."

Her grin turns mischievous. "You trust me not to burn it or not to poison it?"

"I didn't think about poisoning. Is that a thing I should be worried about?"

"We'll see," she says, dropping something in a pot on the stove.

Hopefully, not hemlock or arsenic.

I'm trying to relax, still telling myself that this is okay. Parker invited me in. This is fine. But it's the first time I remember being in someone's personal space in longer than I care to remember.

Curiosity made me decide to stay—wanting to spend more time around Parker, to see who she is now. That and the sense of ease I have just being around her.

Since my knee injury, surgery, and months of recovery, I've spent a lot of time alone. My physical therapist and Jeremy are the only people I've talked to at length. And by at length, I mean short and sporadic conversations.

Now, I'm filling my conversation quota. And then some. For the last twenty minutes, Parker has happily chatted away while she cooks and I sit at her small table and observe. She used to be talkative. But this is a lot even compared to pint-sized Parker. Is she nervous? Excited? On a caffeine high? I'm not sure. But I don't mind the chatter. I find myself smiling while I listen.

Watching Parker is better than Netflix. She moves like a cheerful gale-force wind through the tiny kitchen, banging pots and thwacking her knife into the cutting board, all while telling me every conceivable fact about the Appies.

I can't help but notice she says very little about herself. And doesn't mention Brandon at all.

While listening and watching, I make my own observations. She still loves pink, which is the one color I see throughout her apartment. I guess she likes to cook, which is new. She wasn't kidding about burning cookies when she was little, and I wonder how and when this changed.

I hate that there's a whole lot of blank space in my knowledge of what Parker has been doing for the last ten years. If she kept competing in figure skating. Where she went to college. Who she's dating.

Not that her relationship status is any of my business. It's definitely my fault I don't know any of these things.

A low growling sound has me whipping my head toward

the couch. I don't see anything, but then I hear it again. It sounds like it belongs in some kind of horror movie.

"Do you have a dog?" I ask, still eyeing the sofa.

Parker rolls her eyes. "That's just Mr. Eds. He's a cat."

"You like cats now? And what kind of name is Mr. Eds? Plural?"

"It's short for Evil Demon Spawn," she says, like this is a totally normal name for a cat. Or anything else. "And no, I don't like cats. But I used to volunteer at the shelter, and no one would adopt him. He was set to be euthanized, so I took him in, thinking I could win him over or that maybe he'd be nice out of gratitude. Turns out, I'm not so charming. And he's not grateful. But don't worry. He's an equal opportunity human hater, so he won't come out while you're here."

I sure hope not. Mr. Eds definitely sounds like he lives up to his name. Parker grabs a bag of cat treats from a cabinet, shakes it, then lobs one toward the couch. It lands right by the trunk Parker uses as a coffee table. There's a hiss and then a small black paw darts out and drags the treat under the couch.

"You're welcome, bad kitty," Parker calls in a sweeter voice than the creature deserves.

Mr. Eds hisses in response. Though I continue watching Parker, I keep some of my focus on the couch. Just in case.

"How was your first day?" Parker asks. "Were the guys nice?"

They were, but it doesn't really matter. I'm used to showing up, giving it all on the ice, and going home. Not bonding or making friendship bracelets. But I can tell from Parker's eager face that she's hoping for more.

"It was good. They were fine."

"Man of many words," she says with a smile and a roll of her eyes. "One thing hasn't changed much."

I grunt in response, hoping she'll laugh. She does, and I fight back a smile. "I saw you filming today."

"Yeah—and?"

"It didn't look so bad," I admit. Right after practice, she filmed a segment with Tucker and Dumbo on the bench, holding and discussing a book. It was quick, and looked mostly like they were talking to each other and then faking a fight. "Though I don't get how books are involved."

Her cheeks flush and she focuses hard on the soup she's stirring. "Hockey romance is a big thing. I'm trying to reach a crossover audience of readers as well. But while keeping with our, um, family friendly vibe, just considering our target audience."

I frown, wondering what's in the books that wouldn't be family friendly. And does Parker read hockey romance?

"*Anyway*," Parker says, obviously trying to steer us away from the topic of romance novels. "You should watch some of our videos sometime. Maybe you'd be surprised."

"That would mean actually getting on social media."

"You're such an old man."

"Get off my lawn," I say, and she laughs again. It's so easy with her. Conversation. Making her smile and laugh. Just being present and not feeling any kind of pressure to be or do anything other than me.

"How is it being back in Harvest Hollow?" she asks.

Okay, now we're moving into less easy territory. I shift in my chair. "I didn't think I'd ever come back," I say honestly. "It's an adjustment."

"Your mom moved, right?" she asks.

"Florida." My voice is clipped, and Parker must read my reaction, because there are no follow-up questions.

Instead, she sets a bowl in front of me. I stare down at it

for a few seconds, blinking as I take in the sight and the spicy aroma.

"I know," she says, taking the seat across the small table from me. "It's just cheap ramen and has almost zero nutritional value."

She thinks I'm disappointed? I just sat and watched her chop things and doctor up a cheap meal to make it something else.

"This looks great," I say.

Honestly, it does. What's more, I don't remember the last time someone so much as microwaved a burrito for me. At least, someone who wasn't a paid employee.

"You'll need to stop somewhere later for more protein to feed"—she glances across the table, her gaze sweeping over me as a blush paints her cheeks—"all that."

I chuckle. "My abs really did come up short in your exam, huh?"

My teasing sounds flirty. And I never flirt. I'm not sure what's wrong with me. But something appears to be broken. Parker huffs and tosses a piece of ice at me from her glass. I catch it and pop it in my mouth with a smile.

She bites her lip, her smile fading. "You don't have to do this."

"Do what?"

I watch her across the table that barely fits us both. Parker blows out a breath, then glances out the window next to us that looks down over Maple Street.

"You don't have to try to make me feel better about my stupid, cheap dinner. I'm sure you're used to gourmet everything and perfectly proportioned, healthy pro athlete meals. Not basic ramen."

"Parker." I wait, not speaking until she turns those brown eyes back to me. "You took a dollar pack of ramen and made it an actual meal. I'm kind of amazed, actually. Thank you."

Even though I sat at this table and watched, I'm still not sure how Parker transformed the cheap package of dried noodles into *this*. There's chili oil and garlic, green onion sliced thinly on top, and even a soft-boiled egg. It looks almost as good as restaurant quality ramen. She even served it in unique bowls that look handmade and a set of fancy chopsticks. Not the kind you get free and throw away afterward.

"I mean it." My voice might be a little too gruff.

Which I realize only when she rears back a little, her brown eyes wide. But then her expression softens. The smallest smile appears, dragging my gaze to her lips. I force my attention back to her eyes.

"Really?" she asks.

"Shut up, Pete."

Her small smile blooms into something bigger. It's so strange to see the same smile I remember on a much different face. A *woman's* face.

My stomach twists, a squirmy feeling settling in my belly, the same one I've been feeling all day around Parker.

"Enough talking," Parker says, expertly lifting her chopsticks to her mouth. "Time for eating."

I'm impressed by her dexterity as she expertly delivers noodles to her mouth with the chopsticks. But then, in classic Parker fashion, she slurps the last curly noodle between her lips, giggling. I don't try to look away from her mouth this time.

"Why aren't you eating?" she asks, noting the way my hands are still in my lap.

"Any chance I can get a fork?" I ask. "Chopsticks and I don't really get along."

Parker pins me with a look. "You balance that big body on tiny blades, and you can't use two sticks to pick up food?"

"I can't be great at *everything.*" I smirk, crossing my arms over my chest and leaning back.

Parker only rolls her eyes. "This will not do."

Scooting her chair back, she wipes her mouth with a napkin and stands. But instead of walking over to the silverware drawer, she steps behind my chair.

"What are you doing?"

Suddenly I'm hot all over as Parker leans over me, draping her arms over mine. It's the same electric heat I felt earlier when I practically tackled her through the doorway downstairs. These are all feelings I'd best ignore.

Parker picks up the chopsticks, then shoves them into my hands. "I'm teaching you to use chopsticks. Rest this one on your thumb. Like this."

It's not easy to focus on what she's telling me to do with my fingers when I am all too aware of her body pressed against my shoulders and her breath on my cheek.

This is Parker, I try to tell myself. *Brandon's little sister.*

But I'm not thinking about Brandon or the Parker of the past. My body is on high alert—completely laser-focused on *now* Parker.

The now Parker whose hands are on mine, her fingers attempting to help me grasp the chopsticks correctly. I'd struggle even if I weren't so flustered by her soft skin and the scent of her wafting around me. I can smell the ingredients she cooked with, but also cinnamon cookies—spicy and sweet like her personality. Different from the cloud of cheap brown sugar spray always surrounding her when she was younger. Past Parker always smelled like a half-baked cake.

I make the mistake of glancing to my left, where her cheek is practically pressed to my jaw. Her eyes cut to mine.

She's so close that her brown eyes are out of focus. For a beat, we hover there. It's the closest I've come to kissing a woman in a while. A long while, now that I'm thinking about it.

And I've definitely *never* wanted to kiss someone so much. But it's *Parker*.

A huge piece of the past I left behind. And for now, she'll be a huge part of my every day. At my *job*.

I clear my throat and turn away. The chopsticks fall from my hand and clatter to the table.

Parker's laughter is light, making me wonder if I was the only one who felt that tension between us. I'm almost dizzy with the after-effects of my longing, now mixed with a heavy dose of confusion and a dash of guilt.

Parker gives my shoulders a quick, firm squeeze before stepping away.

"Guess you were right—you can't be good at everything, Barnes. A fork it is!"

———

An hour later, I'm walking back down Maple to my SUV. Alone.

After we finished eating, I couldn't miss the way Parker kept yawning. So, I carried both of our dishes to the sink and said I should get back to the hotel. Parker looked disappointed, but her expression quickly shifted to a believable smile as she walked me to the door.

And then we had a really awkward goodbye. I wanted to hug her, but I didn't know *why* I wanted to and didn't know if she'd even *want* me to hug her. So, I waved like an idiot and bolted.

As I walk by a restaurant now, crowded with people spilling out onto patio seating, I make sure to tilt my face away. It's habit—the downside of sponsorships that plaster my face on magazines and billboards. No one glances my way. Still, I breathe easier when I get to my SUV.

With windows down and classical music playing at a low volume, I cruise back down Maple, glancing up as I pass Parker's place.

Her front window is dark now, and I picture her leaving the dishes in the sink and heading to bed. I really should have offered to help wash up. Next time.

Nope—there should be no next times. Not if I want to avoid another confusing and volatile tripwire of emotion.

But it felt good to be with Parker. Her apartment is cozy—small but airy with its high ceilings and large windows. There were architectural details I don't know the names of, like some kind of fancy molding and what looked to be tin plates on the ceiling.

Parker's whole energy filled the space, making the size seem just right, even for someone like me who barely fit at the kitchen table. It felt welcoming, homey, and so very *Parker.*

The apartment next to it had a For Lease *sign,* a pesky voice reminds me.

Bad idea, a more practical part of my brain answers.

It's probably just as small as Parker's. Nothing like the sprawling house I purchased in Raleigh. But then, I don't like all the space in the mid-century modern ranch my last real estate agent urged me to buy. All that space—too empty and too quiet—closed in around me at night. It was a reminder of how insubstantial my life is: just one big empty box.

It's why I started sleeping in the walk-in closet. I didn't feel the sense of insignificance and claustrophobia. Does it make any sense that I felt less trapped in a small space? No.

But long ago, I stopped over analyzing *why* things make me feel a certain way and focused on how to get those feelings to go away.

I hop on the highway and in minutes, I'm passing the stadium and pulling into the hotel parking lot. The place isn't huge, and my suite is pretty basic, but it's easy. Close. And if I don't plan to stay long, it will do just fine. No need to look at apartments with distracting neighbors.

"Welcome back, Mr. Barnes." The woman behind the front desk smiles a little too eagerly as soon as the automatic doors *whoosh* closed behind me. "Can I interest you in a turn-down service?"

The glint in her eyes promises more than just a turn-down service.

"No, thanks."

I'm pretty sure this is the same woman who fell all over herself this morning when I picked up an extra key to replace the one I somehow already lost. She's not in her work uniform now, something I only notice as she—*oh, jeez*—steps out from behind the desk in some kind of minidress.

I pull out my phone—always a good distraction. Appear busy. Disinterested. Don't make eye contact. Usually, women take the hint.

Or not. Her heels click behind me as I make my way to the bank of elevators.

"Or maybe a drink?" she offers, her voice low.

"I'm good."

"Good? I could make you *better*."

I don't give her the satisfaction of a glance. Instead, I push through the door to the stairwell and start up at a jog. She won't follow me, but she might beat me up if she's persistent enough to take the elevator. And sadly, I know from experience, some of these kinds of fans are.

I move into a sprint, stopping at the next floor to push the elevator button, which might slow her down if she did try to follow.

Three more flights and I'm panting when I swipe my keycard, thankfully finding the small suite empty. I stick the *Do Not Disturb* sign on the door before engaging the safety lock.

I don't take chances. Not when it comes to female hockey fans.

Not *fans*—I don't want to disparage the women who truly enjoy the sport. I like *them*. But I can't stand the obsessive and aggressive fans more into the players than hockey. The ones who are in every city, slinking their way into our events and even into our hotels.

Toeing off my shoes, I collapse on the bed and pull out my phone. There's a text from a number not in my contacts.

Unknown: This is Felix. We met today. Just wanted to say welcome to the team.

I plug in his name even as a few more texts pop up.

Felix: If you ever need a break from all the noise but don't want to be alone, text me.

Felix: Full disclosure—Parker told me to text you. I was planning to anyway, but now I feel like I have to say that she asked everyone. Prepare for your phone to blow up. You've been warned.

I appreciate his honesty, as well as his almost unheard-of use of punctuation. As well as his warning, which turns out to be timely. As I plug in my phone and turn it off, the screen is already exploding with texts.

Leave it to Parker. One thing that for sure hasn't changed is her habit of butting into my life. Like the way she used to give me critiques after every game. She was usually right too. Or the way she would tell me all the things wrong with girls I was dating. She was right about that too.

And as I fall asleep in the empty darkness of my hotel room, my screen lights up again and again with reminders that someone in this world actually cares about me.

Even if I don't deserve it.

CHAPTER 6

Logan

I WALK into the Summit the next day with my completed player profile in hand. Did I fill it out because I was afraid of what Parker might do if I didn't? No.

Did I do it just to have an excuse to stop by Parker's office after practice? I dare anyone to try and prove it.

"Knock, knock, *Boss*."

Parker glances up from her computer, sees me, and drops her phone. I try not to smile as she disappears under her desk. When her head pops back up, she looks flustered, but tries to hide it behind a smile.

"Barnes," she says, eyeing the paper in my hand while toying with a ring on her thumb. "Do you have something for me?"

I hold the profile out, then snatch it back when she reaches for it. "Will this get me out of dancing?"

"No promises. Did you mention that you hate dancing on your profile?"

The truth is—I *don't* hate dancing. I rarely dance, but only because that usually means being somewhere public. And being somewhere public means people are watching me, maybe even filming me. It's hard to let go and enjoy when that's on my mind.

But when I have had the opportunity, the same calm I feel on the ice settles over me when the music pulses loud and I'm able to let loose.

When I woke up far too early this morning, I caved and downloaded TikTok and got sucked into the Appies feed. It's surprisingly entertaining. I can see the stamp of Parker all over it—the creativity and the humor. Years ago, she was always making some kind of craft or project. Now, it seems she's turned that energy to social media.

While some of the videos are dancing, a lot of them are of the guys just lip syncing and there are a lot of them actually playing, sometimes with humorous sound clips over them from shows like *The Office* and *Schitt's Creek*.

Still. Getting sucked in to watching the videos doesn't mean I'm any more eager to be *in* them.

"It's more that I don't like being in the spotlight."

She tilts her head, studying me before dropping her gaze and clearing her throat. Her chair makes an unholy noise as she shifts.

I frown. Why hasn't she had this thing replaced? It's clearly a hazard.

"Logan, I hate to tell you this but you're a professional athlete," she says. "In case you missed it, your life *is* the spotlight."

I take a step closer to her desk, skimming a few of her sticky notes there, all of which seem to be related to video trends I don't know or particularly *want* to know. "I don't mind being in the spotlight for hockey. It's everything else I don't like. Like news stories and gossip sites spreading lies about me."

She goes still. The kind of still that makes me really look at her. Suddenly, she seems flustered. Or maybe nervous. Her pointer finger is still messing with the ring on her thumb, pushing these little beads around on it. She's avoiding eye contact, and her leg is bouncing under the desk.

Is she nervous? Did our dinner last night somehow make her uncomfortable? She seemed fine when I left, but now ... something is off.

Was it something I said?

Narrowing my eyes, I hold out the paper.

But I don't let go when she takes the other side. Parker tugs the paper. I hold tight. Blowing out a breath, she meets my gaze.

"Are you okay?" I ask.

Her laugh is totally fake. So is the smile she gives me right after. "Totes okay."

"Totes?"

Parker tugs the paper harder. I still don't let go.

"Just give me your profile, Barnes. The faster we get this done, the better."

When I don't loosen my grip, she drops her side of the paper and glares.

Yeah, well. Maybe I don't want *fast*. Not when it comes to Parker. I enjoy her company too much.

I always felt most like myself around her or Brandon— and *only* her and Brandon. Until I didn't. With Brandon anyway. Apparently, even after these years, I can still be myself with Parker.

Only now, there's the crackle and spark of something

new. Like the brief moment when I was tempted to kiss her last night.

That is new. And absolutely needs to be avoided at all costs.

For career reasons. And because I don't want to screw up things with the one person I actually enjoy being around. It would be wrong to start something with Parker when I plan to leave. I can't picture her as a casual dating kind of person.

In addition to all those very solid reasons, Brandon would track me down and murder me if I made any kind of move on his sister.

All the more reason I should drop the paper on her desk and head to the trainer's office to get my knee checked.

Instead, I drop into the chair across from Parker's desk, still clutching the paper. "Look. I get that this team is into social media and stuff. I'll do what I have to. But as much as possible, I'd prefer to be in the background."

Parker sighs, relaxing a little. "People are so excited you're here, Logan. They want to see you. It's good for the team. Good for the organization. Good for the town, who still claims you as its hero. The Harvest Hollow Happenings already has several posts with photos of you around town."

"The what?"

"Just this gossipy Instagram account and—you know what? Never mind. The point is—this could be good for you too if you want to capitalize on it. A lot of the Appies have gotten pretty sweet gigs usually not offered to guys in the AHL."

"I'm glad. But I don't need that."

Money isn't a worry for me.

"Playing nice here will also help you get back to the NHL faster," she says.

I'm not sure why I want to deny that this is my endgame.

I mean, who would choose the AHL over the NHL? But I still have trouble saying it out loud. Maybe because it's Parker, and already I'm feeling a surprising attachment to her.

One day is all it took for her to wiggle her way under my skin. Just like she did back then.

I stare at her across the desk—her big brown eyes, dark hair cascading over her shoulders, full lips pursed as we continue our silent standoff.

Okay, so NOT like back then.

I hold out the player profile again but still don't let go when she takes it. Parker glares. The paper starts to crumple a little.

"I don't want to make this a whole battle," she says. "But social media and team videos are in your contract. Trust me when I say fans want to see one of the NHL's best players drop onto our rink."

"*One* of the best?"

Parker rolls her eyes. "I said what I said. Don't get cocky."

"Is it cocky if it's true?"

"Shut up, Wolverine. Give me the paper like a good boy."

She yanks. I maintain my grip.

"Let's make a deal, Pete," I say. "Something I could do as a favor to you in order to stay in the background."

Parker goes completely still. It's almost creepy, like one of those moments in movies where all the animals in the woods stop making noise because something terrible is out there, poised to attack.

I frown. "What?"

"Nothing."

Parker lets go of the paper and pushes her chair back, putting more distance between us. The chair makes several loud popping sounds but, miraculously, it still doesn't break apart.

67

"Parker." She busies herself looking through a drawer, her dark hair falling over her cheek and hiding her expression. "It's not nothing. I may not have seen you for years, but I can still read you better than most people can."

I could swear she mutters *I hope not* under her breath. But then she slams the drawer, and swivels to face me again.

There's color in her cheeks, a cotton candy pink. She's chewing her lip. And her eyes are a little wild.

She looks adorable, but that's not why my heart is thudding like a kick drum in my chest. It's because I have a feeling that whatever she's about to say may not be something I want to hear.

"I might have a deal we could make," she says slowly. Carefully. The verbal equivalent of tip-toeing her way through a den of hibernating bears.

"I'm listening." Terrified, but listening.

Her gaze drops to the desk in front of her, and she starts fussing with the sticky notes, picking them up only to put them right back where they were. I reach out and cover one of her hands with mine. Her fingers are shaking a little, so I curl my hand fully around hers and squeeze.

"Tell me," I demand.

"I ... did a thing," she says, still not looking at me. "Which might possibly translate into a favor."

Well, *that* sounds ominous.

When she doesn't say another word, I give her fingers another squeeze. It's a simple physical contact, but I'm not inclined to let go.

"Twenty questions?"

Her eyes light up, and I see a flash of *then* Parker, back when this was a game she and Brandon and I played. Biting her lip again—this time around a smile—she nods eagerly.

"And if I guess it?" I ask.

Her gaze darts to the side and for a moment, she looks troubled. "If you correctly guess it, I'll do my best to minimize your video time *and* you don't have to be involved with my favor. Unless you want to."

"If I don't guess it?"

"You'll agree to it." Our eyes lock and hold. Hers are swimming with indecision. Nervousness. And … hope?

"No dancing videos?" I ask.

"I can't get you out of *everything*," Parker says. "But I promise I'll do my best to keep you in the background. To make you feel safe."

Safe. That word sends a strange rush through me. It's not like I actively fear much in my life. Even over-the-top fans, I can usually handle.

But I realize *safe* isn't something I usually feel. The mere idea creates a vacuum of longing inside my chest, like some black hole yawning and waiting to be filled. The only times I really felt safe in my life were with Brandon and Parker.

Until that, too, was ripped away by one overheard conversation I'd rather not think about right now.

"Deal," I say. "Question one: does the favor need to be me, specifically?"

If I'm not mistaken, the color in her cheeks deepens a little. "Yes."

Huh. Interesting. My brain scans for possibilities but I can't think of a single thing Parker would need only *me* for.

"Does it have to do with hockey?"

"No."

"Dancing?"

Hesitation. "No?"

"Yes or no, Pete."

She wrinkles her nose. "Dancing is … optional but not required."

This game was a lot easier back in the day when the answers were simpler. When I knew Parker better.

But even now, my ability to read her comes in handy. Something non-hockey with optional dancing. Something that has got her nervous and has to do with me. The last part is the one I'm struggling with.

"Does it involve dressing up?"

Bingo. She looks away from me, shifting in her chair, which groans.

"Yes," she says.

"And does it involve your family?"

She startles, the tiniest widening of her eyes and flex of her hand, still held in mine. "Yes."

Parker and Brandon grew up in the kind of house that could be featured in a show about extreme mansions. Set on a slope in the foothills, it has stellar views of Harvest Hollow. It boasts something like ten bedrooms and the same number of bathrooms. There was an indoor pool and sauna. A full tennis court on the leveled field below the house. I spent more time there than the two-bedroom apartment my mom and I shared that somehow always smelled like feet.

But their awesome house came with their parents. Parker and Brandon's mom was actually okay. Nice enough and friendly enough. Always busy, but with volunteer work rather than two jobs like my mom. Mrs. Douglas did keep my favorite snacks on hand. Always. Which is not nothing.

But their dad only barely tolerated my presence, probably because he didn't know just how much time I spent there. He was almost always at the office.

While I wouldn't call him cruel, he was strict to the point of controlling, with sky-high expectations for both of his children.

And, as I found out the hard way, of their friends.

70

I clench my jaw, banishing that memory. I wonder how Mr. Douglas feels about Parker's current job? My guess: not great.

"Does it have to do with your dad?"

More fidgeting. And this time, a nod.

I'm in the right neighborhood but I'm stumped. I can't possibly imagine what would make Parker nervous, have to do with her dad, and involve optional dancing. My brow is still furrowed as I try to think of my next question.

But it turns out I don't need to.

Looking as stricken as if she's confessing to murder, Parker blurts out, "I told a lie about you. I told a lie and I'm sorry because you just said you hate lies."

I do hate that. But it's different when it's Parker. I know instinctively that any lie she might tell about me wouldn't be to hurt me. Even with this agreement notwithstanding, I know she'd do her best to make me feel safe in anything we film.

So, I'm not scared of this lie. Not angry. More curious than anything.

"Just tell me, Pete."

Squeezing her eyes closed, Parker grips the edge of her desk and says, "I told my dad I was bringing you as my date to his birthday gala."

CHAPTER 7

Parker

WELL, that could have gone worse.

Logan could have laughed in my face. He could have looked disgusted. Or said he finds me so unattractive that he couldn't imagine going on a date with me.

Those are responses I might not have recovered from. I would have ducked under my desk, curled up into a ball, and promptly died if Logan did any of those things. My successor would move into my office and have to use my bones as a footstool.

So, see? It could have gone worse.

But it did not exactly go swimmingly.

"Let me get this straight," Mia says, setting her wine glass down and looking a little too amused. "Logan didn't say a word?"

"Not a single one." I take a sip of my root beer, the only

kind of beer I like. Mulligan's has it on tap, which is why I always insist on coming to this sports bar near the stadium instead of the fancier bars Mia prefers.

"And he just ... got up and left your office?" she asks.

"He did."

"And he's avoided you ever since?"

"I mean, I wouldn't say avoided. He's busy. I'm busy. And it's only been a day, so ... yeah. Fine. He's avoiding me."

My best friend stares at me, and I think she's trying to decide if she's allowed to laugh, or if she has to pretend this isn't hilarious. She must really feel sorry for my humiliation because she doesn't laugh, though she does use her wineglass to hide her smile.

I bet if *she* were the one to ask Logan, he would have said yes. No questions asked. With her modelesque height, dark hair, and bright blue eyes, Mia turns heads in every room. Even since we sat down a few minutes ago, I've seen several men trying to catch her eye.

Yep. If I looked like Mia, maybe things earlier would have gone down differently.

After seeing the blank look of shock on Logan's face when I confessed my lie, I got nervous and kept babbling. I was like some kind of old, rusty fountain that just kept spewing up junky water. I told Logan I wouldn't make him dance with me and promised to pay for his tux (which in all honesty, I can't really afford) and said it was a fake date anyway since I lied. And *then*, I said he'd be saving me from being set up with a guy who only liked me for my boobs.

I cringe now, just remembering that I actually said *boobs* to Logan. I swear when the word came out of my mouth, his eyes twitched and his face tensed, like he was trying to hold back a Pavlovian response to glance at my chest. To his credit, he kept his eyes locked on mine.

I ended the runaway mouth train by reminding him it was not a *real* date, just one night, and that it wasn't marriage.

Yes, I also said the word *marriage*. To a guy who hasn't agreed to go on one date that's not even a real date.

It was like I studied a primer on how to scare a guy off. I could star in the sequel to *How to Lose a Guy in Ten Days—How to Lose a Guy in Ten Seconds*.

Which was worse: talking about my boobs or mentioning the M-word?

Or lying in the first place when he said he hates people lying about him?

I'm honestly not sure.

I don't tell *all* of the embarrassing details to Mia, but it's like she *knows*. Probably because I can hide nothing from her.

She knows how I'm always about one breath away from dropping my practiced poise and slipping into an overflow of the mouth situation. She knows once I start, there's no stopping.

More than all this, Mia knows how I feel about Logan. How I've *always* felt about Logan.

Groaning, I drop my forehead to the table, which I realize too late is sticky. Oh, well. I've already touched down. Might as well stay. Story of my life.

"This is a huge mess," I mumble. "It's a terrible idea. Isn't it?"

Mia's tone softens. "I honestly don't know. I mean, part of me wants you to go for it. At the very least, it would help get Logan out of your system. Finally."

Do I *want* Logan out of my system? That's the question. I somehow doubt spending an evening with him as my date would do anything to quell my feelings. If anything, I might get *ideas*.

"But?"

"But you could also get hurt," Mia says. "Again. And it's been forever since you've dated anyone. Is Logan really the best option for dipping your toe back in the dating pool?"

She has a point. Dating has been difficult for years. And not just for the typical reasons dating can be hard when you're single in your twenties.

No, my reasons are ... unique.

And because our brains are *that* in sync, Mia steers the conversation right to those reasons.

"What if Logan does say yes? And you go and have a great time together. And then at the end of the night, he wants to kiss you?"

The mere idea of kissing Logan makes my entire body flush with heat. I keep my head pressed to the sticky table so Mia won't see my red cheeks.

"It's not a real date," I mumble. "There won't be any kissing."

"Uh huh. But your feelings are real. It would be easy for the lines to get blurry."

I sure hope *they will*, I think. *Blur away, lines!*

"They won't," I say out loud. "Logan dates actual models and people who look like models."

"You're a hottie, Parker. And you two have history, which counts for something. For the sake of argument, let's say the lines *do* get blurry." She pauses. "I'm sure Logan is used to kissing on dates."

At *least* kissing. But I don't want to think about whatever Logan does or doesn't do on his dates with women who may or may not be models.

But to Mia's point, most people would consider kissing at the end of a date normal. Fine. No big deal.

I'm not most people.

"Again, it's not a real date," I say. "There won't be blurred lines or kissing."

Mia's quiet, so I peel my forehead off the table to look at her. The expression on her face says she believes me about as much as I believe myself.

For ninety-nine-point-nine nine percent of twenty-five-year-old women, this whole concept would be a no-brainer. Kissing Logan Barnes would be a fantasy happily lived out.

Unless you're me.

Don't get me wrong—kissing Logan is absolutely a fantasy of mine. One I've had for more years than is healthy.

The issue is that up to this point, kissing *anyone at all* has remained a fantasy. And *only* a fantasy. Because I haven't kissed anyone. Ever.

Not a peck. Not more than a peck. Zero making out at all on my relationship resume.

That's why Mia's question matters.

"I don't know," I answer. Because I really don't know what I'd do if Logan wanted to kiss me.

It's not like I intended to be one of the last living kiss holdouts in the Western Hemisphere. Not kissing anyone wasn't a purposeful choice.

At first, anyway. I was a late bloomer and on top of that, consumed with figure skating for most of my teenage years. While every other girl I know (Mia included) was kissing boys at parties and going to school dances, I was at the rink, practicing. Competing. Traveling.

When I finally gave up on the dream that was never really mine, everyone had left me behind. Not having kissed anyone felt horribly embarrassing as a senior in high school. Like the worst kind of secret.

I had several *almost* kisses—and the experiences were so laughably bad, it almost turned me off on the whole idea.

When someone trying to kiss you suddenly projectile vomits, *barely* missing your face, it will do that to you. And that's just *one* bad story.

That ushered me into my anxiety era. I couldn't go on a date or even *look* at a cute guy without being cripplingly self-conscious about my lack of experience.

Stupid, I know. But no amount of looking back and telling yourself not to care about something can change the fact that you *did* care at the time. It ruined any date or relationship I tried to have through college. I couldn't enjoy a simple dinner with a guy or carry on casual conversation when worried about kissing.

I did the babbling thing times a trillion.

I scared off guys in droves.

It took time, but I dealt with my anxiety—thanks to some online therapy sessions—and made peace with my lack of kissing experience. My anxiety is mild and mostly centered around this one area. Though my therapist also pointed out some unhealthy things related to my dad and expectations that helped as well. My fidget ring helps whenever I'm feeling stressed or anxious. Not just about kissing but anything at all. It's very calming.

In any case, now I've reached the point where I'm more than fine with my choice—and it *is* a choice. I've waited this long, and I'm not willing to settle for just any old meeting of the mouths with a random dude.

But what I do know is that it will be with someone special.

Logan is special, a little voice in my head tells me.

And he *is*, for more reasons than just the whole famous athlete thing, which honestly, I don't care one lick about. Logan is special because he's always been special. Back then and now again. Still. Whatever. The way he still makes me

77

feel when we're together.

But it's not like I have any illusions of Logan sticking around Harvest Hollow. Or wanting something serious. And I'm not interested in casual. So ... yeah.

Kissing Logan is not the best idea to have floating around in my brain.

Mia, however, seems to have other ideas. "You could always ask him to be your kissing co—"

"Stop right there. If you're going to end that sentence saying *kissing coach*, our friendship is over."

Mia smirks. "I was going to say your kissing *cohort*."

Sure, she was.

"This is all a moot discussion since Logan basically ran away when I asked him about the gala. Which leaves me in a quandary. Because I'm *not* going to Dad's gala with Aaron Wagner."

Mia wrinkles her nose. "Gross. No."

"What should I do?" I whine.

"Despite my concerns, I think you should go for it with Logan. I think you should walk right up to him and demand an answer," she says.

I scoff. "Yeah, like that's so easy."

Mia tilts her wineglass toward something behind me. "It is, actually. Because Logan just came in with a bunch of guys from the team."

I whip my head around and yep—there's a conspicuously attractive group of men across the bar. Looks like Van, Eli, Felix, and Alec have brought Logan out. A tiny surge of motherly pride fills me. The guys are bringing Logan into the fold, exactly as I hoped they would.

I don't have time to revel in this because Logan's eyes meet mine across the crowded bar. I'm suddenly struggling to breathe. Without dropping my gaze, he stands.

"Looks like you won't have to go over there and demand an answer," Mia says, smiling smugly as she hops off her stool.

"No," I whisper, unable to look away from Logan's eyes until he's so close I can see the green of his irises. How are his eyes so *green?*

"Be right back," Mia says. "The bathroom is calling my name."

"Don't you dare leave me," I hiss, but she's already gone. I'm absolutely going to rescind her membership in my BFF club when she gets back.

Logan and I are still locked in what feels like an attempt at a Guinness World Record for longest eye contact. He slides onto the stool my ex best friend just vacated, looking comically large on it. Any second now, I expect the stool's legs to snap like toothpicks under the sheer mass of that big body.

"Pete," Logan says.

"Wolverine." I hope I'm exuding calm and control rather than the complete panic happening inside me. All I know is that I cannot let my mouth run away with my brain again.

The tiniest smile lifts one corner of his mouth. "Sorry about earlier." He shifts, finally breaking our marathon eye contact.

I exhale a long, slow breath, feeling like I've been released from a spell now that he's broken eye contact. Under the table, I spin the beads on my ring, letting the movement ground me in the moment.

"I'm the one who's sorry. I shouldn't have lied to my dad. It just sort of happened."

Logan traces a ring of condensation on the table. "I get it. Your dad can be pushy." He smiles. "And you tend to babble."

I gasp in mock outrage. "Do not!"

He doesn't even bother arguing back. "You caught me off guard with what you asked," he says. "I wasn't expecting it."

I snort. "That was obvious when you practically left tread marks on my floor peeling out of there so fast."

Chuckling lightly, he shakes his head. "You don't make it easy on a guy, do you?"

"No one has ever accused me of being easy."

Logan makes a choking sound, and only when I glance up and see the amusement on his face do I realize how that sounded.

I slap a hand over my eyes. "Oh, my gosh. Not easy like —*no*. That is *not* what I meant. Excuse me while I hide under the table."

I start to duck down, but Logan grabs my arm. "Pete," he says, lightly tugging me back up until I'm facing him again—him and his stupid, smug smile.

Ugh! Does he have to look attractive even when he's being impossible?

"I knew what you meant," he says.

"Good."

"And I'd be happy to go with you to your dad's birthday thing," Logan says, making my heart seize right up in my chest. He's still holding my arm loosely and, when I don't respond or move or even breathe, Logan frowns and gives me a little shake. "Are you still with me?"

"Yep. Still here. Just … trying to process."

"Did you really think I would say no to you?" he asks.

I shrug, trying not to get too used to the feeling of Logan's hand on my arm. But I'd *like* to get used to it—that's the problem. I'd like to get used to all of this—seeing Logan every day, having conversations with him, getting lost in his green eyes, seeing that sexy scar move when he smiles, and taking any old touch he'll give me.

But why exactly *is* he still touching me?

I tell myself not to read into this. Not to read into *any* of this. Not his touch. Not him saying yes. Not the two of us sitting at a table where it feels like the whole rest of the room has faded away.

"I definitely didn't get the impression you wanted to go with me when you ran away," I tell him.

"I didn't run away."

"You did. I thought maybe my deodorant failed or I had a whole head of spinach in my teeth—wait, is spinach sold in heads?"

"Nope. Spinach comes in bunches."

"Okay. I checked to see if I had a whole *bunch* of spinach in my teeth. I wondered if horns suddenly sprouted from my forehead or if I'd been diagnosed with a deadly and communicable disease and everyone but me got the memo."

Logan, bless his heart, is doing his very best not to laugh. It makes me more than a little happy to know I can crack the exterior of the man known for his intensity and seriousness.

"Wow. You were busy overthinking after I left."

"Very." I wiggle my straw, wishing I had more than just ice left in my glass. I could use a shot of liquid courage by way of more root beer right about now. "So, why *did* you panic? Was it because I said boobs? Or marriage? Or both?"

Great. Now I've said both words again.

But at least I didn't speak aloud the real question I have: Did you run because the idea of going on a date with me was so horrible?

Logan is full-on laughing now, covering his mouth. "Parker, you are something else, you know that?"

"I get that a lot."

His smile fades, and he studies me. I resist the urge to smooth down my hair or run my tongue over my teeth.

"Your dad won't like me going with you," Logan says, finally.

I frown. "Dad always liked you."

Didn't he? I honestly can't remember a single interaction between Dad and Logan. Mostly because my dad, despite being overly controlling, was rarely around.

Mom liked Logan. I know that. But why would Logan think my dad didn't like him?

"No," Logan says firmly. "He really didn't. And now, neither does Brandon. I'm assuming he'll be there?"

I nod, spinning my ring. "Maybe it will be a good thing? Y'all can clear the air and catch up?"

Logan's face indicates he doesn't agree.

Mia appears beside the table. "Hey, Logan. Good to see you again. I'm Mia, in case you don't remember after you left town without saying goodbye to anyone."

Speaking of not going easy.

I give Mia a look. She only shrugs.

Logan drops his hand from my arm—I miss it the moment he does—and shakes Mia's outstretched hand with an amused smile. "I remember you," he says, getting to his feet. "Good to see Parker has you to keep her out of trouble."

Mia takes back the stool Logan just vacated, shooting me a grin. "Keeping her out of trouble is too high a bar. I'm mostly just trying to keep her out of jail."

I cover my face with my hands. "I hate both of you."

"You love us," Mia says.

I shoot her a pointed look, because there is no good reason for her to mention the L-word in front of Logan. That's even worse than me talking about boobs and marriage! Mia is incurring some serious fines tonight for violating terms of our friendship agreement.

Logan brushes a hand over my shoulder in a way that

sends a thrill zipping down my spine. Then he leans down, his lips right next to my ear. That same feeling now shoots back up and makes my heart feel like it's going to burst.

"I'll call you soon to discuss our upcoming date."

I can't move for a solid ten seconds after Logan disappears, like his whispered words carried some kind of paralyzing agent, leaving me rooted in place.

Mia can't stop smiling, watching me while she sips her wine. "Seems like that went well. I take it he said yes?"

"He did."

"And how are those lines? Crisp and clear? Because from a purely observational standpoint, they seemed a little blurry to me."

"Shut up."

"I wonder how the other guys on the team will feel about this."

My eyes go wide. I didn't even *think* about the fact that so many of the Appies are right across the room. Watching me and Logan. Making who knows *what* kind of assumptions. Probably preparing a host of creative threats and punishments for Logan if he does anything to hurt me.

Working for the team is like acquiring a whole roster of protective older brothers. I may not have dated much since I've worked for the Appies, but I have no doubt if I did, the guy would have to deal with a whole slew of threats.

I already have a *real*, overprotective brother. Brandon is bad enough. And he will *hate* the idea of me bringing Logan to the gala. You know, because of the whole ten-year-grudge thing. I'm honestly surprised Dad hasn't told him yet. I'd know if he had because Brandon would be calling me in an instant to yell.

Mia takes another sip of wine, watching behind me. "Interesting."

"What are they doing?"

"Nothing." Mia gives a little shrug. "They're being totally normal."

That can't be right. I narrow my eyes. "No one's hitting him?"

"Nope."

"Or getting up in his face?"

"No."

"Felix isn't choking him?"

Mia blinks. "Is that something Felix would do? I thought he was the bookworm."

"He is. But it's the quiet ones you've got to watch out for," I tell her.

"They're *all* just sitting quietly." There's a loud cheer behind us, and I recognize several of the voices. "Okay, *not* quietly," Mia amends. "But they're only yelling at the TV, not at Logan." Her expression turns wistful. "Are you sure I'm not allowed to date any of them? I mean, if you're dating Logan ... "

"*Fake* dating. And no. Stay away. I know how this would go—badly. You'd date one of them, break up, and then I'd be stuck like a child in a custody battle. No dating hockey players."

"Who's dating hockey players?" Hazel asks, appearing behind Mia and dragging a stool over. Though we both went to Harvest High with Hazel, we only started hanging out a few months back after my car broke down. Hazel was the one who fixed it. With her petite frame and blond hair, she's smashing all the stereotypes of mechanics. She's awesome.

"No one," Mia and I say at the same time.

"Parker won't let me," Mia adds with a pout.

Hazel gives the hockey table behind me a quick perusal. "Am *I* allowed to date them?"

"Nope."

"Not even the dirty blond who's kind of bouncy?" She has to mean Eli. Smiling, Hazel adds, "He's like a human Tigger."

Definitely Eli. "Nope. Trust me when I say stay away."

"Even if he comes over here?" Hazel asks.

"Especially then."

Eli appears beside our table, and I sigh heavily.

"Hey, Boss," he says. "Good to see you, Mia. And you as well, beautiful stranger."

"This is Hazel, and she's my *friend*. Which means she's under my protection in case you get any bad ideas."

"I never have bad ideas," he says, still smiling at Hazel.

"You *only* have bad ideas," I mutter. But he and Hazel are swapping numbers.

Mia kicks me under the table after Eli bounces back to the hockey guys. "Now you owe me a hockey player if Hazel gets one."

"It doesn't work like that," I say.

"He probably won't ever call. Or text," Hazel says. "But he's still very pretty."

"Keep in mind that he's got the heart of a golden retriever puppy and is about as likely to commit to one woman as a puppy is not to chew up shoes."

"It's so unfair," Mia says. "Now you and Parker are dating hockey guys."

Hazel shakes her head. "Again, not dating. Just exchanged numbers." Then her eyes go wide and she swings her gaze to me. "Wait—you too? Which one?"

"Logan. And it's *fake* dating. It's a whole stupid thing." I briefly explain and try not to scream when she and Mia exchange a look when I'm done. That look says something like, *Suuuure it's fake. Suuuuure, you're not really interested in Logan.*

Mia sips her wine. "We were trying to figure out why the guys aren't giving Logan a hard time about it. Those guys treat her like royalty. I'm kind of disappointed no punches are being thrown."

"Oooh, I want to see punches thrown!" Hazel says. "I need the distraction."

Peeking over my shoulder, I see that Mia's right—everything looks totally fine and normal over there, like nothing's out of the ordinary.

And that's enough to have me worried.

CHAPTER 8

Logan

"Eyes up here, Barnes."

Eli elbows me under the table. I elbow him right back, then glance away from Parker's table. I thought after I came back to the table, they'd give me a hard time. Surprisingly, they didn't. Other than now. But Eli's comment is nothing.

I'm still trying to decide how I walked over there and said yes to a date I know is a bad idea waiting to happen. I glance over there again. The three women are laughing. I find myself fascinated by the way Parker's hair moves when she laughs. Make this—a bad idea already happening.

I turn my attention to Eli. I need to stop thinking about Parker. "You're one to talk," I tell him. "I saw you got that woman's number. Parker's friend."

"Her name is Hazel." Eli grins and takes a sip of beer. "Too soon to text her?"

Alec snorts, then reaches out his hand and snaps his fingers. "Yes. Give me your phone."

I reach out to stop Eli, and the protective reaction shocks me so much, my hands clench. It's a small thing, trying to save Eli from doing something dumb. But I usually don't connect like this with my teammates. I don't get involved. I don't play around. I don't go out with them.

Alec grabs the phone and, muttering and shaking his head, starts tapping away. Yep. Definitely dumb.

"You trust him with that?" I ask Eli, taking a sip of my water. Most of the guys are nursing beers, but I don't like drinking during the season.

Eli shrugs. "He's the captain."

Though he doesn't look up from the phone, I see Alec's lip's quirk. "Thank you."

"But letting him have free reign over your phone is not a requirement," Felix says, then deftly plucks the phone from Alec's hands and hands it back to Eli.

"Hey!" Alec says.

"What did you do?" Nathan asks. The big guy hasn't said more than two sentences tonight—that being one of them.

"I deleted her number," Alec says casually.

"What?" Eli scrolls through his contacts frantically, down, then back up.

"Actually," Alec amends, "I kept it in there, but changed it to another woman's name. Figured I'd toss that needle right into your very plentiful haystack."

"That sounds way worse than what you mean," Felix says.

"I don't have that many women's numbers in here," Eli says, but he's still scrolling. "I'll just go get her number again ..." Eli trails off when he glances over.

My gaze follows. Parker is gone. The others too. I'm disappointed. And instantly concerned. Did they walk to

88

their cars together? Did they ride together or alone? Has the crime rate increased in Harvest Hollow? Does Parker know self-defense? Should I go out there?

I get to my feet. "I should call it a night too."

The guys exchange glances, then Alec grabs my shoulder. "Come talk to me first," he says. He starts toward the bathrooms.

I glance toward the door, which I really want to be walking through right now. "Fine."

Inside the bathroom, Alec washes his hands for at least a solid two minutes, using more soap that I used this morning in my shower.

"What did you want to talk about?" I ask, assuming it's either one of two things: some kind of warning about hockey or some kind of warning about Parker. Maybe both.

Alec tears off a piece of paper towel, then glances up at me with a smile. "Oh. You know what? I forgot. But while I've got you here, I did want to say I'm glad you came out tonight."

Surprisingly, I am too. "Yeah," I say, not sure what else to say.

"Hate to tell you, but you can't be the resident one-word-answer guy. We've got one of those."

"Nathan?"

"Yep. And Felix is a close runner up," Alec says. "This is his first time out with us."

"Really? Huh."

"I think he's got some kind of mystery girlfriend. We've never seen her, but he's always talking about someone named Ivy. Anyway. Good to have you."

I'm thinking about his words and his welcome. Alec, of all the guys on the team, is least likable, only because he's very into Alec. That said, he's surprisingly ego-less on the ice, which I can respect.

I sensed he was genuine when he said he's glad I came out. And I'm still getting over my surprise that I'm glad too.

I'm so distracted that I miss Alec giving me the slip in the crowd. Only when I get back to the table do I realize that the guys have all gone—and left me with their bill.

———

I think that's the end of it. The guys pretended not to give me a hard time about Parker, then stuck me with the bill. Not a big deal.

They're normal in the locker room before practice. Joking, laughter, insults—nothing out of the ordinary. It lulls me into a false sense of safety.

But it all stops the moment we hit the ice.

"Watch it, Barnes." The warning comes right before I'm slammed into the wall.

Which happens in practice. But it shouldn't happen again ten seconds later. And then again a third time.

The guys are hitting me hard in a drill that's no contact. Repeatedly. No smiles. No trash talk. Just narrowed, serious eyes and dirty hits.

When I'm not being knocked around, people are clipping my skates or slashing me with their sticks.

This isn't just about me being the new guy or they would have been doing this my first few practices. Nope—I know exactly what this is about. And her name is Parker.

Too bad they don't understand the situation, I think as Alec slams me into the wall, grinning as I wheeze out an *oomph*. I'd like to knock one of those perfect teeth out of his Disney prince smile.

They could have said something last night at the bar. I honestly expected them to interrogate me. But when I got back to the table after talking to Parker, nothing.

I did think it was a little odd, considering how protective I've seen them all act around her. Since I didn't exactly want to explain about our date—Non-date? Fake date?—I happily let it go and thought nothing of it.

Clearly, I underestimated them. Their silence was more like the ocean pulling back before a tsunami wave.

"It's not … what you think," I grunt when Nathan and Eli come at me from opposite sides at the same time.

But they're gone before I can say more. Then it's Dumbo, followed by Tucker. No one's really trying to injure me, but they're definitely making it impossible for me to be effective on the ice.

Coach Davis barks at us to stop messing around, but he doesn't actually do anything about it. Or seem to care. I even caught him smiling once before he schooled his features into a frown and pretended to look at his clipboard.

Does *he* know?

Truth be told, I knew I should say no to Parker. Saying yes even to get less screen time in videos is a bad idea. I have good reason not to muddy things between us with any kind of date, however platonic or fake she means it to be. Lots of good reasons actually.

Starting with her brother. Though I haven't talked to Brandon since I left town, I know it's only a matter of time before we cross paths. Now, I know we will at their father's birthday if not before. The last thing I want is to give him one more reason to be angry with me.

He never needed to warn me away from Parker back in the day. She was too young for me to even think about it. Four years difference when you're in high school is a total no-go. Plus, I witnessed Brandon's wrath against any guy who dared look at Parker wrong. The few guys who had the poor sense to hurt her feelings? They *really* suffered. I got that message loud and clear without Brandon telling me to leave Parker alone.

Then there's the work thing. I saw how it went when guys on my last team dated a trainer or someone within the organization. After things ended—and they always ended—it made for awkwardness all around. You can't escape and are forced to look that person in the eye every day.

The biggest reason I should have said no has nothing to do with Brandon or my teammates or anything else. I should have said no because I *wanted* to say yes. And wanting Parker is perhaps the most dangerous thing I can think of.

So, why did I walk across the bar last night and tell her yes?

That's something I'd rather not examine too closely.

I survive practice, and the guys are all smiles again in the locker room. Honestly, I expected worse. But when I return from the shower, I see that they weren't quite done.

I sigh and turn to the locker room, where the guys are very conspicuously quiet.

"I got the message," I announce. "Loud and clear. Now, where are my clothes?"

No one looks at me. But there are quiet snickers, and a few guys are suddenly very interested in their phones.

Only Van steps up in front of me, arms crossed over his tattooed chest. "And what's the message?"

"If I do anything to mess with Parker—"

"Anything at *all*."

Shockingly, that comes from Felix—the only one who didn't physically come after me today. I thought maybe it meant he's on my side, but now I realize it was probably just because he was in the goal.

I hold up both hands. "I'm just going with her to a family thing. It's not really even a real date."

Is it?

I'm honestly not sure *what* it is. She called it fake. A favor. We'll stick with that. Because the idea of going on a *real* date with Parker makes me feel unsettled. There's a very real spark of attraction I've felt between us, which I'd rather not acknowledge and definitely shouldn't encourage.

"Why'd she pick you?" Van asks.

"Probably because I've known Parker since we were kids," I say.

The whole locker room goes quiet for a few seconds as the guys process this. I wasn't sure until just now if Parker had told them. Apparently not. I don't know if this information is going to help or hurt.

"Her brother was my best friend growing up," I continue.

"You know Brandon?" Eli asks, looking shocked.

It's obvious by his tone that Eli *also* knows Brandon, who also must not have mentioned knowing me. Otherwise, Eli's welcome probably wouldn't have been so warm when I first got here. I doubt Brandon would paint me in the best light after the way I left.

But then, he doesn't know his own role in why I took off.

Of all my life's regrets—and there are many—ditching Brandon and, by extension, Parker tops the list. At the time, in all my eighteen-year-old maturity, it seemed like the best option. The *only* option.

Now, looking back, I would have chosen differently.

"Brandon and I were best friends and teammates back in the day. We fell out of touch when I went pro." True enough. Even if it's not the whole story. "Trust me—If I did anything to Parker, Brandon would kill me before any of you had a chance."

"Yeah?" Van says. "Well, we'd find a way to bring you back just so we could kill you again."

"And we'd enjoy it," Alec says, the glint in his eyes making me wonder if his shiny outside disguises a very dark inside.

"Noted," I say. "Now, where are my clothes?"

A ball of fabric hits me in the chest, and no one bothers hiding their laughter now as I look at what are not, in fact, my clothes.

"You've got to be kidding me," I say.

Van claps a hand on my shoulder and squeezes a little too hard. "When it comes to the Boss, we are *deadly* serious."

I hold up the crop top and spandex biker shorts, wondering how fast I can make it to my car at a dead sprint.

Fast, it turns out. But not fast enough to miss a lot of snickers and stares. I've never been more grateful that I keep a change of clothes in the back of my SUV. I'm also especially glad my windows are tinted enough to allow me to change in the backseat. The last thing I want is to have to walk in the hotel wearing spandex and a crop top.

By the time I finally get there, I'm exhausted. Physically. Emotionally. Ready for sleep and some quiet.

But the moment I open the door to my hotel suite, I sense something off. An unfamiliar scent, sweet and cloying, hits me first. And something's wrong with the lights. They're … flickering.

I blame exhaustion for it taking longer than it should for me to realize the flickering lights are candles. And the scent must be coming from the woman stretched out on my bed, thankfully under the covers because her bare shoulders suggest she's not clothed.

It takes me another few seconds to recognize the woman who hit on me my very first night here, the one who works at the front desk and clearly can get access to my room anytime she wants.

"Hello, Logan," she says, her voice grating. "Thought I could offer a little distraction after a long day of practice."

Nope.

I'm back out the door almost before she finishes her sentence. My feet are anything but slow as I pound back down the stairs to the lobby, where I locate the manager and then pull out my phone, texting the only person I can think of right now.

———

Felix's place isn't what I expected. Located on the second floor of an older warehouse building, it looks sketchy at best.

Like I might need a tetanus booster at worst.

He texted me a code to get into the building and once inside, I climb a staircase leading up to a hallway with two big metal sliding doors. I knock on the closest one, and it slides open to reveal a woman with long, brown hair and a weary look of resignation.

I take a big step back. After the events of my night, better safe than sorry. "Uh, I'm looking for Felix?"

"Hockey players belong over there." She points to the other door, then gestures to her own with a smirk. "This? This is a sports-free zone."

The second door slides open and Felix steps outside. He smiles warmly at the woman, who narrows her eyes. But I notice she's still smiling. Just a little.

"Sorry, Gracie," Felix says. "This is Logan. He'll be staying with me for a bit."

"Nice to meet you," I say.

Gracie eyes me. "Are you going to knock on my door at random hours and ask me out?"

I cast Felix a glance. He's chuckling, ducking his head and covering his mouth with his hand.

"Um, no?"

She nods. "Then I guess it's nice to meet you too."

"I liked the song you were playing earlier," Felix says. "Is that a new one?"

Gracie's cheeks flush the slightest bit. "Oh, um, thanks."

"If you ever want an audience, I'm right over here. Anytime." Felix hooks a thumb toward his open doorway.

"Thanks for the offer," Gracie mutters, her expression shifting. And then she's ducking back in her apartment and slamming the door.

"You want to explain that?" I ask.

"She's my neighbor," Felix says, waving me inside his door.

I walk inside. "I got that part. I was talking about the weird tension. And what's with her asking me if I'm going to ask her out."

He chuckles and closes the door. "Eli thinks she's hot, so he gets a kick out of knocking on her door 'by mistake.' I've tried to get him to stop but ... well, you can probably already guess how well Eli responds to firm commands. She hates hockey players, for reasons I can't figure out. Anyway, welcome."

If I was surprised by the less-than-impressive outside of the building, I'm stunned by the sleek, modern loft inside. It has high ceilings, an industrial vibe, and looks professionally decorated. And also very, very expensive.

"This place is ... wow. Thanks for letting me crash, man."

"No problem. Sounds like you needed a safe space." He

smirks. "I didn't light any candles to set the mood though. Hope that's okay,"

I huff out a laugh. "No candles. No mood setting. Please."

Laughing, he says, "Fine. No mood lighting. Follow me. You'll be sleeping back here."

Hopefully, Felix won't run his mouth to the rest of the team about what happened at the hotel tonight. I only told him because I wanted to make it clear how desperate I am to find somewhere else to stay—at least temporarily. Though the hotel fired the employee, I didn't feel okay staying there any longer. Too many people have easy access to me.

I follow Felix through the open concept living area, with tasteful throw rugs, a comfortable seating area, and an entire wall lined with bookshelves. There's even one of those ladders on wheels.

"What are the library hours?" I ask. "And do I need to apply for a card?"

Felix smiles. "My library is your library. But no dog-earing pages or breaking of spines."

I don't remember the last time I picked up a book, so he's got no worries there. It almost makes me want to, though. Or want some other hobby off the ice. Other than hockey, it's a little embarrassing how small my life is.

"Her name is Ivy," Felix says.

"Your library has a name?" I remember something Alec said the night before at the bar and laugh. "The guys think Ivy is your secret hook-up."

Felix only smiles. "I know. She's very convenient for getting me out of things I don't want to do. Ivy needs me to spend a lot of time with her."

Though I don't get the reading part, I can appreciate the genius of the idea.

As we walk through the rest of the loft, I'm a little awed.

The place is huge and it's high-end. Simple, but expensive. There's no way any player for the Appies could cover this kind of place on their salary. I'm curious but not about to ask personal details. Especially not when Felix is giving me a whole suite with a private bathroom for me. I'll just be thankful to have a comfortable place where I don't have to worry about finding a woman in my bed.

"There are fresh towels and, ah, toiletries or whatever in the bathroom," Felix says, for the first time looking slightly self-conscious.

"Thanks, man."

"I put a key on the dresser. And I place a grocery order once a week, which happens to be tomorrow. There's a remote for the TV next to the bed. Text me if you need anything." He knocks twice on the door frame and starts to leave the room.

"Felix," I call, and he pauses outside my room. "I appreciate it. I know you don't know me well. This means a lot."

"Shut up, Barnes. Or I'll have to tell the guys you've got a heart under there."

"Got it. And I'll be out of your hair soon."

"There's no rush. Stay as long as you like."

I don't doubt the sincerity in his offer. Felix is a solid guy, and he's obviously got the space for me. But I don't like needing people or being a burden. As soon as I can find another option, I'll be gone.

Felix's bulky form hovers in my doorway. As though he has an uncanny ability to follow my thoughts, he says, "One more thing—about Parker."

I swallow. "What about her?"

"I know you said you were friends back in the day. You seem to care about her." He assesses me for a moment, then runs a hand through his dark hair, tucking it behind his ears.

"Yeah," I say because I'm the genius who can't think of anything else to say.

"Just be careful. If you do anything to hurt Parker—intentionally or otherwise—I think you'll be dealing with a whole lot worse than wardrobe replacements."

I crack a smile. "Like knee replacements? Hip replacements?"

Felix does not smile back. Instead, he nods. "You're getting the picture."

Then he's gone, leaving me wondering if I should lock my door tonight. And maybe drag the chest of drawers in front of my door—just in case.

CHAPTER 9

Parker

He's like any other guy. Just another player.

Telling myself this doesn't ease my nerves as I wait for Logan in my office. Thankfully, I can distract myself by going over his player profile, which he filled out with as many one-word answers as he could. Nothing I didn't already know. Nothing I couldn't have found with a quick Google search online. I think his Wikipedia page is probably more detailed than what Logan wrote.

Getting Logan to talk about himself was always like trying to pull teeth ... from an angry dragon using a pair of chopsticks while wearing mittens. Guess he's still the king of deflection. Recording my normal player profile video is not going to work. I can tell.

Maybe I need to forget doing this the normal way. Thinking outside the box has served me well in this job. The player profile doesn't need to be a sit-down interview, even if that's what I did with most guys. One of the conference rooms upstairs has fabulous light and has worked really well for filming.

But for as long as I've known him, Logan always seems most like himself with a pair of skates on his feet. So, why not film on the ice?

It's perfect. I'm not sure why I never thought of it before. Probably because even the guys who are most introverted or who are the most closed off—hello, Nathan and Felix—gave me more in their profiles than Logan did. And because I'm still on an excited high from my genius idea, I make the mistake of answering my phone on speaker without looking at the caller ID.

"Glad you finally made time for my call." My dad's voice booms through my office, careening like a wrecking ball through the small space.

Is it possible to get instantaneous headaches? I think I just did.

"Dad. Hi."

"We need to finalize details for the gala."

I roll my eyes. Even though he can't see me, the small scoff I hear through the phone line makes me feel like somehow he *knows*.

"What details?" I ask.

"The details regarding your date. I spoke with the Wagners. Aaron was incredibly disappointed, to say the least."

"Then maybe you shouldn't have told him I'd go with him without asking me first."

"His father was also disappointed. And I don't need to tell you how close our families are."

Code for: how important the Wagners are to the company.

"Dad, I am not a puppet or a pawn. You can't use me to keep business partners happy or leverage whatever it is you're trying to leverage with the Wagners. It's like half a step above prostitution."

"Parker!" He sounds disgusted. Not half as disgusted as I feel whenever he does something like this.

"Dad, I will be at your birthday gala. With Logan."

He sighs heavily. But I can almost hear the sound of him regrouping, pulling up the next plan of attack in a file labeled How to Manipulate My Daughter.

"Fine. But coming with a date doesn't mean you can't dance with Aaron a few times."

"No."

"Why not? Surely, Logan Barnes"—I bristle at the condescension in my father's tone—"would be happy to share you."

So many layers of gross in that sentence. Practically a whole layer *cake* of yuck.

I don't bother trying to mask the anger in my voice. "I am not a toy to be shared or fought over. Not by you. Not by Aaron. Not by Logan. And the thing is—Logan knows that. He would *never* treat me this way."

Again, Dad blows right by my protests, and the thing is, I'm so used to it, I don't even flinch. I just keep leaning back in my about-to-break chair, wishing I could end this call. Wishing that ending this call would end this dynamic. But I know better.

"There will be a number of single women in attendance," Dad goes on. "From what *I've* read, Logan seems to enjoy their company very, very much."

The only thing worse than having to see Logan linked with women in the press over the years is to hear my father discuss it.

And whether it's the jealousy burning through me like a stream of liquid fire in my veins or the need to wiggle out from my father's grasp, I find myself clenching the arm of my chair and squeezing my eyes closed.

"Dad, I am not interested in dancing or anything else with Aaron. And Logan is not interested in the buffet of single women you're planning to parade before him."

"This way, everyone wins," Dad says, like he heard nothing I just said. He probably didn't. His ears are all clogged up with ego-wax. "You get to have your little rebellion date and I get to keep the Wagners satisfied."

"No," I say.

"Why not?"

"Why not?" I repeat, my voice pitching higher. Too high. But there's no calming down. I'm burning with an indignant rage. "*Why not* is because Logan isn't just coming as my date. *Definitely* not a rebellion date. He's coming as my boyfriend."

Well, now I've done it. I've shocked Don Douglas into silence. A silence so thick I finally open my eyes to make sure the phone call hasn't dropped.

Only, when my lids part and my eyes adjust, the very first thing I see is Logan leaning in the doorway.

Cold replaces the hot fire in my veins from moments ago. I am an ice sculpture, frozen solid in my uncomfortable office chair.

How much did he hear? *How. Much. Did. He. Hear?*

I jab the red button to end the call.

Then, slowly, I lift my eyes from my phone.

My gaze skims over my sticky-note-covered desk to Logan's arms, crossed over his chest. Up his thick neck, shaved close with barely a shadow of stubble. Past the scar leading from his chin to his firm, unsmiling mouth.

I swallow before I glance over the slightly crooked nose—

broken multiple times but fixed by good doctors—and finally, finally meet his eyes.

A cool green, the color of tropical seas tinged with sunlight, not the deep, rich green of fields or leaves.

I could play this off as a joke or make light of it. I could ask Logan how much he heard or just lay it all out there and explain how I'm still—as a twenty-something adult woman— a woman struggling to escape from underneath her father's controlling hand.

Instead, I just stare, losing myself in his cool, green eyes.

Until Logan raises one brow and speaks first. "Sounds like I got an upgrade. From fake date to fake boyfriend."

I groan and drop my head in my hands. "I didn't mean to throw you under the bus, Logan."

"In this analogy, are you the bus?"

I snort. "My father is always, *always* the bus."

"Oh, I remember very well."

I hear a shift, and without looking up, know Logan has taken the seat across the desk. I peek at him through my fingers. His elbows are propped on his knees, as he leans forward, hands clasped and his gaze pinned on me.

"What do you need from me?" he asks.

I blink. "What?"

Unlike Logan, whose emotions are kept in the equivalent of a mob boss's bank vault, mine are always right out there in front, flashing like a billboard in Times Square.

He must see the confusion on my face, even when only one of my eyeballs is visible, because he says, slower now, "Tell me how I can help with your dad."

Okay—*not* what I expected. While my mind is processing his words, I sit up, dropping my hands to my lap.

I stare. "You want to help with my dad?"

"I want to help *you*, Parker. I couldn't care less about your dad. No offense."

"None taken. Trust me," I mutter. "He is not my favorite person right now." Or most days, if I'm being honest.

Logan shrugs. "If you need me to be your boyfriend, I'll be your boyfriend."

I ball my hands into fists. Then I swallow. Then I remind myself to breathe. My mind has snagged on what Logan said.

If I need him ... to be my *boyfriend*. I really, really like the sound of that.

"Wow," Logan says. "I'm not sure I've ever seen you speechless, Douglas."

I'm not sure I've ever *been* speechless. My mom used to joke that I came out of the womb using fully formed sentences.

But then, I've never heard Logan tell me he'll be my boyfriend. Even if it's pretend.

He didn't say pretend, a naughty little voice in my mind says. *Not pretend or fake. Just ... boyfriend.*

I shut that voice down because whether Logan said *pretend* or not, there's no way he meant he would be my actual boyfriend. At most, he'd be on loan. A rental boyfriend. A temp. Just for the night.

Not *nearly* enough time. But you know what? I'll take one night of being Logan's fake girlfriend for a night than nothing at all.

"Still with me, Pete?" he asks.

"Sorry, it's just—you *want* to pretend to be my boyfriend at my dad's party?"

"I was going to be your date anyway," Logan says easily, like none of this is a big deal. "If you need me, I'll be your boyfriend."

Again, that same part of my brain notes the lack of the

words *pretend* or *fake*. My brain also really likes the phrase *if you need me*.

Oh, I NEED Logan.

"But," Logan continues, while I'm still floundering in fantasy land, "we will have to discuss how to handle this with the team. Because I don't want my clothes replaced with a crop top and biker shorts again."

"The guys did that?" I find myself biting back a smile.

"They did."

"Did anyone get any pictures?"

Logan gives me a mock glare. "Focus, Pete. How will this work? You're the queen of strategy. Do we tell everyone we're together? Is this just until after the party? Tell me how we do this without me getting hazed by the guys after I break your heart."

I snort. "You assume you'd be the one breaking my heart?"

He's right, of course. Anyone could take a look at the two of us and know exactly who would be the dumper and the dumpee in this non-real relationship. Might as well order the matching T-shirts right now. After all, he's already done it once. He has practice. That reminder is almost enough to sober me up. Almost.

Logan smiles and says, "You're right. It would totally be you breaking mine. You're way too good for me."

As if!

Before I can argue or say thanks or respond in any way at all, he continues. "But I think somehow the whole team of guys who call you Boss would still find a way to blame and punish me."

Logan doesn't say a thing about Brandon, but I know we're both thinking of him too. He would absolutely blame

Logan. No matter the circumstances. I shove my brother out of mind and out of this office. *No Brandons allowed!*

"You're right. They absolutely would." I sit up and grab a pink sticky note pad and a pen. "Okay, let's map this out."

Logan rubs his hands together, his eyes sparkling. "Oooh, we're bringing out the big guns now. Not just any sticky notes but the *pink* sticky notes."

"This conversation definitely requires the pink sticky notes. Okay, so—the guys already know we're going together to my dad's thing, right?"

"Hence the crop top. Yes."

I make a mental note to ask Eli if anyone got pictures of Logan in the aforementioned crop top. I'm in need of a new screen-lock image for my phone. I also like to keep things like that on hand just in case a little light blackmail is needed for any reason.

"Then let's keep it simple." I slap the first sticky note on my desk, facing Logan. It says: *Tell the team it's just one date.* "If we don't say anything else, they can go on thinking it's just the one event. They might never hear that you were my temporary boyfriend."

"That works," Logan says.

"As for the breakup after ..." I chew the cap of my pen for a moment.

Logan falls back in his seat dramatically. "One fake date and you're already wanting to break up? I'm crushed."

Oh, there is no way I'd want to break up after one date with Logan. Not in the real world.

But this isn't the real world. This is the plan-my-fake-date world. And a break-up is absolutely essential to this plan. The longer this kind of charade goes on, the more ideas I will get. And ideas are very, very bad where Logan is concerned.

"How about we amicably break up after my dad's gala? If anyone asks, we decided we're better off as friends."

"That works," Logan says, and I swallow down any disappointment that he's not arguing with me about being better off as friends.

Forget the lady doth protest too much. I need the Logan to doth protest more!

See? Already, I'm getting ideas. About a fictional breakup. With my fictional boyfriend.

I pull off the sticky note. I put it next to the first. It reads: *Friendly break-up after party. Stay friends.* "We'll part ways with a handshake," I suggest.

"Handshake, huh?"

"I mean, metaphorically speaking. We don't have to actually shake hands. It's more a figure of speech. But ..."

I pause, then write *Shake hands to end things* on another sticky note and pass it over.

"Hand shaking brings up a good point," Logan says.

He scratches his jaw, looking down at the sticky notes. Then he glances up, and I'm not prepared for the way he's looking at me. His eyes seem darker than they were a moment ago, yet somehow they still twinkle with mischief. His irises are the green of very, *very* bad decisions. My stomach tightens, caught somewhere between anxiety and excited anticipation.

Still, I'm wholly unprepared when Logan says, "We should discuss physical boundaries."

I drop my pen. Then I spend more time than necessary rooting around for it under my desk because I need my cheeks to cool down. My body apparently likes the idea of discussing physical boundaries. Maybe a little TOO much based on my flushed face and the way my pulse is erratically zooming through my veins.

Though I think it's more the idea of *physical* and less the idea of *boundaries* that my body is reacting to. My body is very happy to chuck boundaries right out of Harvest Hollow.

Which is *exactly* why boundaries are needed.

And, as positive as my physiological response is to this idea, my psychological response is weighed down by a lot more trepidation. Because this conversation is skirting pretty quickly toward the whole never-been-kissed territory. I would very much love to skirt very, very far away from this particular region. Perhaps to a whole other continent altogether.

"You okay down there?" Logan sounds far too amused.

My chair groans in protest as I straighten. "Yes. Fine. I'm good." I clear my throat, doing my level best to channel my most professional professionalism. "What do we need to discuss?"

"Just how we'll play this in public," Logan says.

"Okayyyy," I say.

"I mean, if you were my girlfriend ..."

Logan's gaze takes a slow tour of my face, then down my neck—veering back up just before it dips below my collarbone.

Aaron Wagners of the world, take note! A man does not have to have a staring contest with a woman's boobs to make her feel wanted. I feel more desired from one hot but PG-rated look from Logan than I *ever* have.

Not that Logan *desires* me.

I'm sure he's just, like ... scoping out the territory of his potential fake girlfriend. Or something.

"If you were my girlfriend," Logan says then, his voice gravely and low, "there would be a *lot* of physical contact."

I tap my pen on the sticky pad, trying to look serious and thoughtful. Like a scientist doing research. Not as though my insides are melting down like a nuclear reactor with an unstable core.

Is he *trying* to make me react? Logan *did* always like to tease me. Though it was nothing like this.

This feels less like teasing and more like ... flirting.

Wait—is Logan flirting with me?

Doesn't matter! It does not matter if he's flirting because this is serious, fake-dating business. Focus, Parker!

"What kind of physical contact do we need to discuss?" I am proud of how steady and even my voice is. My pen is poised over the sticky note, ready to write. Hopefully Logan doesn't notice how hard the tip is pressing into the paper. Or see straight through me to see how woefully little physical contact I've done in my life. "Maybe you should be specific so we can make an informed decision."

Logan's lips twitch in a half smile. "You want me to be specific about my physical contact with my girlfriends?"

I can't help it. I physically recoil. So much for poise.

"Ew—I mean, *no*. I don't need details about *that*." It takes great effort not to throw up in my mouth at the idea.

Logan laughs, and I want to punch him. "You look like you want to barf. Is the idea of getting physical with me so revolting?"

The opposite, actually. Thankfully, I've regained some small modicum of poise and don't blurt that out.

But not enough poise to keep me from saying, "No! Just the idea of you with all those women is ... unpleasant."

"Calm down. I didn't date *that* many women, Pete."

"Whatever." I wave a hand. "I don't want to talk about your dating history."

Your long *dating history. With women who are or look like models or actresses and make good eye candy.*

"Actually, there's not much to talk about." Logan crosses his arms over his chest.

I raise one eyebrow. An accusing one.

"Ah," he says, nodding. "You've seen pictures in the tabloids. And you assumed any woman photographed with me was *with* me."

"I try not to assume anything." But yes, actually, I did assume the pictures were telling a thousand words I didn't want to read *or* see. "Can we get back to our physical boundaries, please?"

"Absolutely. But, since you brought it up and seem bothered, I'd like to clear the air." Logan waits until my gaze snags on his before he continues. "You can't believe most of what you see or read in the gossip magazines. I really haven't dated all that much. And I've never had a serious girlfriend."

I wave a hand. "Don't care."

Oh, I care. A lot.

And I am more relieved than I'll ever admit knowing Logan wasn't really romantically involved with the women he's been pictured with over the years. At least, not *all* of them. Now I'd love to *never* talk about this subject again.

But Logan keeps going. "I actually haven't dated at all since my injury."

Though math is not my strong suit, I can math well enough to know that's around a year. Logan hasn't dated anyone in a year? For a hockey player, that's sort of like the equivalent of monkdom. Or something. And though it shouldn't matter anyway—because the past is the past and because Logan and I are discussing boundaries for *our* fake relationship—the knowledge makes me feel relieved.

"Good to know," I say. "I also haven't dated in ... a while." I'm not about to get into my string of dating disasters with Logan. Vague is the name of this game.

"Why don't we start with what you're comfortable with?" Logan suggests.

His voice has lost the teasing edge. Now it's almost tender. Which might be more my undoing than the flirty teasing one. Because Logan cares about what makes me comfortable.

Why is that so sexy? I mean, it should be like the lowest of all bars to set. But I've dated enough to know many men do NOT care about what makes their date comfortable. In fact, any time the conversation of physical stuff comes up— which it does for me more than most because of the whole kissing thing—most men run. Or are suddenly horrified.

Or feel the need to "solve" my lack of kissing experience by kissing me right then and there.

So, yeah—Logan actually asking about my boundaries even for a fake relationship is dead sexy to me.

"How about hand holding?" he asks.

"Sure," I say.

While my brain screams, *Yes!!! All the hands! All the holding!*

He points. "Don't forget to write it down."

"Right." I roll my eyes but had totally forgotten about the sticky notes while I was thinking about Logan's big hands. "There will be dancing," I tell him, keeping my eyes on the sticky note as I write *Hand holding—OK.* "I know how you feel about dancing, but—"

"I'd love to dance with you, Pete."

Ugh. Logan really needs to stop saying things like that. And we *really* need to finish and get out of my cramped office before I do something stupid like launch myself over my desk and into Logan's lap.

THAT is definitely not getting written on a sticky note. But I make a mental note: *No throwing myself into Logan's lap.*

"So ... dance touching?" I suggest. When Logan's eyes

gleam with amusement, I stare pointedly. "As in, the kind of touching appropriate while dancing at an event with my *father* present."

He grimaces. "Fine. Appropriate dance touching. What if I put my arm around your shoulders? Or around your waist? Not while dancing. Just ... whenever."

Any time. Any place.

"Fine," I say.

"How about hugs?"

"Sure."

Sure, as in PLEASE let there be lots of hugging.

I keep my head bent as I write, trying to avoid Logan's gaze lest he see all the things I'm feeling broadcast on my face. I move on to the next sticky note.

Who knew we'd need multiple sticky notes to discuss physical boundaries for a fake relationship?

Or that thinking about the most innocent touches from Logan could get me so flustered?

"What about kissing?" he asks.

I knew we might end up here. I did.

But it doesn't stop my pen from jerking across the paper, leaving an ugly line. I rip that sticky note off, ball it up, and toss it in the trash.

"I think that would be a good line to draw," I say carefully, still not looking at Logan.

"A good line as in, yes to kissing? Or as in, no to kissing?"

"No kissing." My voice is firm.

"Not even on the cheek? Forehead? Your hand?"

Every place Logan names suddenly flares with heat, as though his words are enough to create the sensation of his lips pressed to my skin. I'd like to sprawl out on the center of the rink to cool off.

"Fine," I say. "But no kissing on the lips."

113

I pull off the last sticky note, which reads *No kissing on the lips*, and stand. Logan stands too, and I take each sticky note and press them one by one to his chest.

"These will self-destruct in two minutes." I pat his chest for emphasis. And also because it's a very nice chest and I'd like to pat it.

"Noted."

It's long past time for us to record Logan's player profile, so I start toward the door.

"What if," Logan says, moving to block me when I try to step past him, "we *need* to kiss? Like, for the sake of believability?" The teasing note is back in his voice.

"We won't."

I step to the other side, and Logan swerves in front of me again, this time taking me by the arms. Not roughly. But enough to keep me in place.

"But what if we do?" he presses, one side of his mouth curling up.

I wish I also felt the same lightness about this conversation. Instead, I feel the dramatic ticking of some giant doomsday clock. Because we have now entered the talking-about-kissing zone.

"I can't think of any reason we'd need to kiss on the lips, Logan."

"Maybe not a need. But what if it's a *want?*"

This man has zero idea what he's doing to me right now. The closeness of his chest to mine. His strong hands lightly gripping my arms. The flirty tone. The whole topic of this conversation.

The idea of kissing Logan, which obviously, I have obsessively fantasized about since about the time kissing started to sound appealing instead of disgusting.

Essentially, for the last fifteen or so *years*.

I make a scoffing sound and do not meet his eyes. "You're assuming I'd want to kiss you."

"No," he says. "I didn't mean you."

This takes my poor, overstimulated brain a moment to process.

Logan's teasing. I know he's teasing. (Or flirting?) But he is also talking about wanting to kiss me.

I am no longer able to hold my words back, the ones that have been rising to the surface like bubbles in a pot of boiling water.

Jerking myself out of Logan's grasp, I meet his gaze, bracing for impact. "There will be no kissing, Logan. Because my first kiss isn't going to be with someone I'm fake dating."

CHAPTER 10

Logan

PARKER'S PHONE partially obscures her face as she skates backwards in front of me around the rink, filming. "If you could only eat one food for the rest of your life?"

I don't answer right away. Because I'm having a hard time focusing on the questions when I'm still thinking about the last thing Parker said before we left her office.

"Favorite food," Parker says. "Come on, Logan. Stick with me here."

Oh, I'm *with* her. I'm just not at all thinking about my favorite foods. Who cares about food?

What I want to know is how could Parker have made it this long without kissing someone?

Someone so beautiful. So kind. So vibrant and fun. Any one of the guys on the team would probably kiss her.

THAT thought has my ankles wobbling. Not for the first time since we got out here.

No—better not to think about Parker kissing one of the guys. Not if I don't want to get kicked off the team for punching someone in the throat. The force of my reaction surprises me. Jealousy is a new emotion. One I'm still not used to.

"Logan." Parker sounds exasperated now. "Pick a food."

"I don't like any one food enough to eat it forever."

"Fine, Mr. Commitment Issues."

"I don't have commitment issues," I snap.

Parker raises one eyebrow. The corner of her mouth lifts. "Sure, you don't."

Fine. Maybe I have commitment issues. Or maybe it's that no one in my life has ever been committed to me. And I've never had anyone I felt was worth me committing to them.

But even as I think that, I meet Parker's gaze, those brown eyes bright and curious. Probably wondering why I'm being such a jerk. Or maybe wondering what I think about what she said. She didn't give me a chance to respond. Did she want me to respond?

After teasing her about kissing, did I make it worse by saying nothing?

I wasn't sure how exactly to react after Parker shocked me, then ran from her office, calling "Suit up, buttercup. We're going skating."

When I stepped on the ice, meeting a waiting Parker with her phone already out, my ankles wobbled. *Wobbled.* Like some kid who just laced up his first pair of rental skates.

Now, we're skating in circles, with her asking me ridiculous questions like this when all I want is to demand other answers. And it's taking all my energy to keep the tension in my body from snapping me in half.

Why is this affecting me like this? I can't explain it. I just know that I can't stop thinking about it. And how bad I feel about teasing Parker until she had to tell me. So, if I'm mad —it's all directed at myself for pushing her into a corner.

"Fine. You don't have to eat one food for *every* meal," she says. "What's a food you could eat at least once a day?"

"Pizza," I say.

"Solid choice. Toppings?"

"Cheese. And olives if I'm feeling fancy."

She grins. "Olives are your idea of fancy, Barnes?"

I find myself cracking a smile. As usual, Parker is the sun banishing even my darkest clouds. "They're my idea of *pizza* fancy."

"What's your idea of fancy aside from pizza?"

"I'm *not* fancy aside from pizza."

Parker laughs, and the mere fact that I can make her laugh has me grinning right back at her. A little of the tension eases from my shoulders. And a little more as I unclench my fists.

"So, olives on pizza and wearing suits on game day are the only times you're fancy?" she asks.

"Pretty much."

She taps her phone. Probably stopping and starting another video. "What's your idea of a perfect night?"

This sounds very close to asking about a perfect date. Which makes my mind circle back to our earlier conversation. And the sticky notes, which are now fixed to the back of my locker. The rules for our date—or our relationship.

But Parker asked about my perfect *night*, not *date*.

"On a perfect night, I'd have a game—and we'd win, of course."

"Of course. A game and a hat trick?"

"I'll always be happy with a hat trick."

"And after?" she asks.

"I'd go home. With pizza—olives optional." This makes her grin. And her smile makes warmth spread through my chest. "And sitting on the couch in sweats watching footage or TV."

Something I've done almost every night with Felix since I moved in. He and I have fallen into a pretty easy routine. We don't ride to practice together but hang out at night. Watching Sports Center, while he also reads a book. In the mornings, we have coffee and protein. It's almost ... domestic.

So much so that I was almost tempted to take him up on his offer and stay. But I won't be a burden, and I know from experience, the longer time goes on, the more likely this will be the case. Plus, I have an even better place to move into with the best location I could ask for.

Do I still think it's a bad idea to move next door to Parker? Probably. But I find that I just don't care. I like the idea of being closer to her, and I'm not going to examine it too hard.

"Any particular show you binge to unwind?" Parker asks.

"*Downton Abbey*."

Parker laughs so hard she fumbles her phone. I zip forward, catching it before it hits the ice. The phone has a sturdy case—a sturdy *pink* case. Because of course it does.

When we were younger, there was one shade she used to insist was called Parker Pink. The memory makes me smile now.

I hand her back the phone, our fingers brushing. She's still laughing, and the sound of it loosens me up even more.

"*Downton Abbey*, Logan?" she says. "Really?"

"Can't a man like *Downton Abbey*?"

"A man can absolutely like *Downton Abbey*. I just didn't expect *you* to like it." She pauses. "Do you even know what the show is about?"

"A woman named Abby? Who lives down ... ton?"

Parker smacks my arm, but she's grinning. "Logan! You're the worst. You know that?"

"I do."

She messes with her phone for a moment, not looking at me. I allow my gaze to fall on her lips, thinking. Too much thinking. It's like Parker mentioning not kissing has everything in me laser focused only on that.

I really *am* the worst.

She looks up, and I'm glad I'm not still watching her mouth. "For the next questions, how about we try with you skating backwards and me following you."

I pick up speed before spinning to face Parker. She has no trouble keeping up with me.

"So, you still skate?" I ask.

She rolls her eyes. "*Obviously*. I stopped competing years ago. But I get out here when I can."

"Do you miss it?"

"Figure skating?" She makes a face. "Not really. I never wanted to be a figure skater. Though I *am* competitive, so once I got into it, I was all in."

I remember seeing Parker come home from practice, exhausted but glowing and happy. Every so often, we'd be at the rink at the same time, but I wasn't super into watching figure skating then.

Now, I wish I had. I wish I'd paid attention to her practicing on the other side of the rink while we were lacing up. I wish I'd gone with Brandon to see her compete. He invited me a few times. It was obvious his parents made him go, and it wasn't where I wanted to spend my time.

Meanwhile Parker was at every one of our games that I can remember, cheering and trash talking and wearing Brandon's jersey, screaming for us both.

I'm filled with a sudden urge to see Parker wearing *my* jersey.

"I actually wanted to play hockey," she says, a little shyly.

"Really? Why didn't you?"

Her grin is more sad than happy. "My dad."

"Ah."

"How does he feel about you working for the Appies?"

"Hey—who's asking the questions here?" she teases.

"It seems only fair I get a few," I say.

"Fine. We can trade off. Question for a question. You can start, since I've already asked a bunch."

My heart is suddenly beating in my throat, questions like some mob of noisy birds in my head. I spin around, then fall back until Parker and I are skating side by side, stride to stride. I take the outside since my legs are longer, though she hardly seems winded.

"You can go first," I tell her, unable to settle on one thing. Other than the one question I don't know if I should ask about why—or how—she hasn't kissed anyone.

"What's your ideal vacation?"

"I've always wanted to go to Banff," I tell her.

"You've still never been?" she asks softly. "I figured you would have."

She remembers. Of course, she remembers. That's Parker for you.

I shake my head. "I work too much, take off too little. Did you ever get to Bermuda?" I ask.

"Nope," she says. "Still on the bucket list though."

I don't know how we ever got to talking about this back in the day, only that we did. Parker always went on and on about Bermuda—going on about the sun and the colorful houses and British accents—while I wished for mountains and snow and wilderness.

The difference was—her parents could have taken her to Bermuda. If they wanted. My mom barely made rent. The first and last vacation I ever took was my second year going pro. Some of my teammates and I went to this upscale all-inclusive place in Mexico.

I hated it. Too loud. Too hot. Too many people.

"Why didn't you say goodbye when you left?"

The question comes out of nowhere like a battering ram to the sternum. It takes me a moment to find my breath.

At least she didn't go for the bigger question, the one I want to answer even less than this one. This one, I can do.

"I was a punk kid. Hockey was my way out of a place and a life I hated." I don't miss the way she winces at that. "Mostly hated."

"There were some good things." Her soft words are halfway between a statement and a question.

"You were a good thing. You and Brandon."

"But you left us too."

My throat feels thick talking about it, but at the same time, it's a relief. Like draining some festering wound. Doesn't feel good, but letting it out will feel better. Maybe.

"I'm sorry, Parker. If I could do it again, if I could go back and knock sense into my eighteen-year-old self, I would."

She snorts at this. "I'd like to take a crack at him too."

"He deserves it."

"Why haven't you ever kissed anyone?"

Parker sucks in a breath, glances at me quickly, then away. She shoves her phone into some hidden pocket in her leggings. I figured I'd ask this like ripping off a band-aid. But I immediately feel bad.

"Guess this is fair play after my question, huh?"

"You don't have to answer. I shouldn't—I mean, it's not my business. And it's fine. Like, no judgment. I just ... I'm curious." I sound lame. I feel lame. But I also really want to know.

Parker picks up the pace, and I match her speed, wondering if she even noticed. "It wasn't on purpose," she says. "At least, not at first."

I stay quiet through her pause, afraid if I speak, she won't finish.

"Basically, my teenage years were all figure skating, all the time. Practice, school, more practice, competitions, repeat. I didn't have time for anything else. By the time I quit, it was like I was years behind everyone else. It was awkward. *I* was awkward."

"I doubt that," I say, nudging her with my elbow.

This earns me a grin. "Yeah, well. It's true. The older I got, the more it became a thing—in my head anyway. I was terrified of looking dumb or doing it wrong or of someone finding out and making fun of me. It sounds silly now," she says with a shake of her head. "But you know how high school was."

"Dumb."

She laughs. "Yep. I did have some *almost* kisses. They were"—her lip curls— "very, very bad experiences. Laughably, horribly bad."

"Like?"

"Nope. I'm still on your first question. Those are stories for another day. After that, I actually started dealing with some anxiety. About that, but other stuff too."

I try to picture bright, sunshiny Parker struggling with anxiety. It's hard to imagine. But then, I remember what she said about being competitive. And her dad was constantly pressuring her and Brandon. So, okay, yeah—I can see it.

"Anyway, it got to where in college, I didn't date at all because I was too anxious about the whole thing. That ring I usually wear? It's a fidget ring. A lot of people with ADHD use them, but it helped me too. Breathing exercises stress me out, and the therapist I saw for a bit recommended the ring or something like it."

I'm sort of blown away by her honesty. But then, Parker was always braver than me. She spills secrets like they're pennies cast into a fountain to make wishes on.

"I don't have, like, full-blown anxiety or anything," she says. "Not like some people do. Thankfully, mine is mild. But dealing with it still helped me kind of own the fact that I hadn't kissed someone. Now, I don't see it as an issue. I see it as a gift. Don't laugh, Logan."

I frown. She thinks I would laugh at her about this?

"I'm not. I wasn't. I would never."

Parker shoots me a sidelong glance, as though assessing the truth in my statement. She must see that I mean my words, because she goes on.

"I figure by this time, it's a choice. My choice. I get to decide who to give this kiss to." She laughs a little. "That sounds pretentious, like it's some hot commodity every guy would want."

She has no idea.

"I mean, I still won't know what I'm doing. And if I think about it too hard, I start to freak out a little. Just, like, the mechanics of it."

Now my brain is thinking about the mechanics of kissing Parker. Of *showing her* the mechanics.

Waving a hand, she says, "Whatever. That's enough kiss talk. But that's why it's off the table for … this. When I kiss someone, it will be for real. Now you know way more than you wanted to. I hope you're happy."

I don't know what I am. I do know I feel lighter than I did at the start of the night. The anger with myself or the world has fizzled. And I've got the natural high that seems to occur only when I'm around Parker.

Without thinking it through, I speed up, then slice to a stop in front of her. She does a neat little spin and stops too, hands on her hips.

"What? You've got a look."

"No look."

Parker's cheeks are pink. I wonder if it's the exercise or the conversation. Maybe both. When I say nothing, she slides her phone out of her pocket and swipes it open, making a face.

"For a man who doesn't like the interviews, you did great."

"Maybe it's all in the person asking the questions."

I swear the color in her cheeks deepens to Parker Pink. "But good answers means a lot of editing work cut out for me. A good problem to have. This will get broken down into a bunch of videos for TikTok, Facebook, and Instagram, then one longer video for YouTube."

"Do you have to do that tonight?" Disappointment makes my shoulders fall.

It's late. I don't like the idea of her working here alone. I'm also not ready for the night to be over.

"I probably should," she says. "Why?"

"I've got another idea." Before I can rethink or *over*think it, I hold out my hand. "Skate with me?"

CHAPTER 11

Parker

Young Parker is squealing and jumping up and down on her bed. Heart emojis are exploding out of her head as though from a geyser.

Because *Logan Barnes asked to skate with me!!!*

The Now Parker manages a smile with zero squealing. My eyes do *not* contain little red hearts. They're just plain brown eyes as I look at him calmly.

"Why, Logan Barnes, I would be honored to skate with you."

Trying to play it cool like this moment isn't the pinnacle of my life, I slip my phone in my pocket and slide my hand into Logan's.

"You're cold," he says, frowning and giving my hand a squeeze.

His fingers are warmer than mine, which are, admittedly, starting to feel like little ice sticks. Sometimes I wear gloves —fingerless if I'm filming and need to touch the phone screen—but I didn't think about it today. I also didn't plan to be here this long. But I'm not about to turn down skating longer with Logan.

I will turn into a solid ice cube if it means more time with him.

"I'm fine."

Logan only grumbles at this, closing his hand fully around mine.

Bliss! This moment is pure bliss!

The first few laps, we skate in silence. It takes a bit of time to adjust my stride to Logan's. Or, maybe for us to adjust to each other. It was easier when we were just skating beside each other. I know Logan's going slower than his typical speed. Not that I'm slow. But the man is a good head and shoulders taller than I am, so of course, his natural stride is longer.

Maybe it should feel weird to skate around the rink holding Logan's hand, but it absolutely doesn't. Even if this is the first time I've held hands with someone while ice skating.

And not just any someone—with Logan. My childhood crush. My teenage dream. My now … I don't know.

The thought that he initiated this makes me unreasonably happy. Therefore, the thought needs to die.

Don't get your hopes up, Parker, I tell myself, trying to locate some semblance of reason. Logan is more out of my league now than he ever was. Famous hockey studs don't fall for the small-town woman who's never been kissed. No way.

Though honestly … the hockey player plus the never-been-kissed girl-next-door would be a killer Hallmark movie. Not with actual killing. Obviously.

But definitely some kissing.

Just the thought of that has me gazing up at Logan's definitely kissable lips and the scar running from his mouth to his chin. What would it feel like to kiss his scar? To trail my lips along his jaw, exploring and—

"So, you have to do all the video editing yourself? There's no other media person to help?" Logan asks, jarring my mind out of its not-quite-Hallmark-appropriate fantasy.

I make a face. "I wish. Yeah, it's all me. I plan. I film. I edit. I post. I field comments and all that."

"All for the low, low price of … not nearly what they should be paying you?"

"Pretty much," I admit.

"And yet you stay?"

"I love my job. I love it here."

"I sense a but," Logan says.

But I wish I wasn't having to budget so closely. I wish I got more respect, especially for how much I bring to the table and how much I've done to make the team what it is. And at times, Harvest Hollow does feel a little suffocating—mostly because of my family.

"But there are times I think about leveraging what I've done here for something else. Somewhere else," I say. "But I love the guys and the whole Appies culture."

"Did you ever think about skating with a partner?" Logan asks, changing subjects so fast I almost get whiplash.

It takes me a moment to get my bearings. "Pairs? No. It's too hard to find a partner out here. Harvest Hollow has a decent number of hockey players. More now because of this."

I gesture to the Summit and the rows of empty seats, the

Appies banners hanging from the ceiling. Smaller than places Logan's used to skating, I know. But it's a luxury for an AHL team. Just the fact that the space isn't shared and the team gets to practice here too is almost unheard of for the minor leagues.

"There are surprisingly few guys who want to wear tight pants or sequins and twirl. Plus, I can be a control freak, and I don't always play well with others."

Logan laughs at this, a full belly laugh with his head thrown back. It's a full, rich sound, and I can't help but grin in return. Even if he's laughing *at* me. The sound echoes in the empty arena. Other than Javi, who is probably here because he's always here, the facility is empty.

I nudge Logan with my shoulder. "What's so funny?"

He smiles down at me, his green eyes crinkling at the corners. "Just the idea of you not playing well with others. You're like this little ball of sunshine everywhere you go, Park."

The compliment zings through me. It doesn't make sense that my throat gets tight with emotion, but it does anyway. "Thank you."

"You even make guys like me smile."

"Guys like you?" I ask.

"You know—the intense, serious ones."

"You mean the grumpy ones?"

He frowns, but it's playful. "I'm not grumpy."

"Says the man whose nickname is Wolverine."

"I thought you called me that because my name is Logan."

"And how would you describe Logan's character in *X-Men*?" I ask.

"Strong and awesome," he says, just as I say, "Grumpy."

Then we're both laughing. This feels so nice. So much like the times Logan hung out at our place with me and Brandon, the three of us laughing and bickering back and forth. I hope at some point Logan and Brandon can talk and make up or whatever it is guys do after a fight, but even if they don't, I'm not sorry at all to have this time with just the two of us. And if Brandon gets sour grapes about it, then that's on him.

Before I realize what he's doing, Logan lets go of my hand, then maneuvers quickly around me. I'm always surprised by the grace and speed some of these big guys have on the ice.

"I need to make sure I warm up all your fingers," Logan says, taking my other hand. "Can't have one hand going cold."

"For a grump, you sure are thoughtful."

"You're the one who said I'm a grump. Maybe you need to change your stance on that."

"Maybe." I wiggle my fingers a little in Logan's big hand. I hadn't noticed—what with being distracted by Logan himself—but my fingers really were freezing. Meanwhile my other hand is nice and warm. "So, is this where you bring all the girls?"

I mean this to be teasing, but I'm immediately flooded with irrational, raging jealousy at the mere *idea* of Logan skating like this with someone else.

He snorts. "No."

Good. That makes for less people I need to murder.

He tilts his head, eyeing me "Just the ones I'm planning to go on—what did you call it?—a non-date date with. As a non-boyfriend."

I groan and try to pull my hand from his. But Logan holds tight. Then he laces our fingers together so I can't escape. Not that I really want to escape. Especially not now.

I could live and die right here, skating slow laps while Logan Barnes holds my hand.

I mean, eating and using the bathroom would be tricky if I refuse to let go of his hand. But as Jeff Goldblum's character said in *Jurassic Park*, "Life finds a way."

I'd *definitely* find a way if it meant more time with Logan like this.

"Are you going to give me details, by the way?" he asks. "I don't even know when the party is."

"Right. Details are kind of important. It's Friday."

"This Friday? Like, four days from now?"

I wince. "Yes? And like I said, I'll pay for your tux rental. This is a favor to me, and I don't want to put you out."

Logan squeezes my hand. "You're not putting me out. And I have a tux."

"You do?"

He smirks, again giving me a sideways look. "Had to get one custom made. Off-the-rack suits won't fit over all this."

The mere idea of Logan in a custom-fitted tux is enough to make me stumble a little, my blades going a little wonky as I skate over a rough patch on the ice. Total rookie move. Thankfully, Logan doesn't seem to notice.

I force lightness into my voice. "All *that*, huh? I hadn't really noticed. Hockey uniforms are so bulky. Hard to tell what's underneath."

Okay, THAT didn't come out the way I intended.

Logan really looks at me this time, his smirk even smirkier. "You spend a lot of time thinking about what's under my uniform, Pete?"

Now I am. Though thanks to several endorsements with major brands, I am already *very* aware of what's underneath the Appies T-shirt Logan's currently wearing.

"Nope," I say. "I am all business. Not thinking about that at all."

"Except when you grope my abs."

I lean over to punch him in the shoulder. I'm sure it hurts me more than it hurts him, what with all those solid muscles. "You were supposed to forget that ever happened!"

"I definitely didn't agree to that."

"So, why did you need a fake date slash boyfriend?" he asks. "You can't say no to your dad?"

"Wow. Way to make a woman feel independent," I say drily.

Logan squeezes my fingers, and though I'm not cold, the touch makes me shiver.

"I remember how your dad was. If he's still the same—"

"He's worse. Ask Brandon." I wince as soon as the words are out of my mouth.

In what seems to be typical Parker fashion, I've stuck my foot in my mouth, skate and all. Bringing up my brother, aka Logan's ex best friend, is a touchy subject at best. But I don't bother to apologize. Maybe if I pretend I didn't say anything, Logan won't notice.

"Does your brother hate me?" Logan asks.

I think carefully about how to answer this. "If by hate, you mean he obsessively and secretly follows your career while talking about how you could improve, then sure."

"He follows my career?" Logan's gaze snaps to mine.

"We both have. Always."

I hope this isn't admitting too much. I'm doing my very best to keep my words measured.

What I really want to do is demand Logan tell me the exact reasons why he left. Why he never spoke to me or Brandon again. His apology was sincere, but I still have questions. A lot of them.

I get why he wouldn't necessarily keep in touch with me. It would have been weird for a rookie NHL player to be texting a high school girl.

But Brandon? The two were inseparable since the first day they met at pee wee practice. It's bugged me forever not to know what made Logan ghost us like this. And I hate that I'm thinking about such a sore subject now when I should just be focused on how it feels to have my hand in his. To laugh. To act like the past ten years of nothingness didn't happen.

Logan picks up his speed. I match his pace again, though I'm starting to feel the burn. My legs are screaming, *No! No! No!* While the rest of me, the Logan-fueled part of me, is chanting, *Yes! Yes! Yes!*

I'll be sore tomorrow, which is sad considering how many years I spent hours on the ice daily, working every muscle nearly to the point of collapse.

"And you?" Logan asks carefully, definitely not looking my way this time. "You don't hate me?"

It was never *hate*. Complete and total heartbreak? Sure. More like crushing bitterness as the guy I kept on a bedazzled pedestal showed off his crumbly clay feet.

I might have even said I hated him a time or two when talking to Mia and Brandon. I definitely screamed that I hated him into my pillow. But even then, I knew that wasn't the emotion I felt. I'm pretty sure they knew it too.

Maybe I'm naive to think he'll tell me more in his own time. But I'm not going to push him. Not more than I have already tonight.

"Oh, I definitely hate you," I tease. "And I plan to exact my revenge through making you dance like a circus monkey in my videos."

He groans. "I thought part of our agreement was no dancing if I go with you to your dad's thing."

"I said *less* dancing. Not no dancing. I've got special plans just for you, Wolverine. You just wait."

Logan's head whips my way, and before he can stop me, I yank my hand from his and take off, laughing as I go. I find my max speed and ignore the protests of my screaming muscles.

It doesn't take Logan long to catch me. And, like a total show-off, he passes me, then whips around to continue skating backwards in front of me. When he grins, my stomach doesn't just flip. It executes a complicated set of gymnastic maneuvers that leave me breathless.

"Is this how it's gonna be, Pete?"

I grin. "Can you handle the heat?"

"I'm better with cold than heat. But I can hold my own. The question is—can you?"

And with that, he flips around and takes off, tossing me a look that reads pure challenge over his shoulder.

Challenge accepted.

And though I can only catch Logan when he lets me, we continue playing a game of tag until I practically collapse, leaning against the wall near the players' bench, breathing heavily. Okay, fine—I might technically be panting.

Logan slices to a stop beside me, spraying my legs with ice. He hardly looks winded.

"Show off," I say.

"Sore loser," he says.

"Definitely sore. Or I will be tomorrow."

"Too sore to keep skating? Because I have an idea."

I probably should stop. But I've never been big on *probablys*.

"I love ideas," I tell him.

"Be right back."

Logan disappears through the tunnel, and I take a seat on the players' bench. I catch sight of Javi standing not too far away in the stands, smiling and shaking his head. I wonder how long he was watching. "Be careful," he mouths to me. I smile and nod in response, but honestly, it's far too late for *careful* now. I'm pretty sure my childhood crush has matured into a whole full-blown infatuation.

Or worse.

When Logan returns, it's with gloves, sticks, and a puck. His grin is so big and so boyish that I can't help but smile in response.

"Get out here, Pete. You wanted to play hockey? Let's play hockey."

He doesn't need to tell me twice.

And while there was something magical about skating hand in hand with Logan, having him teach me puck control and how to line up a shot is excellent. I also do not mind even the smallest bit when I need help with my hold and he comes up behind me, placing his arms around me to adjust my grip.

"Slide your hand like this," Logan says, moving my gloved hand.

"I feel like I'm wearing the equivalent of clown shoes, but on my hands," I say.

"These are a little big for you, but the principle is the same." Logan is all business now, adding another version of him to like.

Grumpy Logan is great. Happy, smiling, laughing Logan is fantastic. But all-business Logan practically spooning me as he shows me how to properly grip a hockey stick is my new favorite.

"Your hand should be over top. You see that part of the

glove between your thumb and forefinger?" he asks, point-ing. "That should line up with the top of the stick. That's it. Good."

I consider faking to get him to stay put behind me, wrapped around me like a Logan-scented cloak, but I can't bring myself to do it. Plus, I'm excited to move on from puck control and start shooting.

We do that next, and I'm terrible but determined. The moment I sink my first shot, albeit in a net unprotected by a goaltender, I squeal. Logan gives me a gloved high-five.

"Nice one, Pete."

"I had a good teacher. When can we work on hitting?"

He chuckles and shakes his head. "We're not wearing pads. Plus, I don't think that would be a good idea."

I crowd him, knocking his stick with mine. "You scared?"

"No."

Logan skates to the goal, retrieving the puck and skating around the back of the goal. Though I probably shouldn't, I take this as a challenge and come after him, trying to steal the puck. It looks so much easier than it is. I've always known this, logically speaking, but it's a totally different thing to actually be on the ice with someone like Logan. He might be bulky, but he's full of grace and expertly skilled at keeping the puck just out of reach.

So, I decide to play a little dirty. Who cares if we don't have pads? It's not hockey without hitting.

That's what I'm thinking when I try to slam Logan into the wall.

Try being the operative word. He barely budges, and I almost eat it, falling forward on my skates. Logan gets a wicked gleam in his eye, and the next thing I know, I'm the one being slammed—a gentle slam—against the wall. My stick *thwacks* against the plexiglass as Logan's body presses into mine.

Holy hockey, Batman.

"You see, Parker?" he says, his breath hot on my cheek.

"See what?"

The only thing I see is his face, inches from mine. The only thing I feel is his chest, rising and falling against mine. The only thing I smell is his clean, masculine scent. The only thing I hear is a ringing in my ears that grows louder as we stay suspended like this.

The only thing I want to taste is his lips on mine.

And for approximately ten seconds (ten seconds that *feel* like forever), I think I'm about to taste just that. Logan's gaze drops to my mouth. His smile falls away as his expression turns serious. His green eyes darken.

He hovers, so close but not quite there.

But he's thinking about it. Hard as it is to believe, he's thinking about it.

It's a testament to the man he is that Logan doesn't make a move. Not after what I told him earlier. Or maybe for other reasons. Maybe I don't care.

If I were a different woman, maybe I'd take control and close the distance between us.

But I'm suddenly very aware of my inexperience.

My stupid anxious thoughts crowd in, making me worry about how exactly to line up our lips and if I need to tilt my head.

As if my loud, tangled thoughts telepathically reach Logan, his gaze meets mine. He looks startled. Stunned, really.

Then the weight of him lifts away, making me want to cry out. But he's off, zooming across the ice to line up a perfect shot. Like nothing ever happened. Like it was all in my head. Like he isn't affected in the slightest.

But I know he was affected enough not to finish whatever he was going to say moments ago.

The puck hits the back of the net, and Logan turns to me with a small smile. "Ready to call it a night, Pete? Some of us need sleep so we can get up early for practice."

And some of us may never sleep again with the thought of this almost-kiss running through our heads.

CHAPTER 12

Parker

THERE'S LESS than two weeks before our first preseason game. So, the next few days are a blur of meetings and filming and editing and posting a million social media things. It keeps me from thinking too hard about Logan.

And that moment on the ice where I swear we almost kissed. Or the time at my house when I felt the same tension crackling in the air between us. Oh, and let's not forget Dad's gala.

Which is tonight.

Arriving at my office early with a list a mile long of things to do before I finish the day, my head is buried in my phone. Which is why I don't register the very important change until I sit down.

Immediately, I scramble to my feet and back away slowly.

"You're not my chair," I say.

The strange chair, obviously, does not respond.

A sense of panic unfolds. My old office chair was barely holding on. It complained loudly every time I moved. The lever to adjust the height broke off a year ago, which meant I looked not unlike a child sitting at an adult's desk. There was one metal piece that always stabbed my shoulder if I made the mistake of leaning back. More than once I begged Javi to put in a request for a new one, and more than once he looked sad and mentioned budgets and blah blah blah.

Now, I stare at what is clearly a very fancy and expensive and *pink* chair. I don't trust it. This level of fancy doesn't belong in my windowless office. And I didn't know luxury office chairs came in such a fun color. Something is afoot.

"Where did you come from?" I ask the chair, clearly not learning my lesson after it didn't answer my first question.

Honestly, I half expect the chair to come equipped with some kind of AI, which will answer me in a robotic voice, describing its hero's journey from fancy factory to here.

Coach Davis pops his head in my doorway, and I jump. "Did you ask me something?"

"Oh, sorry," I say. "I was just talking to … myself. Are we getting some kind of office upgrades?"

He lifts his baseball cap, smoothing his hand over the wispy white hair underneath. "Not that I know of. Why? Do you need something?"

I glance at the chair again. It's like a Cadillac of office chairs. Scratch that—it's more of a Lexus. Just looking at it, I feel my spine start to realign.

"Don't worry about it. I'll ask Javi."

Coach nods and scurries off.

Maybe my requests finally came through? Maybe I got a bonus I didn't know about? Maybe there's a chair fairy that somehow hasn't gotten the same mainstream recognition the tooth fairy gets?

If the chair was delivered to my office by mistake, I should enjoy it until the person who was supposed to get it figures out the error and comes looking.

But who else in this building would want a *pink* office chair?

I give the chair another few seconds of suspicious eye contact before sitting again. Where I normally lower myself carefully, knowing any day now, the legs on my worn chair will give out, this one eagerly accepts my weight.

The chair is, in a word, *glorious*. If I could choose two words, it's *glorious* and *heavenly*. Truly. I can imagine a whole row of these chairs just beyond the pearly gates and streets of gold, extending as far as the eye can see.

My eyes flutter closed as I lean back, sinking into the soft leather that feels almost like a caress. In a non-creepy and non-sexual way of course. Just in a super luxurious office chair kind of way.

"I might be in love with you," I whisper.

"Oh, really?"

At the sound of the very male and very familiar voice, my eyes fly open. And then, for reasons that must date back to prehistoric times and not logical, modern ones, I dive under my desk to hide.

"Sorry, Pete," Logan says. "Didn't realize you scared so easily."

I uncurl myself from the protective ball my fight, flight, or curl up in the fetal position instincts sent me into, then peer over my desk, glaring at the smug face eyeing me.

"Barnes," I growl, smoothing my black pants as I stand. "You can't sneak up on me. We have a strict knocking policy."

"I was walking by and couldn't help but overhear. My question is—were you talking to me or the chair?" he asks.

"The chair. Definitely the chair." Still glaring, I sink back into its cocooning softness. "Fancy Chair would never appear out of nowhere and scare me. Fancy Chair has some respect for boundaries."

"Fancy Chair?" Logan asks. "You couldn't think of a more creative name?"

"Maybe later. For now, Fancy Chair will do."

Logan crosses his arms over his chest and gives me the tiniest smile. Though it's small, it sure is smug. "I'm glad you like it."

It takes my brain a minute to catch the meaning behind his words.

I immediately jump out of Fancy Chair. "Wait—this is from *you?*"

Logan shrugs, still with that same tiny smug smirk. A *smirg*, if you will. Surely, he didn't buy me a new office chair.

Wait—DID he buy me a new office chair?

"Yours was a death trap," he says, as though this is a completely reasonable argument to make here.

He's not wrong. But it doesn't mean he can do *this.*

"And I'm sorry, but I don't want to see you maimed or worse by a subpar piece of furniture," he says. "Accept the upgrade, Pete."

"Nope."

I start to roll Fancy Chair around my desk, shoving it toward Logan while silently shedding goodbye tears.

So long, Fancy Chair. We had it good for a while, didn't we?

Logan reaches out, and with one big hand, stops the chair from moving forward. I lean into it but am no match for Logan's strength.

"It's yours," he says.

"I can't accept this. It probably cost a few hundred dollars."

"Try a few thousand." Felix appears behind Logan in the doorway.

"What?" My voice is barely a whisper.

I gape at Felix, who's casually leaning on the doorframe. Then I gape at Logan. Finally, I gape at Fancy Chair. A few *thousand* dollars?

The other day, I saw an older car on Facebook marketplace for two grand. Sure, it was rusted and had a million miles and the muffler was falling off, but it was a CAR. A chair can't possibly cost that much.

Can it?

Like I've been burned, I yank my hand away from Fancy Chair and step back. With a heavy sigh and an eye roll, Logan pushes the chair forward, backing me into the small area behind my desk.

"Thanks, man," he says to Felix. "Super helpful."

"What?" Felix asks. "Buying gifts is totally acceptable when it's for your *girlfriend.*"

For a few long seconds, Logan and I both freeze—eyes locked on one another's. The guys have barely teased me about Logan, and he hasn't mentioned finding crop tops in his locker again. Things haven't been weird. I assumed that meant they didn't ever hear about the upgrade from date to *dating.* I mean, why would they? Our sticky notes said we wouldn't tell the team more than they needed to know.

But Felix just called me Logan's girlfriend.

Don't like it too much, I tell myself. Felix probably just read too much into the situation. Maybe Logan buying the chair made Felix think things are official. A two-thousand-dollar chair will do that.

But I'm *not* Logan's girlfriend. So, *why did he buy me a two-thousand-dollar chair?*

"It's a great chair, Parker," Felix says, his words snapping both Logan and me out of our *girlfriend*-induced trance. "Keep it."

"She might not have fought me on it," Logan says, returning the chair behind my desk. I stay pressed against the wall, "if you hadn't told her how much it cost. It wasn't a few thousand dollars, by the way."

Felix coughs something that sounds like *two thousand*.

I narrow my eyes at Logan. "I can't accept this," I tell him, forcing my gaze to his green eyes. "Take it back."

Instead of doing what I ask, Logan spins the chair to face me and, before I can protest, bodily forces me to sit. I try to wiggle away, but his hands are a firm and unrelenting weight on my shoulders.

"Logan!" I protest.

"Shhh." He's leaning down over the back of the chair now, his breath fanning over my cheek. "Just accept Fancy Chair," he whispers. "Don't think about the money."

Oh, I'm not thinking about the money. I'm thinking only about Logan's proximity to me. His lips, which are inches from my skin. His hands, so strong and steady on my shoulders. The heat of him.

Is the man coal-powered or something? He's like a furnace.

"So," Logan says, his hands giving my shoulders a squeeze that morphs into a light massage. "Are we agreed?"

"Hmm?" This comes out of my mouth as less of a word and more a low groan as he kneads muscles I didn't know were sore.

"You'll keep Fancy Chair. And not worry about the money."

The word *money* rings like a Pavlovian bell. I start to struggle again. "I *have* to worry about the money," I say, fighting against Logan. He doesn't budge, and I'm trapped here in a delicious dungeon.

"There's a no-return policy," Logan says. "If you don't accept it, I'll have to give it to someone else."

"Take the chair, Boss," Felix says from the door. "You deserve it."

"Shut up, Goalie. Mind your business," I tell him.

Felix only chuckles. Logan leans closer, and I freeze like a little baby fawn as a wolf stalks through the grass nearby.

"The chair is yours," Logan says. "A gift. Accept it. Stop being stubborn and prideful."

Is that what I'm being?

Maybe. But more than that, this is an act of self-preservation. If I let Logan buy me chairs, what's next? My heart is already stuck on the man. I can't let him do things like this. It'll only make me like him more.

"I'm yours, Parker." Logan makes his voice sound like a cartoon character, clearly pretending to be the voice of Fancy Chair.

He's being silly. I know it.

But hearing Logan say he's mine?

The phrase *I cannot even* was literally borne out of some moments like this.

I cannot.

I cannot *even*.

Logan seems to take my incapacitated state as surrender because he pats my shoulders twice and moves away. "Good girl," he says.

I barely manage to hold in a whimper.

"Later, Boss," Felix says, and the look on his face is so

knowing I make a mental note to kick him right in the shins next time I see him.

"I'll pick you up for our date at six-thirty," Logan says. Then he winks and is gone, leaving me in the soft embrace of Fancy Chair.

"I am in so much trouble," I whisper. "So. Much."

———

Turns out choosing what to wear for a *fake* date is just as difficult as it is for the real thing. Which is why I make an emergency call to Mia a few hours before Logan is picking me up for the gala. When there's a knock at my door, I've got three different dresses still on coat hangers looped over my neck.

"I've narrowed it down to three choices, and Mr. Eds is *no* help. Which dress says …" I trail off as I open the door.

Because it's not Mia on the other side.

It's Logan.

I'm so grateful I didn't finish my question, which was to ask which dress would make me look irresistible.

"You're early," I blurt, rubbing my eyes, like this will make him disappear. "And you're in … track pants?"

Not that Logan doesn't look good in track pants. Or any pants for that matter.

Something I shouldn't be thinking about now because I'm totally blushing.

"Don't worry. I've got my tux." Logan takes in my current status, wherein I'm impersonating a clothing rack. "And you're wearing but not wearing two—no, three—dresses. You were asking your evil cat to help you with fashion advice?"

As though he can understand what Logan just said, Mr. Eds lets out a low growl and then a hiss from wherever he's hiding currently. Last I saw, he was lurking behind my fake fiddle-leaf fig.

"Mia's on her way to help."

"Guys have it a little easier. Less decision fatigue with a suit."

A laugh bubbles out of me. Something about Logan using the word decision fatigue is just too much. Or maybe it's nerves from thinking about Logan all day and now actually seeing him.

"Do you want my opinion?" he asks, then holds up both hands. "I know better than to offer one if you don't."

Do I want Logan's opinion?

Yes. No. I don't know!

I finally manage to nod. Logan steps closer, and I do my best not to spontaneously combust as he examines the dresses. Or what he can see of them, considering they're layered over me. He reaches out, his fingers brushing the material of each dress in turn. He may not be touching me, but I swear I feel the brush of his fingertips everywhere.

"The pink," Logan says finally, dropping his hand and stepping back.

"Why that one?" I ask, genuinely curious.

If I'm being honest, it's my very favorite of the bunch. And not just because it's my favorite color. I love the fitted bodice and the loose skirt that twirls around if I spin. It's fun and sexy without being too much. Plus, it's soft to the touch.

Logan's smile is slow, and it toasts my insides like a marshmallow in front of a blowtorch. "Because pink is your favorite color," he says. "Right?"

"Yes," I manage, struck even more dumb by the fact that Logan knows this.

"So, choose the pink. You'll feel good wearing what makes you happy."

"Pink it is."

I'm still trying to recover from this whole encounter when I realize something.

He's standing outside my apartment door, which shouldn't be possible. Mia's the only one besides me who has keys to both sets of doors: the one downstairs that sticks and my actual apartment door.

"Wait—how'd you get in?"

Logan pulls a set of keys from the pocket of his track pants and jangles them in front of me. "I used my key."

"You have a key?"

While I watch, still trying to puzzle through this conundrum, Logan turns to the door just next to mine—the one I'm just now realizing no longer sports the *For Lease* sign. Which I always thought was dumb anyway, considering no one could wander in off the street to see it.

Logan turns a key in the lock. The door swings open, and Logan waves an arm toward the empty apartment.

"Surprise! I'm your new neighbor. Feel free to bring by freshly baked cookies as a welcome gift. I prefer chocolate chip. No nuts."

Only then do I notice the bags behind Logan.

Bags. Keys. *Neighbor?*

Before I can pass out from shock, the door downstairs opens, and Mia walks inside. She pauses, eyebrows shooting up when she spots Logan. Then she takes me in, still draped in dresses.

"Looks like I'm late to the party," Mia says, starting up the stairs.

"Logan's moving in next door," I say slowly, my voice sounding more than a little shell-shocked.

Mia's grin turns wicked as she reaches the landing,

pausing to look between the two open apartment doors. "Is he now?"

"He is," Logan says, hoisting two of his duffel bags up and tosses them inside his apartment. "Though his furniture won't be delivered until later this week."

"You're serious?" I ask, peering around him to scope out the apartment that appears to be a mirror image of mine, only facing the back rather than Maple Street.

"I didn't like staying at the hotel," he says. "No privacy. Felix let me crash temporarily, but I need my space. Plus, I like the location. And the neighbors."

Mia's grin could rival that of the Grinch, looking down over Whoville on Christmas Eve. "How convenient. Y'all could carpool to work and everything. Anytime you need to borrow a cup of sugar, you can just walk right next door."

I meet Logan's amused green eyes. He holds my gaze, and I swear, my knees wobble.

"I do often find myself in need of sugar," he says, and how does this manage to sound so incredibly flirtatious?

It's too much. I was already a mess with our fake-date-I-really-wish-was-a-real-date just hours away.

Without a word, I grab Mia by the elbow and forcibly drag her inside my apartment.

"See you at six-thirty!" Logan calls before I slam the door and lean my back against it.

Mia takes one look at my wide eyes and panicked expression and bursts out laughing.

"It's not funny," I hiss. "Logan is moving in next door." Horror dawns on me as I think about the layout of the two apartments. I looked at both before moving in and chose the smaller one facing Maple Street. "We're going to share a bedroom wall. Mia—*we're going to share a bedroom wall.*"

She only laughs harder.

"You are the absolute worst," I declare. "You can go. I don't need your help any longer."

"I'm sorry," Mia says, wiping tears from her cheeks and making a valiant attempt to stifle her laughter. "But Parker? I'm pretty sure you need my help more than ever."

———

I am no less nervous when Logan knocks on my door again, exactly on time. Mia gives my cheeks a little slap. Harder than necessary if you ask me.

"Hey," I protest, stepping out of reach.

"It'll put natural color there. Since you insisted on not letting me do your makeup." She rolls her eyes.

Mia, in addition to graduating at the top of her law school class, is one of those people who understands terms like contouring and knows what kind of brush is for foundation and which is for whatever else women use brushes for. Whereas I'm a pretty strict moisturizer, mascara, and *maybe* eyeliner kind of girl. Years of wearing caked-on performance make-up for skating competitions will have that effect on a person.

Logan knocks again and I startle, knocking into my dining table.

"Just a sec!" Mia calls. Then she takes my hand, her voice softening. "You're going to be great. You're going to have fun."

"What if I—"

"Nope." Mia shakes her head.

"But what if he—"

"No what ifs. Go. Be yourself. Enjoy. And don't spend the night worrying about whatever thoughts are racing through your mind right now."

"But what if he wants to kiss me?" I whisper too quickly for Mia to interrupt.

"If he does, and you want to, then do it." Mia shrugs. "If not, don't. And you have nothing to feel weird or ashamed about. You've waited this long; you can wait for it to mean whatever you want it to mean. Or you can decide to heck with it and kiss the hot hockey player just for fun. Your lips. Your choice."

And before I can overthink anymore, Mia lets go of my hand and throws open the door to reveal Logan. The man might look most at home in his hockey gear, but he looks like he was born to wear this tux.

He looks so good, in fact, that it takes me several seconds to realize he's got on a pink bow tie and matching pocket square—the exact dusky pink of my dress. The flowers in his hand are an explosion of pinks from pale blush peonies to vibrant fuchsia roses.

I realize I'm standing here silent, staring everywhere but Logan's face. When I finally drag my eyes up to meet his gaze, he's staring right back at me.

I can't decipher the expression in his eyes, but whatever it is, it's intense. My heart trips over itself, and I'm suddenly more nervous than I've been all day, which is saying a lot. I take a hesitant step back, my brain working overtime to find any excuse not to go.

I have cramps. A migraine. A sudden and crippling case of vertigo. My nonexistent goldfish died and required a burial at sea.

Anything at all to get me out of this.

But Logan steps forward, holding out the flowers. "These are for you," he says.

I take the bouquet, jolting a little when his fingers brush mine. He shoves his hands in his pockets, stepping back. I drop my nose to the flowers to avoid looking at Logan. I inhale deeply.

A little too deeply, apparently, because then I sneeze, sending a shower of petals to the floor.

"I'll take those," Mia says, plucking them from my hand. She heads to the kitchen and, not finding a vase because I don't own any, she sticks the bouquet into a glass pitcher I sometimes use to make sun tea.

My eyes find Logan's again, and his expression is no less intense but a little softer now. The small smile he gives me loosens up my nerves just a bit.

But would it kill the man to tell me I look beautiful? Isn't that just plain good manners?

Unless he doesn't think I look beautiful. Unless he hates the dress and regrets getting dragged into this event. Unless—

"Stop with the what ifs," Mia whispers in my ear. Louder, she says, "Stand together. I need to take your picture."

"Mia," I protest, but she gives me a shove toward Logan.

"Not optional. *We are taking pictures.*"

I doubt Logan wants to pose for pictures like we're going to prom, but I'm also secretly grateful for Mia's bossiness. Because even if this night is a disaster and I never stop being nervous and Logan wants to leave early and regrets coming, I'll at least have photos to help me relive this moment for years to come.

I stand next to Logan, leaving a few inches between us. I clasp my hands in front of me and know I'm standing as stiff as a department store mannequin. Mia glares over her phone at me, but before she can say anything, a strong hand wraps around my torso.

Logan tugs me to his side, that big hand fitting perfectly in the curve of my waist. The scent of him overwhelms me, and I swear my vision goes a little fuzzy. I probably should have eaten beforehand. This is far too much Logan on an empty stomach.

"That's better," Mia says, snapping a few pictures.

"It's one of the rules," Logan says in a low voice. "Putting an arm around your waist."

"Yes, it is." Those rules are both going to save me and be the death of me.

I try to remember how to smile, but I'm too aware of Logan's arm around me, his fingertips moving lightly over the soft material of my dress.

When he leans close, his lips brushing my ear, my breath hitches.

"I'm glad you wore the pink," he murmurs, and I don't miss Mia's smug smile as she continues taking pictures.

My heart vibrates like the plucked string of an instrument. It's not quite him saying I'm beautiful, but it's *something*. "Yeah?"

"But you need to stop looking so miserable or I'll have no choice but to take it personally."

A laugh bursts out of me, and Logan's arm tightens around my waist. "That's better," he says. "Can't have my Parker unhappy."

My Parker?

He may not have told me I look beautiful, but this is somehow ten million times better.

CHAPTER 13

Logan

I SPEND the entire drive to the hotel where the gala will be held drowning in regret.

Not because I said yes to going with Parker—though I suspect that will come later—but because I didn't tell her how beautiful she looks. I'm not sure beautiful is the right word, and part of my problem was just that. I had no words when she opened the door. None.

I could only stare. Parker is the perfect combination of girl-next-door and dead sexy. She is too beautiful for words. At least, not any words I know. Even if I had a stellar vocabulary, the sight of her made me lose even the most basic single syllables.

And then I felt weird complimenting her. I don't want her to think she only looks beautiful when dressed up or something. Because the truth is, Parker looks every bit as beautiful walking around the Summit in her work clothes or or in leggings and a pair of skates. I actually prefer her in skates. Maybe even to the pink dress she's wearing now.

But seeing her all dressed up—dressed up for *me* ...

Yeah. I'm still overwhelmed and trying my best to appear perfectly normal when all I want is to reach across and take her hand.

Then maybe pull the car over and kiss her the way I've been wanting to for days now.

Instead, I run through the checklist of why that's a bad idea: first and foremost, the fact we're on a fake date, not a real one. I'm a fake boyfriend, not an actual one. I don't think I'd even know how to be a real boyfriend, so there's also that. Brandon. Parker's father. The guys on the team.

None of those thoughts make a dent in my desire. But when I remind myself I plan to be gone as soon as humanly possible, THAT thought sobers me.

Strangely, the thought of leaving Harvest Hollow doesn't fill me with a sense of relief. Not like it has before. Not like when I was dreading this move, even though I assumed it would be temporary. Now, the thought of my time here ending makes me feel ... conflicted. And the very last thing I want is to be conflicted about this town. I can't already be feeling tied to this place.

Or, I think, *to its people.*

"It's not too late," Parker says, startling me out of my downward thought spiral.

I frown. Glancing over, I see her white knuckling her sparkly purse. "Too late?"

The smile she gives me is shaky. "To back out. You can drop me at the door. I'll uber home. I know I strong-armed you into this, Logan."

I place my hand over hers. Touching Parker is dangerous

—something I realized earlier when Mia took our pictures. The moment I put my arm around Parker, I was immediately hit with the urge to crush her against me. Even just touching her hand with mine seems to spark something to life.

"There's nowhere I'd rather be," I tell her. "And no one I'd rather be with."

Okay, maybe the first part wasn't completely honest—I'd definitely rather be going somewhere I won't have to see her brother and dad. But the second sentence was a little *too* honest. I need to make sure I'm not giving Parker any ideas. I remove my hand quickly, clenching the steering wheel because *I'm* the one getting ideas.

"Are you sure?" Parker presses. "Because—and don't take this the wrong way—you seem stressed."

I don't say anything, and Parker angles her body toward mine. I resist the urge to look her way, keeping my eyes on the road instead.

"Is this because of my dad and Brandon?"

That's definitely a part of it. But it's my own struggle to tamp down the feelings that keep rising up. Feelings I shouldn't—I can't—act on.

"I'm not looking forward to seeing them," I admit.

"I know my dad is a jerk, and I understand about Brandon. Though he'll get over it. You were best friends."

We were. But right before I left, I realized friendships are a lot more complicated than that. And he's not the only one who has something to get over before we could be friends again. I have my own hard feelings Brandon doesn't know about.

"Does Brandon know you're coming with me?"

"He does," Parker says.

When she doesn't elaborate, I say, "And?"

She sighs. "He had a few choice words about it via text.

But look—it's fine. I don't care what he or my dad thinks. You're with me tonight, Wolverine. I've got your back. Okay?"

I can't help but smile at the ferocity in her words. And at the idea of Parker protecting me—the big, bad-tempered hockey player.

When I don't answer, she leans over and pokes me in the shoulder. "*Okay?*"

"Okay."

"I'll stick to you like glue," she says, and her words sound somewhere between a threat and the sweetest promise.

To tell the truth, it sounds awesome.

———

One thing I did not expect was Harvest Hollow's version of a red carpet entrance, complete with the press. I shouldn't have been surprised, considering Parker's dad. I mean, I assume the man is as self-important now as he was then. Given the birthday *gala* and all.

Parker comes to a dead stop on the sidewalk. If the valet hadn't already left with my SUV, she looks like she would consider hopping back in and peeling rubber to get out of here. Ahead of us, photographers and reporters crowd against the rope barrier while guests pause and pose for photographs. For a town this size, it's a *lot* of press.

"Oh no," Parker says. "I didn't know about this. Maybe I should have, given my dad, but I didn't."

No one has seen us. Yet. There's still time to leave or find a back entrance.

Or not.

This is Harvest Hollow. It's not a big city. These are local reporters, not paparazzi and celebrity gossip magazines.

We'll be just fine. People will likely make assumptions. But it wouldn't be the first time I've been publicly linked with someone when it wasn't true. If a woman so much as stands close to me and someone snaps a picture, I'm practically engaged.

But Parker looks so anxious. And that's the last thing I want her to feel right now. I'd rather wipe the stress from her face, to ease the tension I can visibly see in her shoulders. I like being private, but I'm also used to this enough not to care.

"Are you that embarrassed to be seen with me?" I tease.

She smacks my arm. When she smiles, I feel like I've done my job. At least a little.

"No! It just derails the plan of this being low-key if pictures are splashed all over the *Harvest Times* and wherever else. It just means more people we have to explain things to when things ... you know, end."

Parker's voice goes a little quiet. But then she shakes her head a little.

"What about you? I don't want to mess up your reputation or anything."

I snort. "I should be so lucky. With a little investigative journalism, they'd quickly find that you're way too good for me, Pete."

It's true. *So* true. For a fraction of a second, I wonder how things would be if I *were* the kind of man who could spend my life with Parker.

Her lips part, her mouth seemingly caught between a smile and dropping open in surprise. A flush rises in her cheeks, a deeper and prettier hue than her dress. I'd like to keep that blush on her face all night.

So, I keep going. "You're, like, twenty-thousand leagues out of my sea."

"You're an idiot," she says, but she's giggling now. "But are you sure it won't be a big deal for you?"

"Nope. I can't top the bad press I've had lately."

It's died down some. But after the fight with the fan … it seemed like every media outlet wanted to dig up more dirt on me. Old photos were reposted, even if they were just pictures of me looking angry in a game or looking angry in a club. Anonymous sources opined about how I'm not a team player. Blah blah blah.

I can't see how this—even if it did get reported—could be bad for me.

But I'm not surprised Parker is worried about *my* reputation—she's always been more concerned with others than herself. It's not me she should be thinking about. Online trolls come out of the woodwork hungry for blood when hockey players are linked with women. And they don't go after the players.

This gives me the slightest pause. But then again, these are small town reporters, here to fuel Mr. Douglas's sense of self-importance.

Still.

I'll text Jeremy later and give him a heads up just in case someone tries to sell a picture to a bigger news outlet or something. Wouldn't be the first time. Since I don't have a PR person, my agent will be the one people might ask for a comment.

"We don't have to stop for photos if you don't want to," I tell her.

Her eyes brighten. "Really?"

"Yep. Keep your head down and tilted toward the building. I make a good human shield. The question is—how fast can you walk in those heels?"

"Fast enough," she says.

"You sure?" I ask, just to get a reaction.

I get one. She mock glares. "I'm faster in heels than you are in skates, Barnes."

I laugh. "Come on." I slide my hand into hers, and when she looks at me in surprise, I shrug. "Hand-holding. It's in the rules. Ready?"

She nods, and we set off. But Parker was perhaps a wee bit overconfident in her heel-walking abilities. We're halfway through the group of photographers, who are still taking pictures and calling for us to stop, when Parker stumbles.

Immediately, I drop the hand I'm holding and slide my arm around her, steadying her. She giggles, grabbing at me and swinging her smiling face up to mine. I try to angle my body so I'm blocking her from the photographers.

"Don't you say a word about me walking in heels," she says.

"Wasn't going to. I was going to say something I meant to tell you earlier. You look beautiful, Pete."

Her lips part in surprise, but she quickly shifts her expression, narrowing her eyes. "You're so full of it, Barnes."

I'm not though. Not about this.

"Ready to go in?" I murmur, again leaning down to speak right in her ear.

She turns then, probably to read my expression. But I'm still right there, which puts our faces—and our lips—just millimeters apart.

The noise around us becomes static. The flashes of cameras blend into a blur. For what feels like a small eternity, there's just me and Parker.

Her eyes, trained on my mouth—*hungry*. My own, I'm sure reflecting the exact same desire.

This is Parker. *Pete*. But trying to remind myself of this fact has no impact.

The pull between us makes me sway on my feet.

I lean closer, but instead of taking her mouth the way I'd like to, I press a quick kiss to her temple. "Another rule," I whisper. "Kissing but not on the mouth."

The moment breaks. Sound returns. There are more shouts than before. More questions. More photos.

Parker gives me a smile, but she still looks dazed. "You're really going to milk this fake boyfriend thing as much as possible, huh?"

"Hey—I'm just following the rules."

She shakes her head at me. Keeping her hand in mine, I lead us to the entrance. Men in suits hold the hotel doors open for us without making eye contact.

I'm still catching my breath, still recovering as we walk inside. So, I don't mind at all when Parker stops outside the restroom and says, "Give me a sec?"

Still. I don't like watching her walk away.

"Of course."

I take this time while I'm leaning against the wall, watching the door to text Jeremy: *I'm at an event with someone and there were photographers. You might get some calls. Take care of it?*

A thumbs up emoji is the only response that I get. Glad I'm paying Jeremy the big bucks.

I probably won't need to worry about it. What I do need to worry about—and worry a *lot*—is keeping myself in the right frame of mind tonight. The frame of mind that this isn't even a real date and I'm definitely not Parker's real boyfriend.

Even if I most definitely enjoy pretending to be.

CHAPTER 14

Parker

This isn't a real date. Logan is not my real boyfriend.

I think this to myself. Then I whisper it. And then, because I'm totally alone in this bathroom, I say it again with force while staring into my own eyes in the mirror.

"This isn't a real date. Logan is not my real boyfriend. None of this is real."

Yeah—no. I can say it all I want. But the words are not making a dent in the part of me that feels like this is all very, very real. At least, real to *me*.

Either way, the truth behind this arrangement is not sinking in. Not even close.

How can it? I mean, when Logan is teasing about the rules, touching me, and whispering in my ear that I'm beautiful ... yeah. There is a definite brain to body disconnect happening.

The best I can do is enjoy the night and hope I'm not left shattered when Logan leaves *again* sometime in the not-so distant future. Thinking of him eventually leaving doesn't even sober me up. I am punch drunk on Logan.

Giving my cheeks a little slap—*thanks for the suggestion, Mia*—I stride out of the bathroom.

I'm not prepared for Logan leaning against the wall outside, staring intensely at me the moment I exit. I'm not sure I fully got to appreciate him in his tux earlier. I was too nervous and worried about how I looked. Now, as I take him in, I feel the need to pinch myself. Or maybe give myself another—harder—slap?

A slow smile breaks over his face as he peels himself off the wall and moves my way with panther-like fluidity. My steps falter—stupid heels—but Logan is right there, steadying me.

"Thanks," I say, giving him a sheepish smile. "I'm better on skates than in heels."

"Me too."

I can't help but laugh at this, and a few people just entering the hotel glance our way. With Logan holding my arms, the two of us standing much too close, I'm sure we look like a couple having a private moment in a side hallway.

It *feels* like we're a couple having a private moment.

"We better head inside," I say.

Logan offers me his arm, and I'm only a little disappointed he doesn't take my hand again. On the plus side, I get to feel his firm biceps underneath my fingers. Zero complaints on that front. Would definitely recommend. A glowing Yelp review will be forthcoming.

"I have to warn you," I tell Logan as we enter the room already filled with people. "My dad will still probably try to pawn me off on some son of a businessman."

Logan frowns. "You're not a pawn, Parker."

Be still, my swooning heart.

I think I need to raise the bar for what inspires swooning. Not being a pawn should be the baseline of common decency.

"Tell that to my dad," I say.

"Happily."

I have a sudden vision of Logan pulling a nobody puts Baby in the corner kind of moment. Yes, that would be epic. No, my dad's birthday gala is probably not the place.

I pat his chest with my free arm. Also very deserving of a Yelp review. "I appreciate the sentiment, Wolverine, but keep your claws in. I've got this. Plus, remember my promise to stick to you like glue? It serves a dual purpose. Dad can't hand me off to some other guy if you're with me all night."

"So, I should stay with you all night. Got it."

I know he means stay with me all night *here*, at the party. But a wicked little part of me is picturing me and Logan kissing outside my door later tonight. And because this part of me has a very active imagination, it's now picturing Logan kissing me pressed up *against* my door later tonight.

Which reminds me—my door is right next to Logan's door now. Because we're neighbors. How is *that* going to work?

"Do you have any furniture?" I ask, scanning the crowd for my dad. Best to make a doting daughter appearance early.

"What?"

"In your new apartment. How are you going to sleep there if you don't have furniture yet?"

He shrugs.

"You can't just sleep on the floor, Logan. You need good sleep. Your body is your paycheck."

He chuckles, then brushes a lock of hair back from my

cheek. It's too quick for me to relish in the feel of his finger-tips on my skin. I want to shake that stubborn hair loose so he'll do it again.

"I'm glad you're worried about me, Pete. But I refuse to be objectified—my body is much more than a paycheck."

I pinch his arm. "Shut up. You know what I meant. Oh! There's my dad. Let's get this over with. Deep breaths."

I'm saying this as much for Logan as myself. I would really like to enjoy what will likely be the ONLY date I EVER go on with Logan—*reminder: it's not a real date*—and to do so, we need to get the not so great stuff out of the way first. Namely: seeing my dad and Brandon. I warned Brandon to be on his best behavior, but at some point, he and Logan probably need to talk.

Dad catches sight of us as we approach, and I really hope Logan doesn't notice his slight sneer. Mom's reception, thankfully, is a whole lot warmer.

"Parker," Dad says.

"Happy birthday, Daddy." Reluctantly, I let Logan go just long enough to give Dad and Mom quick hugs and kisses.

I go right back to clutching Logan's arm, feeling relief move through my body like an electric current once I'm secure at his side. What does it mean that I feel more comfortable with this man than I do with my own parents—or at least, with my dad?

"You remember Logan," I say pointedly.

I place a hand on Logan's chest again. It's a gesture that I hope communicates something like: *This man is under my protection. If you mess with the bull, you get the horns. Proverbially.*

Or, on a more basic level: *Mine.*

"Mr. Douglas," Logan says.

I can tell from the length of the handshake and the clenching of jaws that one or both of them is squeezing too

165

hard. I would bet money Dad started it, and Logan's not going to back down.

Men and their stupid battles of the handshakes. Can't we all just get along? Can't we???

I nudge Logan a little with my elbow and he releases my dad.

"Mrs. Douglas," Logan says, and my mom surprises me when she steps forward to wrap him in a tight hug. I think Logan's surprised too, based on his expression.

The hug is a little awkward since I'm still holding Logan's arm. But I promised to be glue, and I meant it. Especially when we're in firing range of my family.

"Please, call us Don and Janet," Mom says.

I almost snort at Dad's expression. Clearly, he is not on board with the first name basis idea.

Mom gives Logan a warm, genuine smile when she pulls back. "It's wonderful to see you again, Logan. Too bad Brandon isn't here."

I glance between her and Dad. "Brandon's not here?"

"Something came up with work," Dad says. "I needed him to go to New York."

"But it's your birthday," I say.

"Which means obviously I couldn't go. It's fine," Dad says, waving dismissively. "This needed to get done. Brandon and I see each other all the time."

I'm sure they do. But while this whole event is a little excessive for a birthday, I find it sad Dad basically forced Brandon to choose work over family. My brother is already in danger of becoming a fully-fledged workaholic just like Dad. Not JUST like him, because Brandon is warm and kind and fun. Or he can be. There's still hope for him yet, but this kind of thing does not bode well.

The only positive thing about Brandon's absence means

one less awkward encounter with a hostile member of my family. I glance at Logan, whose expression is totally neutral. I mean, HOT neutral because the man is never just *neutral*, but he looks neither pleased or disappointed by this news.

Just as an awkward silence descends on our little group, a man with a shock of white hair and a thin mustache edges his way into the conversation. I'm not mad at all when Dad turns to give the man his full attention.

"Don't be a stranger," Mom tells Logan with another smile.

Then she joins my dad, and it's over. I breathe an audible, dramatic sigh of relief. If I were the type to carry a handkerchief, I'd wipe it across my brow.

"I'm sorry," I say when my parents are out of earshot.

"You can't apologize for other people, Parker."

"No, I know. It's just ... you deserve better."

Logan pins me with a look. "So do you."

His words warm me, but I can't hold his gaze for long. I look away, watching as Dad curls an arm protectively around Mom. She drops her head on his shoulder. "Dad is tough to deal with. But he has some good qualities. He really does love my mom. That's not nothing."

"It's not," Logan agrees.

"Enough about my parents," I say, smiling at Logan. "Now that we've faced the familial inquisition, we can actually have fun."

Logan gazes at me with a smolder full of promises he has NO business making as a fake boyfriend. "Who says I'm not having fun already?"

As far as adhesive goes, I'm about as effective as an off-brand glue stick. The kind that barely holds construction paper together and frequently serves as a snack for children.

Because within half an hour, I've lost Logan. Completely and totally lost. There is no sign of the man anywhere. And trust me, I've looked. It's not like he's hard to miss either—he's a big dude.

A big dude who might have left the building right alongside Elvis.

I know Logan is a celebrity and I should have expected that everyone and their half-brother's cousin from Idaho would want to talk to him. But I vastly underestimated the way he'd get swarmed. The last I saw of him, he was shooting me an apologetic look and being dragged off to discuss sports with Larry. I also forgot the team owner would be here. My dad may not be a huge hockey fan, but Larry throws his money around, and being a shareholder at Ever-Tech is one of those places. I'm not surprised he stole Logan, but I sure wish Larry would bring him back.

By now, Logan could be in another state. On another continent. In space.

What I know for certain is that when Aaron Wagner appears in front of me like some kind of ghastly apparition, I really regret not being Logan's superglue.

"May I have this dance, madame?" Aaron asks in a terrible French accent. He sounds like Martin Short doing a bad impression of Lumiere from *Beauty and the Beast*.

I briefly consider saying, "My breasts don't dance," since Aaron directed his question toward my chest, but decide against it. I do cross my arms, providing some small amount of protection from Aaron's slimy gaze.

"I'm actually here with someone."

"Yeah?" Aaron makes a show of exaggeratedly peering around the room. "Where is he?"

"Obviously not here," I mutter.

I glance over Aaron's shoulder and wish I could make Logan appear with only the concentration of my mind. But I'm no better at moving objects with my mind than I am at being glue.

"Come on," Aaron says, tugging at my arm. "It'll be fun."

About as fun as getting pelted with vinegar-filled water balloons. Ew! That is a viscerally terrible idea—but still preferable to dancing with the man now trying to man-handle me out onto the dance floor.

It's just my luck that the full band—because of course my father has a full band—stops playing a fast-paced Bruno Mars cover and moves into Ed Sheeran.

Awesome. Now Aaron Wagner is going to ruin Ed Sheeran for me forever.

I pull my arm away from his just as a warm hand slides around my waist, gently maneuvering me backward into a firm chest.

I know this chest! And I know this scent. More than either of those things, I recognize the immediate sense of peace I seem to feel in Logan's presence.

"I don't mean to butt in," Logan says, and it's clear from his tone he's not the least bit sorry and absolutely meant to butt in, "but I need to have the first dance of the night with my girlfriend. It's a requirement."

Girlfriend. This all may be fake, but hearing Logan call me his girlfriend *does* things to me.

I am a stick of butter left outside on a summer day. A warm, buttery puddle.

I mean, I know Logan's words are just a ploy to get Aaron

away. They're what we agreed on in the rules: one night of being boyfriend and girlfriend.

But in my heart of hearts, I'm burying this treasure of a moment for a rainy day. I'll unearth it later, when I've lost all joy in my life so I can remember that brief point in time when Logan Barnes called me his girlfriend.

I can't bring myself to look at Logan's face. And not just because it would be awkward with how close he's standing behind me. I'm afraid if I look at him right now, I'll be a goner.

Aaron smiles, looking like a little dog baring its teeth. "Sure, man. I didn't realize Parker had a boyfriend. Or that it was *you*."

He looks like he's about to say something insulting— either to me or to Logan or possibly to us both—but thinks better of it. Who knew the man had more than one brain cell? There are at least two in there.

"Maybe I'll catch you later, Parker?" Aaron says, for once making eye contact with my eyeballs instead of my chest.

Maybe he has three brain cells.

"I don't think so," Logan says smoothly. Calmly. Politely. But there is an edge of a threat underneath his words.

Silly me, I never thought hearing a man threaten someone could be sexy. It absolutely is. It is the *sexiest*.

"Surely, you could spare Parker for one dance," Aaron says with a sneer.

"I don't share," Logan says, and the rough edge to his voice makes my insides quiver. "But the choice is not mine to make."

I think of Logan's words earlier, how he said I'm not a pawn. His protectiveness combined with his respect for me is like the ultimate gold standard for men.

It is in this moment that I realize I might be a little bit in love with my fake boyfriend.

"Parker," Logan says with deliberately slow enunciation, "do you want to dance with this person?"

Not even a little bit. "No, thank you."

I almost expect Aaron to say something about what his father or my father will have to say about this, but he doesn't. He just disappears into the crowd. Hopefully to never return.

I count to five, taking in a long, deep breath before I turn around. What I don't do is step back, and neither does Logan. This means we are really, really close. Most definitely girlfriend close.

Or ... fake girlfriend close?

"Would you like to dance?" Logan asks.

"I would like nothing more," I say, not even caring a little how desperate this might sound. After all the things Logan just did and said, forget restraint. What's the point?

With a devastating smile, Logan places his hands on my waist. I wrap mine around his neck and relax into him. It was a close call, but Ed Sheeran was spared. I'm glad because I wasn't at all looking forward to removing his songs from my playlists after Aaron ruined his music forever.

The trimmed hair above Logan's collar bristles against my fingertips and I find myself sliding my fingers up his scalp. Might as well milk this moment for all it's worth.

"Thanks for rescuing me," I say. "I thought I lost you."

"I couldn't escape Larry. He needed to parade me around like his personal show pony."

I make a face. "Ugh. Larry. I'm sorry. I didn't do a very good job at being your glue."

"I don't plan to let you go again," Logan murmurs close to my ear. "This time, I'll be *your* glue."

"Okay," I say, listening to the steady thump of his heartbeat. "I can live with that."

The reality is that after the brief time we've spent together tonight, I'm not sure I can live *without* it.

Sorry, Logan. You might have intended to be one-night-only glue, but you're actually the forever kind. A new, lab-tested and irreversibly permanent glue.

"Is this appropriate dance touching?" Logan asks, and I laugh.

"Yes." I chew the inside of my cheek until I'm sure I won't blurt out that I'd happily settle for something *less* parent's birthday party appropriate.

I'm surprised how smooth Logan is. Even though this is just a slow dance, he's doing more than swaying. And if I didn't know any better, I'd say he's enjoying himself. Not as much as I'm enjoying it, obviously.

Logan smirks. "You're not secretly filming this for social media, right?"

"That you know of."

His piercing green eyes lock on mine. "There's something to be said for just living in the moment. Not filming it. Not posting it. Not sharing it."

"Despite my job, I actually agree."

"Then, let's be in the moment, Pete."

Logan pulls me closer, lifting a hand to cup my head, nestling me against his chest. His fingertips trail over my neck before coming back to rest on my waist.

I close my eyes, getting lost in Logan's scent and the safe feel of being held right here.

Logan's right about being in the moment. This is one of those where I wish I could hit pause. The kind of moment I want to revel in, burrowing down like it's a warm, comfy bed where I can shut out the whole rest of the world.

I want time to spin out slow and thick and sweet like taffy. I want to stay right here for an eternity of seconds, my cheek on Logan's firm chest, his hands warm and strong on my waist, his fingers moving lightly over the fabric of my dress. When I shiver, Logan spreads those big hands wide over my back, nestling me even closer.

"Cold?" Then, with a note of teasing in his voice, he says, "Or scared?"

"Neither. I'm happy."

"You shiver when you're happy, Pete?"

"Wouldn't you like to know."

"I would, actually," Logan says, and then his voice changes. It's sincere and impassioned. "We've lost years, and that's my fault. But I want to know what I missed. To know who you are now, Parker, and who you want to be. Not to start over but to start fresh."

The words make my eyes prick with tears. They sound like a confession, and not the close friends kind.

But am I delusional to think Logan could want more?

With *me*?

It's not lost on me that Logan is saying this when I can't see his face, as though hiding allows him to be brave.

His words sound like … *feelings* words. Like something you say at the start of a relationship. Not simply rekindling an old friendship.

Or maybe it's been too long since I've been in a relationship. My radar is broken. Maybe my wishful thinking is hearing what it wants to hear. What it's always wanted to hear.

"I'd like that too."

"Like what?" he asks, the teasing tone reappearing in his voice.

"What you said."

"What did I say?"

"You're going to make me repeat it?" I ask.

"Seems only fair," he says. "I said it first. Repeating it sounds a whole lot easier. And"—he tilts his head, lowering it so his lips brush my cheek—"despite what you might think about athletes and egos, we're just one harsh word away from curling up in the fetal position."

I can't help but laugh. "Somehow I doubt that."

"Well, maybe I'd just like to hear how you feel," he says. He clearly shaved before tonight, but there's still the slightest scratch of his stubble on my cheek. It makes the moment feel more real. "I'd like to know what you want."

How I feel? What I want? Now *there's* a pair of loaded questions.

I try to pluck the perfect words from my mind to confess how I feel without laying myself completely bare. Without opening myself up to a whole world of hurt I have no doubt will eventually follow this night.

It's been too magical. Too *not* fake. Too close to what I really want. Too good to last.

Everything in me wants to open up again. Except the part borne out of the hurt Logan caused when he left. That part wants to raise the drawbridge and add some crocodiles to the moat in front of my castle.

I ignore the scared part of me. I choose bravery instead. I choose to be reckless. I choose hope.

"I'd like to start fresh too," I tell him. "I want to catch up on what I missed, to fill the gaps, to get to know the Logan of *now*."

He doesn't say anything for a long moment. "I'm not sure you'll like the Logan of now."

"I do like the Logan of now," I tell him. Perhaps a little *too* firmly. But I hate hearing him sound unsure.

174

Logan slides his hands up my back slowly, then down again. I do my best not to react, but another shiver moves through me. I know Logan feels it when he chuckles. His breath on my neck makes me shiver again.

Even if my words hadn't said it all, the way I react to even the simplest touch from Logan is a bold confession about how happy he makes me. With all my might, I shoot a wish into the universe that I won't regret opening myself up to Logan a second time.

CHAPTER 15

Parker

AN HOUR LATER, we still haven't left the dance floor. After our initial slow dance, the band picked up the tempo and I fully expected Logan to lead me away for drinks or the buffet. Instead, I was totally shocked when he smirked (like he knew just what I was thinking), twirled me expertly (like this is something he does all the time), and then proceeded to show off his moves (like his life depended on it).

And let me tell you—the man has *moves*.

His hips? They don't lie. His feet? Not guilty, because they have got *serious* rhythm. His groove thing? Thoroughly shaken.

The best part—besides simply watching Logan—is the way he keeps touching me. Even in the faster songs, we never go more than a few seconds without him taking my hand or holding my hips or brushing his fingers along the bare skin of my shoulders. The only time we're more than a few inches apart is when he pauses to take off his jacket and throw it over a chair.

"For a man who doesn't like dancing, you sure do it well," I tell Logan now, leaning closer so he can hear me over the instrumental version of "Uptown Funk."

"I never said I didn't like dancing," he says, arching an eyebrow.

"Yes, you did!"

He shakes his head, the smallest of smiles lifting one corner of his mouth. "I said I came here to play hockey, not dance. And I told you I don't like the spotlight. I never said I don't like dancing."

I think back to our conversations, realizing he's right. "Well, you certainly gave me the *impression* you don't like dancing."

"It just takes the right partner."

Though the song is fast, Logan pulls me close with both his hands on my hips. I slide my hands up his chest and around his neck. Our eyes lock. The other dancers disappear. The music fades.

I'm no longer at my father's birthday gala. I'm not even in Harvest Hollow. Logan and I are tucked away inside our own little wrinkle in time.

As the moment stretches, so does the intensity. Something is building between us, gathering momentum like a boulder hurtling down a hill. I can sense the cliff's edge just before I go flying over.

And that's when I step back, pulling away from Logan as reality snaps back into place like a rubber band that's been stretched too far.

"I need some air," I say.

I don't dare meet Logan's eyes as I dart from the dance floor, trying to catch my breath and shift my trajectory.

Fake, I remind myself. *Fakity fake fake fake.*

The problem is ... Logan's not just leasing real estate in my mind. There is no renting to own. He's like the guy who buys up a whole side of the board in Monopoly and plants a hotel on every spot.

He catches up to me at the bar, where I'm gulping down a bottle of water. He grabs one for himself and then places a hand on my lower back. "How about we get some food and find a quiet corner?"

My stomach growls an enthusiastic yes.

But a quiet corner? That sounds downright dangerous.

Still, I nod, and after Logan reacquires his jacket, we beeline toward the food. The buffet is a lavish affair, complete with carving station and the fanciest of finger foods. When we've loaded up plates, Logan tilts his head toward a far corner of the room. But he doesn't stop at one of the linen-covered tables like I expect. Instead, he leads me outside to a patio garden.

As the doors close behind us, the music, lights, and voices fade. Only a few couples and small groups are outside, faces cast in shadows. A few gas fire pits are lit with groups of chairs and large potted plants creating semi-private seating areas. Logan leads me to a back corner with a small loveseat tucked away behind a vine-covered trellis.

Yep—totally dangerous.

"How did you know this patio was even here?" I ask.

"Lucky guess."

As Logan sits, I realize just how small this loveseat is. I'm practically in his lap. Hopefully, the dim lighting will hide the flush in my cheeks. I'm pretty sure it's not going anywhere.

I give up on my food after a few minutes. It's awkward

balancing my plate on my knees, and I find that sitting so close to Logan, on top of all the touching we did while dancing, has my stomach tied up in a whole tangle of knots. I set my plate down on the small table next to us, surprised when Logan does the same. His plate, however, is empty.

I laugh. "You don't play around."

"Dancing made me work up quite the appetite."

Logan shifts closer to me, lifting one arm so it rests behind me, his fingertips lightly grazing my bare shoulder. I shiver, and he smiles.

"Happy or cold?"

"Both?" I say, rubbing my arms.

In seconds, Logan has removed his jacket again, draping it over my shoulders and pulling the lapels together in the front. I hold my breath the whole time until he puts his arm back around me, this time tugging me closer.

Then he goes and ruins it.

"You said I could ask about your terrible kissing stories another time. Does this count as another time?"

Really? Right now, this man wants to hear my horror stories? Way to ruin the mood, pal.

I glance up at him. We're seated so close I can't hold his gaze for longer than a second or two. "You really want to know about all that?"

"I do. I mean, if you don't mind talking about it, that is."

Do I mind?

My kisslessness isn't my favorite topic of conversation. But I'm not embarrassed. None of these stories have anything to do with *me*—other than the common thread that I sure know how to pick 'em. And that I never did end up getting kissed.

I turn until I'm facing Logan. He mirrors my position, then pulls my legs over his lap, resting his hand on my calf.

THAT won't be distracting at all. I nestle a little deeper into his jacket, pulling it tighter around me. His warm, masculine scent surrounds me, putting me even more at ease.

"Okay," I tell him. "But remember—you asked for it."

I decide to start with Joey Walton.

"My sophomore year I went to a party. Just one. It was an end of the year backyard cookout kind of thing. Joey Walton had been flirting with me all night and at this point, everyone had a boyfriend but me. So, I figured, what the heck."

Logan's starting to look like he wishes he hadn't asked. He's doing the muscle clenching thing in his jaw. I realize I've barely seen it since his first day here, back when he found out his contract included TikTok.

"Are you okay?" I ask. He nods, but that muscle keeps right on clenching. "Anyway. I guess Joey had just watched *Spiderman*—the one with the upside-down kiss—"

The tension leaves his face now as Logan groans. "No. No, he didn't Tobey Maguire you."

"Yep. Well. He *tried* to Tobey Maguire me. He led me out to this old tree house and then climbed the rope ladder—"

"Stop it."

"—and he hung himself upside down. Then he tried to pull me in for a kiss but ... the wood holding the ladder was rotten. It fell with him still hanging from it by his knees. He broke his arm and his collarbone."

Logan gapes at me. "Is it bad to laugh? I feel bad laughing."

"Laugh all you want. Joey ended up falling for a volunteer at the hospital. She went to Stony Peak High and was doing service hours to look good on college applications. One thing led to another, and they got married a few years ago."

"Wow." Logan shakes his head and runs his hand lightly up my calf. A cascade of goose bumps follows his touch.

"Okay, you're right. That's terrible. But like, epically terrible. Other than him meeting his future wife—which is a surprising twist. That's got to be the worst."

"That depends on the criteria you're using to judge," I tell him. "Comparatively, that one's pretty tame."

Logan's jaw drops, and I press on, recounting the many tales of my terrible almost kisses. Like Bruce Fiander, a guy in college whose breath smelled so much like dog food that I panicked when he got close and pretended to faint. Which made *him* panic and desert me in a restaurant parking lot. A class act.

There was Jeff Zacharias my junior year of high school, who decided to start by kissing my neck but somehow got his braces caught in my sweater. We ended up having to cut him out of it, ruining my very favorite sweater. Then he needed an emergency orthodontist appointment to remove the remnants of cashmere from his mouth.

His parents tried to make *my* parents cover the bill, which turned into a whole thing. Mrs. Zacharias has been shunned on any committee my mother has run ever since.

And I can't forget Matt, who had an allergic reaction to my perfume so severe that before he even made contact, his lips swelled ten times their size. They looked like two sausages stacked on top of each other.

"How many of these stories involve someone needing to go to the hospital?" Logan asks.

"I'd say about sixty percent. I did wonder briefly if I'd been cursed."

"I mean, you have to consider it." Logan shakes his head. "You're right—those stories are … something."

"Oh, I'm not even done," I tell him. "This last one is by far the worst. If you still really want to know."

"Tell me. It's kind of like a car wreck I can't look away from."

"It was Cameron Dunn in the observatory with the candlestick," I say. Logan stares blankly. "Sorry—Clue humor. In reality, it was Cameron Dunn in the university library with the stomach flu."

Logan covers his mouth, eyes wide, and shakes his head.

I laugh. "Don't worry. I jumped out of the way before he —" I pause, trying to find the least disgusting way to tell this part. "Suffice it to say, I dodged a very special kind of bullet. If you get my drift."

"I wish I didn't. I really wish I didn't. I can see how this all might scar a person."

"I wouldn't say I'm scarred, per se, but all the awful almosts *did* give me pause. A *lot* of pause. And it helped me decide to hold out for my first kiss. Which ... brought its own set of challenges."

"That sounds ominous," Logan says.

I hesitate, suddenly unsure how much I want to say. The ridiculously embarrassing stories are one thing.

The rest ...

But, for the first time, I actually *want* to talk to someone other than Mia about this. It feels cathartic or freeing. And Logan hasn't for one second made me feel naive or silly or ridiculous about this. He also hasn't stopped running gentle fingers up and down my calf, so that's extra motivation to extend the conversation.

I draw in a breath, then dive in. "Since most people expect at the very *least* to kiss someone on even a first date, I started being up front. Just so there weren't any surprises. Mia says it's not anyone's business but mine. While I agree, it just feels right to be honest that I'm not going to kiss a guy on a first date. Expectations matter. It's also sort of a test for me to see how they respond. Most guys, as it turns out, react ... poorly."

Logan's jaw starts clenching again.

"What does that mean?" he asks in a low voice. One that sounds threatening and protective and makes the tiny hairs on my arms stand up.

"Guys usually fall into one of two camps when I say I haven't kissed anyone before. The first seems to think there's something wrong with me. I've been called a prude—among other things."

Logan looks downright murderous now, which makes me feel all warm and happy. Guess I'm into homicidal urges now. I hold up a hand before he can interrupt and say whatever he seems poised to say.

"I know that's their issue, not mine. And not having experience doesn't make me a prude or naive or anything else. I like to think that I'm just ... *choosy*."

I smile, which seems to ease Logan's tension the slightest bit. Which is probably good because he's really not going to like what I say next.

But when his hand makes its way up to my knee, resting there and giving me solid comfort, it's just the push I need.

"The other camp of guys seem to take this as a personal challenge. Like they wanted to be the first to ..." I search for a word or phrase, then wrinkle my nose when I come up with the best one I can think of. It's crass, but it really is the most fitting. "Like they wanted to mark their territory."

The expression on Logan's face shifts to something so terrifying that I'm honestly shocked.

"It's fine," I say, reaching out to squeeze his hand. "I mean, it's not *fine*. It's honestly terrible, but *I'm* fine. I can look out for myself."

I squeeze Logan's hand again and can practically feel the

tension radiating from him like summer heat steaming off the pavement. I need to bring him back down, so I grasp for the only potentially humorous story I can think of.

"I only had to use pepper spray once. Did you know it affects the person spraying too? Especially if you're in a car."

Logan groans, looking caught somewhere between laughing and throwing furniture. "That's terrible. You actually had to use pepper spray?"

"I know it sounds extreme but when I said no and he didn't—"

"No," he interrupts. "If some guy didn't listen to you saying no to kissing or whatever else, I fully support the use of pepper spray."

"Just not in a car," I add, smiling.

Logan doesn't smile back, and I worry I've really ruined this date.

Fake date.

Whatever. Real or fake, I ruined it by oversharing.

But then Logan lifts my hand to his mouth. Our eyes meet, and he asks, "May I?"

I swallow past a very inconvenient lump in my throat. "Yes."

What I'd like to say instead is *always. Anywhere.*

The kiss he places on my knuckles is achingly tender. I don't know how it's possible to feel so much from a kiss on the part of your body that has so few nerve endings. But I'm feeling A LOT.

"I'm sorry, Parker," Logan says then.

"You have nothing to be sorry for. You're not, like, the representative for all men."

With his free hand, he drags a hand down his face. "I know. I just hate thinking about any guy treating you like that. You deserve better." He pauses. "Also, if you have a list of their names and last known addresses—"

I cut him off with a laugh. "Nope. Not worth it. We're turning that bad boy image around. Speaking of ... want to tell me why you got into a fight in the grocery store with a fan?"

Groaning, Logan leans back, covering his face with both hands. This means I'm not holding his hand anymore, and I try not to feel disappointed by this. But then he drops his hand to my calf again, and all is right with my world.

"Anything but that."

Well, okay then. He opened that door nice and wide for me. Still, I hesitate for a moment before asking, "I know you chalked your leaving up to being a stupid kid, but I know there had to be more. Did something push you to go? To cut us out of your life?"

Logan stiffens and his fingers tighten around my calf. He glances at me quickly, then away, attempting a small smile that looks more like a grimace. "You don't pull any punches, do you?"

Instead of telling him not to worry about it or giving him an out, I chew the inside of my cheek and wait. Even though we briefly talked about him leaving and he already apologized, I still don't understand what prompted his sudden departure. I know it couldn't have just been to get a fresh start.

Logan sighs, absently running a hand through his hair while his other slides up my leg, finally resting on my knee. He still doesn't look at me.

"As you know, I spent a ton of time at your house when I was a kid. Mostly because things at home weren't good."

This much I know, though Logan talked very little about his home life. His dad was never in the picture. From what I

185

gather, his mom was disinterested at best. Looking back now with older eyes, I might be a little less forgiving and call her neglectful.

"You and Brandon always made me feel welcome," he says. "Your mom too."

"She still loves you."

And she's not the only one.

I tell that pesky voice to shut it.

Logan shifts, angling my legs a little on his lap. I smooth down my skirt and pull his jacket tighter around myself.

"Your dad on the other hand ... I always knew he wasn't my biggest fan. It's not like he flat-out said anything, but I could tell."

I didn't ever notice, but I remember Logan mentioning this when I first talked to him about the gala. "As we've discussed, my dad can be kind of a jerk."

"Which I expected," Logan says, his voice sounding tight. "And so I wasn't surprised right after graduation when I overheard him saying I was a bad influence on Brandon."

I lean forward and take Logan's hand. I squeeze, but he doesn't squeeze back. "I'm really sorry, Logan. For what it's worth, I disagree."

He meets my gaze. "It's worth a lot." Then he sighs, glancing away again. "What *did* surprise me was hearing your mom and Brandon agree with him."

I gasp, already shaking my head. "No. They didn't. They wouldn't!"

Would they?

But the sad smile Logan gives me assures me that they would and they did. I'm shocked at how fast my protectiveness swells. Followed quickly by anger.

I squeeze Logan's hand again. "What did they say?"

"Your mom wasn't cruel or anything. She just said they

should look at it more like Brandon having an opportunity to be a good influence on *me*."

Not terrible. But not great either. I can tell from the way Logan's hesitating that my brother must have said something much worse. I wish I could take back my question. I should have asked Logan about his life in Raleigh or pretty much anything other than this.

But at the same time, now I *need* to know.

"And Brandon?" I ask quietly.

Logan goes back to the jaw-clenching from earlier. Even so, I still catch a glimpse of the boy he was, the boy who was hurt by people he trusted.

"Brandon said it wouldn't matter much longer because the two of us didn't have anything in common other than hockey. He said once I left, we'd probably never talk again. Your dad said something along the lines of 'the sooner the better' and I walked right out then. That was it."

Without overthinking, I lean forward and pull Logan into a hug. It's awkward with my legs in his lap, and I'm practically bent into a pretzel but *I don't care*. All I want right now is to hug away the stupid things my family said. Not like I can.

But I hug Logan as if that's possible, as if I could squeeze this bad memory right out of him.

I'd also like to stab Brandon with a fork. A plastic one because I'm not *really* a violent person. But the heavy-duty plastic kind because I still do want it to hurt.

While my brother has always been able to stand up to Dad in a way I'm just learning how to do, Brandon also wanted to—*wants* to—impress him. I seriously doubt he meant what he said back then. It was probably just one of those times where you agree with someone just to get them to back off or shut up. I bet it would kill him to know all these years he's been mad at Logan, that Brandon's own words were the impetus for Logan's departure.

"I'm sorry, Logan," I say into his neck, which smells so distractingly good it's hard to focus on what I'm apologizing for.

Oh, right. My terrible family.

"You don't need to be sorry," Logan says. "You had nothing to do with it. I'm just sorry the way I reacted hurt you. I'd do it all differently if I could."

"No more apologies to me," I tell him. "You should really tell Brandon."

"I'd rather not."

"But he'd understand. I'm sure he'd feel terrible. You were good friends once. I have no doubt you could be at least peaceful acquaintances again. If not friends."

"While I appreciate it, I don't need you fixing this. Okay? Brandon and I will talk."

"Promise?" I ask. Maybe it shouldn't be so important that they work this out. But it is.

"Eventually. I had planned on it. Though I still might not explain the whole story. It's old news."

Logan's jacket slips from my shoulders then. As the cool night air hits my skin, I'm instantly cold.

Logan pulls his jacket back up over my shoulders, then shifts me so my arms are still around his neck but I'm in his lap, not leaning over. It's definitely more comfortable. And warmer. And it's LOGAN'S LAP.

So, you know. A place I've always wanted to be.

And yet, I'm suddenly feeling shy. The whole night we've been touching more than ever before. We've talked about more intimate things too. Overall, it feels like we left the metaphorical kiddie pool and dove straight into the Mariana

Trench for a free dive. I'm not sure how long I can keep holding my breath.

"Is this okay?" Logan asks, his hands still moving up and down my back. "I don't think you made a sticky note about sitting in laps."

I most definitely did not. And the reminder of the rules is exactly what I need to sober me up from being Logan-drunk. As gracefully as I can, I hop off Logan's lap and hold out a hand.

He raises a brow but lets me pretend I pull him to his feet when clearly, I don't have the strength to move this boulder of a man anywhere.

"You know what we need right now?" I ask.

"I can think of a few things," Logan says, and the look in his eyes makes my pulse skyrocket.

"Was one of them dance therapy? Because that's definitely what we need. Come on, Wolverine. Time to boogie."

CHAPTER 16

Logan

SOME PEOPLE TALK MORE when they get nervous. Parker gets quiet.

I've witnessed her nervous babbling before, so she can definitely go that route. But when she's really, *really* anxious, it's like someone drops a soundproof glass jar over her. Total radio silence.

And somewhere between getting the car from the valet and nearing Maple Street, Parker clammed up.

Glancing over as I pull into the parking spot I'm paying an arm and a leg for, I see Parker staring straight ahead, toying with the strap of her small purse. It's the only movement I see from her. Is she even blinking?

After the ease and comfort we usually fall into, I don't like thinking she's nervous.

I'll admit—I'm feeling a little unsure myself.

Is anyone *ever* totally confident at the end of a date? It's like stepping into a room with ten unmarked doors, all leading in different directions. They could open up to reveal the end of night and an amicable goodbye—or a more permanent one. A door might open and extend the evening a little longer—or a *lot* longer. The doors might lead to a long future. Or a goodbye.

In addition to the stress of making the choice of what door to open, the person you're on a date with also must pick a door. Ideally, you choose the same door. In the past, this wasn't a big deal, because if I dated, things were clear up front.

But not with Parker. This is new territory for me, and I'm not sure how to navigate it.

What if Parker and I don't want to walk through the same door?

To be fully honest, I don't know what happens next. And based on Parker's silence and the way she's now chewing on her lip, I don't think she's so sure either.

Tonight has been, hands down, the best date of my life. Not even seeing Parker's dad look at me with disdain or having Larry parade me around like his personal circus monkey could dampen the evening. Parker's light eclipsed any of those low moments, banishing them into shadows.

That is one thing that hasn't changed about her. She illuminates whatever space she's in. She illuminates me.

What also hasn't changed, no matter the feelings I seem to have caught for Parker, is the big expiration date stamped on my time in Harvest Hollow. Which means I should just let this night be what we agreed on: a single night of being a fake couple.

The idea sours in my stomach.

I turn off the SUV and climb out, jogging around to open

Parker's door. Taking her hand, I help her down. Until I say goodnight and goodbye to being her fake boyfriend, you better believe I'm going to get the most I can out of the rules we agreed on.

She looks over at me with surprise, the lights outside the car illuminating her features with a soft glow. I smile, and she returns it weakly before dropping her gaze, almost shyly. I keep a firm grasp on her hand. It's in the rules!

We amble through the parking lot, headed toward Maple Street and our building. Slow, like neither of us is ready for the night to end. Like we're both hoping these few blocks will stretch out longer somehow. Marathon length, maybe?

The shops are all closed up for the night, and the lights strung across the street give our stroll a whole *vibe*. I want to enjoy this moment the same way I've enjoyed all the moments tonight—being completely present. Right after I texted Jeremy, I turned off my phone, never taking it out of my pocket again. Instead, I snapped mental pictures of Parker smiling, Parker dancing goofily to the orchestral version of Outkast's "Hey Ya," Parker gazing up at me with her brown eyes crinkled in laughter. I've savored the feel of her in my arms, the warm cinnamon sugar scent of her skin.

But it's hard to relish in *this* moment when she's still so unnaturally, un-Parker-ly quiet. "What's going on in that head of yours? Your thoughts are almost as loud as the computer in your office."

She huffs out a laugh, shaking her head. Then goes quiet again. "I had a good time tonight," she says finally.

"Are you letting me down easy, Pete? Because that sounds like the start of the end of every bad date ever."

She grins—a real one this time. "No! I really mean it."

"Good. Because if you're done with me after one night, that would make me a pretty terrible fake boyfriend."

Her smile falters. I want to punch myself in the face. Why did I say *fake?*

Because I'm a coward who hasn't decided what I want. Because I've never felt about a woman the way I feel about Parker.

Even after one fake date, I know. This is something different. She's different. And maybe I'm starting to want something I've never wanted. Something I never thought I'd have.

"You are the very best fake boyfriend I've ever had," she says softly.

I squeeze her fingers, letting my thumb skim over the back of her hand. "And exactly how many fake boyfriends have you had?"

"None." Then her eyes go wide. "That's not true! I had a fake boyfriend at camp once!"

I grin. "You did not."

"I did! I went to this great sports camp near Asheville. Hiking, canoeing, horseback riding—all that stuff. The guy's name was John. This other guy wouldn't stop trying to ask me to go out with him—"

"Where exactly does one 'go out' at camp?"

Parker waves a hand. "Nowhere. It's an expression. Though some people did 'go out' down by the creek—aka, kissing and … stuff. Anyway, the point is—John offered to be my fake boyfriend so the other guy would leave me alone. He sold the idea like he would be my bodyguard of sorts. Very convincing."

I'll bet he was. "And how'd that work out for you?"

"The other guy stopped bugging me. And John confessed his *real* feelings for me at the very end of camp." She bites her lip and then smiles. "We wrote letters for almost a year before we fell out of touch."

I can't help but ask the question burning in my mind like

an Olympic torch. More like, making *me* burn with jealousy at the thought of Parker with some guy—which is stupid considering we're talking about the distant past.

This does not seem to matter to my irrational jealousy, which is crackling and roaring.

"Did you and John ever 'go out' down by the creek?" I demand, feeling stupid even as I ask. Parker already told me she hadn't kissed anyone. And even if she did—this is *middle school*.

Still. I find myself clenching my teeth until she answers.

She shakes her head, and even in the dark, I can see the blush climbing her cheeks. "Nope. But we did hold hands."

"Like this?" I lift our joined hands.

She gives me a look. "I'm not sure of any other way to do it."

Clucking my tongue, I say "Oh, Pete. You think this is the only way to hold hands?"

"There are more?" she asks.

I tug her to a stop in a pool of shadows under the General Store's awnings. Then I unlink our fingers and then press our palms together, hooking all my fingers around her hand. "For starters, this is called the Palm Curl."

She giggles, the sound tiptoeing through my chest. "You're making that up."

I am. And clearly, I'm not doing a very good job.

"No, for real." I readjust so our hands are pressed up against each other, flat with fingers straight like we're holding a high-five. "This one is the Mirror or the High Five Hold."

Again, Parker laughs. I will make up stupid hand holding names all. Night. Long.

Now I link our fingers the way they were before. "This, of course, is the Classic."

I'm running out of ideas, which means running out of time. We're about thirty seconds from our apartments. And I'm not ready.

I manage to come up with a few bizarre other hand holds. There's the Backhand, where you—shocker—press the backs of your hands together. The Around the World, in which you hold the hands-on opposite sides of your body. The Brady Bunch, where all four hands link together.

"This is the Scarf," I say to a giggling Parker. Draping one hand over her shoulder, I wiggle my fingers until she lifts the hand closest to me and links our fingers.

"Wow," Parker says. "All these years, I had no idea what I've been missing out on."

"You learn something new every day, Pete. But don't go sharing these with just *any*one."

More like: don't go share these with *any other person at all.*

"So, do you have a favorite?" I ask.

Parker slips her hand in mine, linking our fingers. "The Classic. You?"

I run my thumb over the back of her hand. "Same."

She smiles but then starts walking again. Disappointment is a swift kick to the gut. But she doesn't let go of my hand, so at least there's that.

Holding hands, I've decided, is severely underrated.

The night was pleasant when we left, but there's a chill in the air now, and I can feel Parker shiver. This time, I know it's not from happiness. I pull her closer. She lets me, and I don't miss her tiny sigh.

Words gather into a flash mob in my brain. Too many things I want to say. Too many things I probably shouldn't say.

Now, *I'm* the quiet one.

We reach the door, and I manage to finagle the keys

without dropping my arm from Parker's shoulders. When the door opens without so much as a protest, Parker looks up at me.

"I meant to ask you before—did you do something to the door? It hasn't been sticking. I wasn't sure if that was just because the temperatures are dropping or if you did something."

She narrows her eyes at me, like the idea of me sneakily fixing a broken door is akin to stealing Halloween candy from little kids.

She's smart to be suspicious. I hired a guy to fix the door, unbeknownst to Parker or the owner of the building. "Maybe."

She shakes her head. "You got me Fancy Chair. You fixed my door."

"Now it's *our* door."

"*Our* door. And you teach me all the secret hand-holds I've been missing out on all these years. You're really something, Logan."

Her tone is light. But I glance her way when we're about halfway up the stairs, and her eyes are bright. Like she's trying to keep tears from spilling over. At the landing, I pull her into a hug, dropping my chin on top of her head. I don't know what's going on in her head, but if it's anything like the confusion in my own, it's a lot.

I can only *hope* it's something like what's going on in my head.

Parker's hands slide underneath my jacket, fisting the fabric of my shirt as she burrows into me. There's an edge of desperation in this hug.

It's nice to feel needed by someone. Especially by someone I know would be there for me as well. I might be almost thirty, but I really have no one like this in my life.

And it's only since I've come back to Harvest Hollow that I've realized how much I've been missing real connection.

Parker sighs, and I run a hand up and down her back. "Hey. Are you okay?"

I can feel her nodding against my chest. "I'm perfect. This night was perfect."

Almost perfect.

The only way it would be *more* perfect is if I could work up the nerve to ask Parker if she wants things between us to be *not* fake. Because nothing about tonight felt like pretend at all—except when either one of us brought it up.

There is definitely something real here. But I just can't stop circling back to the harsh facts: I hope to be gone in a matter of months.

But even if I go, does that have to matter? Couldn't we talk about how things could be? Living in different places doesn't have to mean an end. And it wouldn't need to be forever. But the idea of the future suddenly hits me like a slap in the face.

Parker's hands loosen on my shirt. But instead of pulling away, she slides her palms up my chest, curling them around my neck. She angles her head back, and when I meet her eyes, the look there makes my heart hammer.

She bites her lip. Looks at my mouth. Back to my eyes. Down again.

I wait, and these are the longest moments of my life. I know she wants her first kiss to mean something. And she flat-out said she didn't want to kiss me when this was fake.

All it would take from me is a word to say it's not fake. That this means something. Everything. The words are lodged in my throat as the moment stretches.

Then Parker is lifting up on her toes. My lids start to fall

197

closed, waiting. Ready. But her lips brush my cheek, not my mouth, as she leans forward to whisper in my ear.

"Logan, will you ... will you tell me what you would do?"

Tell her?

Parker correctly reads my hesitation as confusion and moves closer still, her lips grazing my ear. "Tell me in words how you'd kiss me. If this were a real date."

She gives a soft laugh then, one I recognize as embarrassment because I know her so well.

"I mean, if you *wanted* to kiss me."

If I ...

Does this woman honestly not know? After this whole night together, is it possible she doesn't know how I feel?

Maybe not, but if she's confused, it has to be because of the fake label still stuck to everything. I'd like to rip that label right off.

But that's not what she asked for. She asked me to tell her how I'd kiss her. And she's still waiting for my answer.

Parker must think my lack of answer is a no—a *no I won't* or a *no I don't want to kiss her*—because she stiffens and starts to pull away.

I don't let her. Instead, I draw her closer. Now I'm the one leaning forward, finding her ear to speak soft and slow. At least, that was my intent. But it takes me a moment.

I swallow thickly, then clear my throat. Still, my voice is shaky. "You know I'm not so good with words, Pete."

But then Parker places a kiss, feather soft, on my jaw. "I trust you," she says.

Turns out, that's all the permission I need.

CHAPTER 17

Parker

THIS IS either the best or worst idea I've ever had. Ask me again tomorrow.

I'm still sort of frozen in shock from what I just asked when Logan starts to move. I suck in a breath.

He keeps his rough cheek pressed to mine, his lips close to my ear. But his hands glide slowly up my back, his palms spread wide and his fingers tiptoeing their way up my spine. Still, Logan doesn't say a word. But his breath catches when his hands reach the top of my dress and move to the bare skin of my upper back.

Then he speaks, his voice raw and rough but so, so soft.

"I wouldn't rush," Logan says, and I'm not sure if the full-body shiver is from his words or his breath on my ear or from his rough hands moving slowly on my skin. "I would take my time with you."

I bite my lip as Logan's fingers slide underneath the straps of my dress. This shouldn't be so sensual. He's touching my upper back. My trapezius muscles. The scapula bones I've always thought looked way too much like stunted chicken wings. Nothing sexy or sensual about that. Total neutral zone.

But there is nothing neutral when it comes to Logan. The man could touch my heels, calloused from years of being in skates, and even those deadened nerves would start singing an opera.

One of Logan's hands slips back down my spine, spreading his fingers wide when he reaches my lower back. With gentle pressure, he shifts me forward until there is no space between us. He glides his other hand up my neck and his fingers move into my hair.

If I hadn't seen Logan on the ice, I'd never believe this big man could possess so much grace and control.

I can't help but let out a little sound when his fingertips press into my scalp, massaging. Stroking. Logan tilts his head, the tip of his nose brushing my jaw just below my ear.

"I would make sure you felt safe," he says then. "Safe and *wanted*."

The words *safe* and *wanted* seem to float through the air before wrapping around me like a warm cloak. I want to tell Logan that he's always made me feel safe. But my brain snags on *wanted*.

Because … despite the soft caress of his fingertips on my scalp and the way his nose is gently tracing the line of my jaw, I don't know if I'm *wanted*. Not really. Not by Logan.

I mean, yes—right now, he's making me *feel* wanted. But does Logan want me? Or is this all part of the dangerous game of make-believe we've been playing all night?

I was the one who made the rules. I was the one who

called this fake, who lied to my dad about Logan being my date and then my boyfriend. I did that. But now I've trapped myself in a place where I don't know what's really real. Not for sure.

Logan is definitely making me *feel* wanted.

Logan's mouth replaces his nose on my jaw. It's not a kiss, exactly, but more of a caress with his slightly parted lips.

While I do feel completely safe with Logan, I have never felt more like I've just been thrown out of a plane. Because whatever protective harness I'd kept strapped tight around my heart to keep it in place is gone, and I am flying or maybe falling, suspended over something unknown.

This man has my heart. It's his. I think it always has been. And there is nothing more dangerous than that.

I could step away. I could fake a smile and tell Logan, "Wow, thanks for a very informative and educational kissing tutorial. Sleep well!"

I could run.

I could protect myself.

I don't. I stand there, eyes closed and breaths coming fast and shallow, as Logan moves his mouth along my jaw, then trails his lips down my neck.

"I would explore," this man holding my heart says then. "I would savor you."

He drags his nose over the spot where my neck and shoulder meet, and goose bumps shoot across my skin. *Savor*, indeed.

I've read a few romance novels. Okay, fine—more than a few. My fair share, if I'm being honest. The best ones make me hope for love, but also for meaningful friendships and relationships.

As much as I love reading romance, there are a few

phrases authors use that I simply cannot handle. The one that makes me immediately roll my eyes is a character saying they felt their ovaries explode.

Yeah, right. Ovaries. Exploding.

First—ew.

Second—*what woman is aware enough to feel their ovaries?* Or maybe I'm just NOT aware of mine.

Third—out of all the anatomical parts of the body to feel desire, why ovaries? I mean, sure, I get the whole thing about a man being so amazing, a woman might think about marriage and babies.

But to feel your ovaries explode? Hard pass.

Only ... I think I get it now. I do.

It's still a stupid phrase. I will still roll my eyes every time I read it. But I am one hundred percent sure that for the first time in my life, I *feel* my ovaries. And they are doing something that feels a whole lot like a whole carton of fireworks on the fourth of July.

I am in so much trouble.

"Before I ever got to your mouth," Logan whispers against my skin, "I would kiss you here."

Logan presses an open-mouthed kiss to my throat, right over my pulse. His lips are perfect. The pressure is perfect. Everything is *perfect.*

A straight line of desire shoots directly from that spot on my neck to my mouth. I am actively fighting the desire to tug Logan right up to where I want his lips the most—on mine.

Forget what I said about no kissing. That one brief brush of his lips is enough to make me want to toss all good sense and all self-preservation out the window of a hundred-story building.

Almost.

But not quite. Because I *don't* grab Logan's face and drag

his mouth to mine. I keep standing. Keep breathing. Keep fisting my hands so tight in his dress shirt I'm gonna leave permanent wrinkles not even dry cleaners will be able to remove.

Logan chuckles then, like he knows exactly what's happening in my head. I'm sure he does. It's not like I am in any condition to hide my reactions to him and what he's doing. I can't even be mad about his amusement at my expense.

Laugh away, buddy. So long as you don't stop.

"Are you still with me, Pete?"

"Mm-hm," I manage.

"I'm glad. Because we're about to get to the good part."

The *good* part? Hasn't all of this already been more than good? These tiny touches, Logan's words—all of it has been making *good* obsolete.

Speaking of hands, the one on my lower back shifts, and one finger traces a path up my spine. Logan moves his other hand too, cupping the back of my head as those soft lips kiss me again in the same spot on my neck. Then a little higher, following the exact path I so badly want him to take.

The path leading to my mouth.

"You smell so good," he murmurs, his mouth cresting over my jaw to press a kiss between my cheek and my chin. "I could spend the whole night just kissing you. Just this."

So many words to unpack. *Could,* not *would*—does that distinction matter? It feels somehow like it very much does.

But ... *a whole night just kissing.* That sounds ... like a dream I'd like to pull straight from sleep into the waking world.

I mean, I can see spending an entire night kissing Logan. Especially if it's anything at all like this buildup. Most people seem to treat kissing as a means to an end, like it's just the starter's pistol. But Logan is talking about kissing for kissing's sake, and I am here for that.

I would respond, but it's taking all my brain function not to melt into a puddle of Parker right here outside my apartment door.

Logan's lips travel up to the apple of my cheek, his nose brushing lightly against my eyelashes and causing a cascade of heat to blaze through every part of my body. He kisses the tip of my nose then, a playful little kiss that makes me smile.

That's when his lips find the very corner of my mouth, kissing the edge of my smile.

I draw in a breath—one very close to a gasp. So close. He's SO CLOSE.

It's not just my ovaries threatening to explode. My entire body is a fuse, burned down to its end.

And maybe it's thinking about what's at the end of the fuse, maybe it's sensing Logan's hesitation as his mouth hovers near mine, maybe it's the tiniest scrap of self-preservation I have left that starts to drag me back to myself.

"I want to break the rules," Logan murmurs then. "All of them."

It's like I've been thrown straight from a sauna into an ice bath.

His words remind me that we have rules. The rules for *fake* dating.

Which is what we are doing: faking.

Maybe Logan wants to break all the rules, but that doesn't mean he wants something *real* with me. He's probably just caught up in the moment because I was dumb enough to ask him to describe kissing me.

Yep—I walked myself right into this.

I am *not* faking. And if I don't want to die from wanting someone I don't and can't have, I need to end this. *Now.*

It hurts the way pulling a bandaid off slowly hurts as I force myself to unclench my fists from Logan's shirt. So many parts of my body form a mob, an organized union of protest as I take a giant step back, leaving his warmth, pulling away from his touch.

His hands drop to his sides. His lips part with a question he doesn't ask. But it's his eyes that make my heart trip. The expression in Logan's eyes looks anguished. Regret for what just happened? Or disappointment I'm ending it now?

Don't worry about Logan, I tell myself. He's a big boy. He's fine. He can find any other woman in the world to kiss and *more than* kiss with.

The thought of Logan with someone else is all the sobering up I need.

I force a grin, knowing full well it's unhinged, and I look like some kind of serial killer.

"Thank you again for tonight," I say with a forced politeness and cheer. "That was very ... educational."

And then I hold out my hand. Logan stares, blinking rapidly, like he's trying to figure out what changed in the last minute. It's some small consolation that he seems every bit as affected as I feel.

Seems. He *seems* affected. I'm sure that's not the case, as we didn't even kiss on the lips. Why would this have any effect on a man like Logan? Right—it wouldn't.

Logan frowns. I shake my hand at him dramatically.

"We agreed to end the night with an amicable breakup and a handshake. Remember? I made a sticky note."

I say this as though writing something down on a pink sticky note carries all the seriousness of the Geneva Convention.

It *needs* to be that serious. We have to take a big step back before we take too many steps forward and cross some line we can't come back from. A line I can't come back from. I'm sure Logan would recover just fine.

I wiggle my fingers at him. "Come on, Logan. It's time for our amicable breakup by way of handshake."

Logan's frown deepens. Part of me wants him to just smile, wiping away whatever just happened. To shake my hand and walk away.

Part of me is screaming for him to grab me and do all the things he just described. To fight for me. To see through the act I'm putting on, to slay the fear driving me to run right now. To actually kiss me.

To want me for real.

When he still doesn't move, I take his hand, then shake it. Almost violently.

"Best fake date ever," I say, almost choking on the words.

And then, while he's still standing with a frown darkening his features and confusion in his eyes, I turn away, quickly unlock my door and disappear inside, leaving Logan standing alone in the cramped vestibule.

CHAPTER 18

Parker

I STAND JUST inside my apartment, trying to teach myself how to breathe again, for far too long. Long enough to hear that Logan doesn't move for a long time either. Long enough to hear him finally—*finally*— unlock his door. Long enough to hear that door close with a quiet noise that sounds a whole lot like disappointment.

I'm sure I'm imagining it.

Logan isn't on the other side of the wall choking on regret and cowardice like I am. If anything, he probably regrets that he ever got roped into my fake boyfriend shenanigans in the first place.

I squeeze my eyes closed and clench my fists. I am now expertly equipped to write a dissertation on how to screw up a fake date. Tonight could be used as a template on how NOT to do it.

My thesis statement would read something like: When fake dating someone, the more real feelings you have, the worse the fallout will be.

In the opening paragraphs, I would put forth the idea that fake dating a person you've actually had—or currently *have*—feelings for is a bad idea. Choose a person you'll never be attracted to. Ever.

For supportive evidence, I'd discuss the impact of things like dancing together, having conversations about real things, and laughing. All of which can impact one's feelings.

I would conclude with a warning not to ever, *ever* ask your fake date to describe how he would kiss you.

And that the worst thing you can do is try to revert back to the established rules, pretending like nothing at all happened.

Which is, of course, exactly what I tried to do.

I'm not an actor. As I've previously established, all my feelings show on my face. I know Logan has to suspect how I really feel. Not fake feel. *Really* feel.

And I can't be mad he didn't actually kiss me or protest when I ended the night with a handshake. I can't be hurt he didn't knock on my door instead of going into his apartment. Logan did exactly what I asked of him. The consummately perfect fake boyfriend.

Finally, after spending way too long in the same position, I peel myself off the door, drop my purse, and head to the bathroom to wash off my makeup.

I am such a baby, I think, scrubbing my face maybe a little too hard. The cowardly lion looks like a dashing hero compared to me. Because when faced with how to end what was a really great night, I just ran. Metaphorically *and* literally.

Mr. Eds growls from under my bed as I kick off my shoes and unzip my dress.

"Are you chastising me or trying to tell me it's going to be okay?" I ask. He hisses in response. "Chastising me. Got it. So, you think I should have gone for it? Either telling him how I feel or, like, really *going* for it and kissing his face off?"

Mr. Eds doesn't respond to this, which I'll take as a sign he wants to hear more. I hang up my dress, running a hand over the soft pink fabric, thinking of all the times tonight Logan's hands touched it.

Maybe I should take it to one of those places that preserves wedding dresses. I could make a little plaque for it: *This is the dress I wore the one time I dated Logan Barnes. The night that ruined me for all other men forever. This dress is the reason I'm an old spinster cat lady.*

"Not that there's anything wrong with that," I say out loud.

People can live perfectly fulfilled single lives. And those who choose to have cats are of superior intelligence, in my opinion. Cats are independent and brilliant and can display very human emotions.

Except for mine, who displays demon emotions.

As if to illustrate this, Mr. Eds takes a swipe at my ankle while I'm pulling on my pajama pants. "Hey!" I protest. "Knock it off."

He only growls in response. It's then I hear something on the other side of the wall and freeze. It was a dull thud, like the sound of someone dropping something heavy. Or falling down?

Logan. I'd been so caught up in rehashing my stupid mistakes that I forgot about his bedroom being next to mine. Feeling like a total creeper and not at all sorry about it, I press my ear to the wall.

If this were a newer building, I might be able to hear more. But these walls are plaster. It makes hanging pictures a pain and eavesdropping almost impossible. I can only make out quiet, unidentifiable sounds. But Logan is definitely over there.

How am I going to sleep with him however many inches of plaster (and possibly some asbestos) away?

I'm not. That's how.

Also, what is he sleeping on? These hardwood floors are original and in need of a good refinishing. More than once, I've gotten splinters from walking barefoot. Logan cannot sleep on splintery floors!

I'll have to offer him my couch. There is simply no other choice. It's a moral imperative, to quote *Real Genius*—one of my favorite movies and one of Val Kilmer's finest works, only beaten by *Tombstone*.

Val Kilmer quotes aside, the point is—even if I screwed up my chance for more than friendship with Logan, friends don't let friends sleep on hardwood floors. I think I saw that printed on a welcome mat in the home section of the General Store.

I'm shuffling to the door in my slippers, all set to invite Logan to sleep on my couch *as a friend* when Mia calls. I answer as I reach my door.

"Can't talk. I'm about to—"

"Ohmygoshdidyouseethisyet?" Mia, despite being super composed most of the time, has a habit of speaking in one long multisyllabic word when she's super excited.

"Slow down. You're doing that fast-talking thing."

"Sorry. Are you okay?"

"I'm … fine?" Other than berating myself for being too dumb and scared to be honest with the man I think I'm in love with.

The man who is standing outside my door, hand raised to knock. My heart careens through my chest, landing somewhere in the vicinity of my stomach. Logan smiles, a little sheepishly, looking practically edible in joggers and a fitted tank top that is arguably sponsoring the best gun show this side of the Appalachians.

And that's when Mia practically shouts in my ear, "You're all over the internet. As Logan Barnes's new girlfriend."

———

"Drink." Logan presses a warm mug into my shaking hands.

The smell of cinnamon hits me, and I glance up at him. "You made me tea," I say. "You know *how* to make tea?"

He snorts, then sinks down on the couch beside me, leaving no room between us. "Please. I'm an athlete, not an imbecile. I can boil water."

"But dropping the bag in the hot water takes real dexterity and precision," I deadpan, then shake my head. "And after you missed that shot in practice yesterday …"

"There she is," Logan says. "There's my Pete."

My Pete. I wish. But apparently, it's only true in the tabloids.

I take a sip of tea, which Logan somehow got the perfect temperature for drinking. To be honest, I'm not sure I noticed him making tea. I've been too busy over here listening to the sound of my life burning down. Logan could have been dressing Mr. Eds up in baby clothes and teaching him to fetch and I wouldn't have noticed.

"Talk to me," Logan says.

I eye him over my mug. "You are remarkably calm."

"I'm used to dealing with the press and the gossip sites. You're not."

"How does one … get used to this?" I ask.

Logan leans back, one hand trailing through his dark hair. "I guess it's like the saying about boiling a lobster. Or is it a frog? Whatever. The water heats up so gradually that—"

"You don't notice you're dying? That sounds pretty terrible."

He smirks. "Okay, so not the best analogy."

"Or maybe it's perfect. It's right on the nose." I shake my head. "It's not okay to live this way, Logan."

His smile falters. "I really am okay with my life," he says, with more than a touch of defensiveness in his voice. "I knew what I was signing up for when I got drafted. *You* didn't agree to this, which is not okay. I didn't think it would bleed over into your life with one night."

But didn't I sign up for it? When I announced to my dad that Logan was my date and then my boyfriend—without his consent, mind you—I walked right into this life. Which I apparently didn't think through at all. I was more worried about the team messing with Logan or about my own real feelings tripping me up—as they have actually done.

I wasn't thinking about the fact that *TMZ has my photo on their website.* And never mind that I look good. "A regulation hottie," as Mia said. I'm totally going to print out the photos later so I can have copies.

But that doesn't mean I *like* the attention.

Despite the unnerving feeling of being suddenly famous (ish), this is a lovely and terrible distraction from the realization that I might be in actual LOVE with the man whose big thigh is currently touching mine.

"What do we do?" I ask, staring into the bottom of my mug.

I should have some ideas, being that I'm a social media strategist. But I deal more with trends and engagement, not with the PR side of things. And even if I might be able to think about that stuff if it were the Appies we were talking about, I cannot begin to consider this with my own life. I'm way too close to it.

And way too emotionally wrecked.

"There are options," Logan says. "Say nothing at all is the first. Neither confirm nor deny. Though that sometimes drives the interest and curiosity higher."

"Would we do that with the people in our actual lives?" I ask, wide-eyed. I'm trying to picture me saying, "No comment," to someone like Van or Eli. Or the Appies staff.

I squeeze my eyes closed. Despite there being no official fraternization policy, I can't help but feel like this isn't a good career move for me. I picture Larry's frowning face, and his walrus mustache twitching.

"Next option?"

"We tell the truth. Or a version of it," he amends. "What we agreed on in your office would work. We're old friends who went on a date. Tried things briefly. We decided to stay friends. End of story."

Somehow, I don't think that would be the end of the story, but it sounds better than option one. I'm about to ask for any other alternatives when Logan's phone buzzes on the coffee table.

His expression darkens. "It's Jeremy. The last person I want to talk to." Sighing, he glances my way. "But he could probably help."

"You want help from the guy who let you sign a contract that included performing in TikTok videos without telling you about it?" I ask.

"Fair point. Still. This is the kind of thing he navigates. Might as well get his take."

"Does he know this was a … fake thing?" It's still hard to get my mouth around a word as untrue as *fake*.

"No. I mentioned I had a date tonight. I didn't think it would blow up like this, but I told him just in case."

Interesting. I mean, it probably means nothing. But still —interesting.

Logan leaves the phone on the table and puts it on speakerphone. "Hey. I'm here with Parker. You're on speaker."

"Great," Jeremy says, and I can picture his slimy face smiling slimily. "The happy couple."

I roll my eyes, and from somewhere under the couch, Mr. Eds growls. Maybe he's a good judge of character after all. Or maybe he still just hates everyone equally.

"We were just discussing how to handle this," Logan says. "What's your read?"

"How to handle what? There's nothing to do but embrace Logan Barnes snagging a girlfriend from your hometown who's as hot as—"

"*Jeremy.*"

Logan's voice is like a samurai blade. I'm shocked his phone doesn't slice in half from the force of it.

Sorry, he mouths to me. When I only shrug, Logan grins. It's pure mischief.

"He's not wrong," Logan whispers.

I elbow him in the side, even as I bask in the compliment. *Newsflash: Logan Barnes thinks I'm hot!!!!*

"The point is—this is the best possible thing for your career right now," Jeremy says, sounding like he's not drinking cinnamon tea. More like a triple shot of espresso.

"No—playing good hockey is the best thing for my career," Logan says.

"Oh, sweet Logan," Jeremy says, and I'd like to shove the man into a supply closet alone with Mr. Eds. "If this were just about your skills, you wouldn't be stuck in Harvest Horror right now. Rebuilding your career is about your reputation and image as much as your skills. You're not seen as a team player. The fight with the fan made you seem like a liability. And banishing you to the AHL is your penance. I don't need to tell you this is your chance to prove your personal life won't negatively impact the franchise."

Logan leans back and tilts his head up to the ceiling. I try not to get distracted by his neck—the way his Adam's Apple bobs when he swallows, the faint flicker of his pulse, the shadow of stubble gathering strength to turn into a category five o'clock shadow.

Focus, Parker!

All of this can't be news to him. Or maybe he's just used to thinking like a hockey player, not like a team owner. Or a social media strategist—which is what I am. Hearing Jeremy's words seems to have shaken me back into biz mode. I welcome the shift, because it clears my head a little for the first time since Mia called.

I lean forward and set down my mug next to the phone. "So, what's the best play here for Logan's career?" I ask.

"Parker," Logan says, a note of warning in his tone.

But Jeremy interrupts. "Simple," he says. "Don't break up."

CHAPTER 19

Logan

PAIN YANKS ME FROM SLEEP, and it takes a few groggy moments with my eyes still closed to register where I am and what hurts.

Especially since a *lot* of things hurt. My back, for one. My head is also throbbing, just behind my eyes. A telltale, up-too-late and need-coffee-stat headache.

But what woke me is unfamiliar—this pain is needle-sharp, stabbing my chest in a steady rhythm. *Stab. Stab. Stab.*

When I open my eyes, I am face-to-face with a black feline of monstrous size.

My very first realization that I'm on Parker's sofa—hence the aching back. This is quickly followed by the memory of everything that happened with Parker last night, which is likely the reason for my headache.

These thoughts though are quickly eclipsed by a more

immediate worry. Because a cat whose name is a shortening of Evil Demon Spawn is currently parked on my chest.

How in the world does this cat hide underneath furniture? He looks like he could eat furniture for breakfast. Is he actually a domestic cat? Or some kind of bobcat house cat hybrid?

Despite his sheer size, he doesn't look nearly as intimidating as he sounded when growling at me the time I was here for dinner. His greenish eyes, fixed on mine, actually seem kind of friendly. Or, at least, not murderous. Though I've never owned a cat, I know enough to recognize that kneading his paws on my chest is a good sign. Even if it hurts. So is the rumbling purr I hear.

"Hey, there, pretty kitty," I say in a soft voice.

I'm not sure if Parker is up yet, and I don't want to wake her if she's still sleeping. I also would prefer not to upset the cat status quo. I prefer this pleasant version of Mr. Eds to the evil demon spawn version.

Also, if it came down to it, I think he could take me.

Without moving my head, I let my gaze move around Parker's apartment. Early morning light filters through the blinds. There are no sounds other than the cat purring. No sign of Parker.

Which might be good, as I need to unpack the events of last night before I see her again. After Parker shook my hand and bolted like a frightened bunny, I paced my empty apartment. Then I changed out of my tux and paced some more. I dropped my bags in my empty bedroom, listening like a creeper for anything I could hear on the other side of the wall. Nothing.

Parker and I might have agreed on our cordial handshake breakup, but our contract is as flimsy as the sticky notes she wrote it on. Frankly, I'd like to burn them all up. I could, since they're in my locker at the Summit. Before now, I've never thought of myself as sentimental. But I couldn't bring myself to throw the rules away.

Even if I'd like to break each and every one.

That was actually why I was standing outside Parker's apartment door when she flung it open last night. I came back because I didn't want to let the night end without kissing her. Or asking her if she wanted me to kiss her for real.

I didn't want to sleep without telling her that, for me, none of it was fake.

Have I figured out any of the details about how this would work with me leaving Harvest Hollow in the near future? No.

But I decided that Parker was worth the risk.

Then, it all came crashing down before I had a chance to say a word.

To be honest, I wasn't shocked that someone (or several someones) sold photos of Parker and me to bigger news sources and gossip sites. I knew the moment I saw the press at her father's party that there might be an issue. I just didn't expect it to happen so fast. Or for the story to spread so quickly.

I've been out of the news for a while. They got bored when I didn't get into any more fights with fans at the grocery store and when I stopped going out. And, of course, when I stopped playing hockey to rehab after my knee injury. With as fast as the public moves on to their next non-interesting story to obsess over, I didn't think me dating someone would be cause for this much attention.

I was wrong.

All the major outlets picked it up. *People* even had a brief article about it with a photo of Parker and me looking like a very real couple. All of which I would have known if I hadn't turned off my phone after texting Jeremy.

I'm not sure what exactly made this story like some kind of gossip catnip. But as Jeremy said, she is like the girl next door. And she is hot. But hot in a wholesome way. Not hot in the real housewives of hockey kind of a way. Parker is *real*, and considering I've honestly never had a real girlfriend, I guess I can see how this is news.

Oh, the irony—considering it was a fake date. And now, thanks to Parker agreeing with Jeremy that continuing to date me will help my career goals, we're still together.

Real, so far as my agent and the world knows. *Fake* in actuality.

And that's what I need to talk to Parker about this morning. Because yeah, maybe I'm still planning to leave Harvest Hollow as soon as I can get called back up. But location shouldn't predetermine the success or failure of something like a relationship. No matter where my home base is, I'll be traveling much of the year anyway. Distance and separation will always be an issue. We can talk through that.

Parker is worth trying for, worth trying to figure out all these complications.

If she wants the same thing—and that's what I don't know. I was sure I felt something. The attraction making my chest tight didn't seem one-sided.

But after Jeremy mentioned us not breaking up would help my career, Parker agreed really quickly to keep this going. After we hung up with Jeremy, Parker said she'd love to see me get back to the NHL, and if she could help me get there by being my fake girlfriend for longer, she would.

My *fake* girlfriend.

Whereas I was about to suggest we go for it for *real*.

We're clearly not on the same page. I'm not sure our books are in the same bookstore.

And now I'm confused and sleeping on her couch with a FOMS (feline of monstrous size) kneading me with his needle claws.

I need to use the bathroom. And I definitely need to stretch out my back and neck, which feel a little like they've been slammed in a set of industrial doors. Better than sleeping on the bare floor in my apartment but only a little.

"Can I move you? Will you be a nice kitty or are you going to eat my face?"

I shift slightly, testing the waters, and those claws dig in. Hard. The purring stops, replaced by a guttural growl. Fabulous. At that moment, I hear keys in the door. The claws go deeper, and I grunt.

Parker tiptoes inside with a cardboard box in her arms. When her eyes meet mine, she freezes. And then she sees the giant lump of cat on my chest and gasps.

"A little help, please. How do I get him off me?"

"I have no idea," Parker whispers, her gaze darting between Mr. Eds and me. "I've never seen him *on* a person. This is ... unprecedented."

Carefully, Parker steps inside, closing the door and setting her box on the table. The whole time, Mr. Eds doesn't take his eyes off mine. It's eerie. Isn't there some old wive's tale about cats stealing your breath? Or your soul?

Looking at Mr. Eds, I'd believe either one.

"Hey, Mr. Eds," Parker says in a sugary sweet voice. I almost laugh, but the green eyes inches from my own stop me. "Can you be a nice kitty?"

I groan as the cat stiffens, digging in his claws. "That's a resounding no. He is a very, very bad kitty. Or else he doesn't like being associated with a talking horse."

Parker stops just a few feet away like she's unsure how to proceed. "He doesn't like *anything*."

"For a few minutes, he seemed to like me. Then he decided to attach himself to my chest by way of his talons."

Mr. Eds decides at this very moment to remove his stabby little razors from my pectorals, and in a flash of black, he's gone.

"Wow," Parker says. "That was ... "

She trails off when her gaze lands on my chest. Then her mouth curves up in a smile, and it's the best thing I've seen all morning. So far.

Pointing, she says, "You still seem to, um, have a cat on you."

I sit up and then pull my shirt away from my body to look. Sure enough, black hair in the shape of a large feline is right in the center of my white tank.

"Is Mr. Eds going to be a dealbreaker to this fake relationship, Wolverine?" Parker teases.

There it is again: *fake* relationship. Is it just me, or is Parker overly eager to keep saying the word? I swear, my head gives a little throb each time I even *think* the word.

"I require more caffeine for this conversation," I grumble.

"Then I've come to save the day." Parker hoists up the box she brought in and sets it on the coffee table.

Excusing myself, I head to the bathroom while Parker unpacks whatever is in the box. From the smell of it, pastries and coffee.

Parker's bathroom is tiny, just like mine, but with pink practically bursting from the seams. Pink bathmat. Pink shower curtain. Pink towels. Even a pink toothbrush. Because I'm curious—*not* nosy—I peek in the shower and find that even her shower gel and shampoo are pink.

It makes me smile. But then I think about her pink dress

last night and how good she looked. How good it felt to spend the evening with her, being introduced as her boyfriend, getting to have my arms around her, to dance with her, to hold her hand whenever I wanted.

And now … where does this leave us?

I return to the living room and stop when I see what looks like half a bakery set out on Parker's coffee table.

"I wasn't sure what you liked nowadays," she says. "So, I bought apple muffins, apple cider donuts, apple strudel, and apple tarts."

"This baker definitely has a type."

She rolls her eyes. "You can't have forgotten how obsessed Harvest Hollow is with its apples. Also, do you think it's an accident that the name *Appies* is so close to *apples?*"

I snort. "I thought the name was short for Appalachian, like the mountains."

"It is. But I don't think it's a coincidence. Anyway, if you're feeling non-apple-y, I have croissants—chocolate filled and regular. I know you're supposed to be eating all the healthy things, but whatever. As you already know, that's not what I serve."

I smile and take a bite out of one of the pastries. I already forgot all the names she listed, but it tastes like a flaky apple pie and is most excellent. I practically inhale it and go for the donut next. I could really get behind this apple thing.

"Wow," Parker says. "Guess you're not against sweets."

"I'm supposed to keep to a pretty strict regimen. But I burn something like 3,000 calories a day during the season. So, I think it's fine to balance it out with the occasional donut."

"My, my. You really *are* the bad boy of hockey. Eating the occasional donut. Scandal!"

Next, she pulls several to-go cups from the box, and the scent of coffee almost knocks me over. My head gives one big throb.

"I also didn't know what kind of coffee you liked or even if you liked it. You didn't drink coffee back in the day. But"— she tilts her head as she studies me with a small smile— "based on the way you're practically salivating, my guess is you do."

"I very much do."

"Well, I've got an Americano, a cappuccino, and a pumpkin spice latte. Plus a variety of creams and sugars. Pick your poison."

I notice there's a fourth cup, one she didn't gesture to. "And what's that one?"

"That's a chai latte," Parker says. "For me."

"And what if chai lattes are my signature drink?" I deadpan.

Without any hesitation, Parker pushes the cup my way. "Then it's yours."

And this is a perfect illustration of the problem I'm facing. Parker is so good at doing what's best for other people. So giving. So generous.

If I want her drink, she'll hand it over. If a friend needed a kidney, she'd be at the hospital within the hour, setting up tests to see if she matches as a donor.

And if a hockey player needs a girlfriend to help his image, she's all in.

But what does *Parker* really want?

And then, the question I really want to ask but can't bring myself to: Does she want *me*?

I push the cup back toward her. "I was kidding, Pete. The Americano sounds great. Thank you." I pause. "You

223

shouldn't give up what you really want just because someone else asks you to."

Her brow furrows. "Are we still talking about coffee?"

"Don't worry about it."

I grab another donut and make a mental note to leave a couple of twenties for Parker. It will have to be somewhere sneaky where she won't notice and try to return it immediately. Coffee and pastries aren't cheap. Taking a slow sip of the Americano, I consider how to bring up what I want to bring up.

I've never had a conversation like this one. I've never wanted to have this kind of conversation. And given the examples of relationships I've seen in my life, I don't have much to draw from.

Few other players I know are settled in a committed relationship. And if they are, they keep their girlfriends and wives and kids private—far removed from the hockey world. I have my mom, who didn't settle down with any one man after my dad left. She seemed to value variety over commitment, though I think she's been with the same guy for a while now. I wouldn't know, as she's somewhere in Florida. Our only contact really is the checks I still send her every month.

Parker's parents are the only close-up I've had to a long-lasting marriage relationship, and I don't want what they have.

How do I do this? Besides the fact I don't know what I'm doing, the whole fake aspect has muddied the waters.

Parker dives in before I can figure out what I'm doing. "So, last night, huh?" She gives a long, low whistle. "Talk about a first date. A first *fake* date," she amends. "Leading to a longer-term *fake* relationship."

And there she goes again. I frown and set down my coffee. "You don't need to *pretend* to be my girlfriend."

She shrugs, clearly missing my emphasis on *pretend* and instead focusing on the part requiring her to play along. "I know. But it will help your career. And"—she lowers her voice—"keep this on the DL, but you're my favorite hockey player. I have a vested interest in seeing you on the ice with the NHL again."

While this might have been enough to warm my heart or just stroke my ego before, now I want something more from Parker. I want to *be* more to her than a hockey player. Also, she has to be aware that me getting back to the NHL means me leaving.

Does she *want* me to leave Harvest Hollow again?

"I've seen you play, you know," she says, looking far too pleased with herself.

This confession is enough to make me forget the uncomfortable questions I'm asking. "You have? When?"

"Twice in Raleigh. Once in Atlanta." She clears her throat. "Once in Denver."

Raleigh and Atlanta are driving distance. Still not *close*, but not outrageous. But ...

"*Denver?*"

She grins. "What can I say? I happened upon a great plane fare. Mia came with. Kicking and screaming, but she came."

I lean back on the couch, processing. Parker came to see me play. All these years when I had cut her and Brandon off, she made the effort to come see me play.

"Did you wear my jersey?" I ask.

I can't *not* ask. And yeah, maybe it makes me a brute or an egomaniac or whatever. But I *have* to know.

Parker's smile is soft. "Of course. I've only *ever* worn your jersey, Logan."

Calm down, son, I tell myself. Plenty of fans wear my name across their backs. Jeremy, who intercepts my fan mail, told me more than one woman has sent a picture of my name tattooed on her body.

But this is somehow more than permanent ink on skin. (It's also decidedly less creepy.) Parker, who had every reason to hate me after the way I left, snuck off to my games and wore my jersey. I barely refrain from asking her to put it on right now.

Focus, Logan.

"What if *I* don't want to do this?" I say, swinging the focus back where it needs to be. Immediately her face falls and I feel like a jerk.

She recovers quickly, her expression shifting to the one I see most often at work—poised and professional and a whole lot less *Parker*.

"I get it. I mean, it's a little hard to believe someone like you would be with—"

"Stop."

Before she can close her mouth, I reach over and take her hand. This shuts her up. For a second.

Then she smiles and says, "The Classic hand hold."

I chuckle, having completely forgotten about my lame hand-holding thing. It makes me ridiculously happy she hasn't forgotten.

"Parker, I wasn't saying I wouldn't want to be with *you*."

"Then what are you saying?"

"I don't know about the whole *fake* thing."

She tilts her head. "Why not? Celebrities do this all the time, right? And I've already said I don't mind."

Yeah, Logan—why not?

Though it should be easy to just say the truth—that I'd like something real with Parker, something that has nothing to do with my public perception—I can't make myself say the words.

I feel totally ill-equipped for this conversation.

"We'll need to look at the rules again," I say, disappointed in myself for not telling her to forget the rules and then *showing* Parker how I feel.

Dropping my hand, Parker stands and stretches casually. A little *too* casually?

"The rules are fine."

I stand. "I'm not sure they are. Not for something more than a night of you being my girlfriend."

"I'm not sure what would need to change," she says.

Neither am I, exactly, but I do know it will need to be more if we actually want anyone who sees us on a semi-regular basis to believe it. Despite the influx of caffeine and carbs—or maybe because of it?—my brain is mush.

"I think we'll need to discuss how to be more convincing," I say. "Or how to behave at work. With the team. All that."

Everything I'm saying is true, but I'm also not sure why I'm pushing this. To spend more time with Parker? To suss out what she really wants by pushing the fake angle? That doesn't even make sense. Unless pretending could segue into *not* pretending. Or at least help me figure out what Parker wants for real.

"Fine," Parker says, playing with her thumb ring. She didn't wear it last night but it's back in place now, which strangely makes me feel more at ease. "We'll discuss it in my office after filming?"

"Filming? You're working today?"

She gives me the kind of chastising look that will serve her well one day if she ever has kids. "You're working today too. You've got practice in an hour and then we've got our first big batch of filming after. Don't tell me you forgot. Make sure you're ready and pretty for the camera."

I glower, and she laughs. Then, she hops up to the door and swings it wide open, gesturing me toward it.

"If I didn't know better, I'd think you were trying to get rid of me," I say, grabbing the Americano.

Or trying to get out of this conversation?

Her laugh is too loud. "I need to get ready. And so do you."

She's not wrong. But just like last night when we said goodbye, it feels like Parker is running away. Pushing me away as she goes.

I pause in the doorway. We're standing close enough I can see the lighter brown flecks in her eyes, almost gold.

"I think the guys will ask questions," I tell her.

"Felix already thinks I'm your girlfriend. What about the rest of the guys?"

"I don't know. But we should probably make sure we're on the same page about what this looks like." I lean closer and lower my voice. "Because if you were mine, I'd be sure everyone knows it. There would be no question in anyone's mind."

Parker seems to sway a little on her feet. Her eyes seem fixed on a point behind me. I fully expect her to shove me out the door. To keep pushing me away, to keep running.

Then her gaze flicks up to mine. "And how would you do that, Logan?"

Lifting my free hand, I tuck a strand of hair behind her ear. My fingertips sweep over her cheekbone, then along the line of her jaw. I watch color rise in her cheeks. I make note of the way her breathing quickens.

Fake, indeed.

"Many ways," I tell her, dropping my hand. "I'd make sure people knew you were mine in so many ways."

And it's in that moment I decide to do just that. I might be a chicken and totally inexperienced in terms of how to have a relationship, but I'm going to make Parker mine. Maybe I won't shove off the fake title yet; instead, I'll use the guise of fake to get close for real. To make sure Parker knows what it would be like to be mine.

Parker blinks then, and as though waking from a dream, she shakes her head slightly and takes a big step away from me. Again.

"Save it for my office, Barnes," she says sweetly, and then slams the door in my face.

CHAPTER 20

Logan

IF I HAD any hopes that the guys wouldn't have checked the internet before practice, they're dashed immediately. But I'm surprised that instead of the guys trying to replace my clothes or something worse, I walk in to claps and cheers and slaps on the back.

They've even taped a whole group of congratulations balloons to my locker. Well—congratulations balloons and one that reads *Get Well Soon*. I hope that one is an accident and not a veiled threat from Nathan, who's the only one not smiling and clapping.

Still, I open my locker carefully, keeping an eye on the guys just in case they have something else planned.

"Why do you look so paranoid?" Eli asks.

"I figured if you guys heard, you might react differently."

"If Parker was going to choose someone—other than me, of course—we're glad it's you," Alec says.

"She never would have chosen you, man," Van says, and then an argument breaks out about who Parker's hypothetical second choice would be.

Felix steps up close, adjusting his goalie pants. "I think if it were anyone other than you, this would have gone a whole other way."

"But why?"

The only reason I can think of is that the guys might want to curry favor from someone who's played at a higher level for years. Not that I have much sway right now with anything at all.

Felix gives me a look, like this should be obvious. "Because we like you."

"Oh. That's ..." Not what I expected. And it has me feeling slightly overwhelmed. In a good way. "That's cool."

Of course, like me or not, this doesn't mean they don't give me total hell the minute we're on the ice. Still, I can tell it's in good fun. And they respect Parker enough not to say anything about her that would require me to murder them.

"Boyfriend, eh?" Van zips by me on the ice, smacking the back of my thighs with his stick. "I didn't know you knew what that word meant."

He's righter than he knows. Considering my lack of ever actually *being* a boyfriend—including now. Since my boyfriend title is actually fake. For now.

I ignore Van. Which is to say, I don't slam him into the wall. But he distracts me just enough for Alec to steal the puck.

"Where's your head at, man?" Alec teases, leaving me standing on the ice like an idiot. The smile he throws over his shoulder tells me he didn't even need to ask.

I briefly consider giving chase, tripping him, then skating right over that pretty face.

"I think we all know where his head's at," Eli says, grinning. "And it's right up there."

He jerks his head up. And sure enough—there's Parker. Leaning over the metal railing, filming. My pulse ratchets up, and I quickly glance away.

I haven't seen her since she shoved me out of her apartment this morning. When I knocked on her door to see if she wanted to ride together, she had already gone. Which I tried not to take personally. Or as some kind of sign of something.

To tell the truth, I have no idea where we stand or what we're doing. Only that I'm going to steer this ship out of the fake zone.

I remember my first day of practice, seeing Parker up on the catwalk. It feels like ages ago. Or maybe it's just that so much has changed. Even things with the team feel different. It's almost like my life has been made up of disjointed pieces, and they're now starting to slide into place. I feel … solid. This is something I'm not sure I ever knew I was missing until now.

As I go after Alec and the puck, my eyes keep going back up to Parker. I'm sure the catwalk is structurally sound. The stadium is fairly new, and I bet it was built with exacting safety codes.

Still—does Parker *have* to be up there?

I'm already having a hard time focusing today. Obviously. But worrying irrationally about Parker getting hurt makes it worse.

"She's not going to fall." Felix doesn't look up as he says this, blocking Alec's shot and sending the puck my way.

"I'm not worried," I mutter.

There's no way Felix knows the double meaning his words carry. But I can't miss it.

Parker's not going to fall—for you, an ugly little voice in my head tells me. I have a sneaking suspicion it sounds so ugly because it's the truth.

While I'm all-too aware there are many women who would want me just for my looks or the money or the fame, I'm not sure any of those are reason enough for Parker.

And what else do I have to offer someone like her?

I'm a guy who has commitment issues, maybe some mild anger issues, and a job with a grueling schedule. Not to mention no track record of long-term relationships. My house is devoid of people, pets, and house plants. I barely even have any furniture in Raleigh. I'm not there enough to care, and I don't care enough to even keep a succulent alive.

The weird thing is that when I ordered furniture from a store in Asheville that will deliver here and set it up, I bought more for my apartment than I own in my *house*.

FOCUS.

I pass the puck to Nathan, the one guy who keeps his mouth shut. Always.

Except now, of course. "Yeah, we can tell you're not worried," Nathan says. "That's why you keep looking up there, looking scared."

It's the most words I've ever heard him say in a row.

"You'd better be worried. Someone like the Boss?" Eli flies by, stealing the puck from Nathan and sending it over the ice to Alec. "She'd be *all* I thought about."

I barely hold back a growly response telling Eli he *better* not be thinking about Parker.

"Aw, Eli. You're a closet romantic," Alec says. "How sweet."

Eli grins. "My romantic isn't hidden in the closet. It's right out in front. And if it were *me* with Parker—"

"It's not you with Parker," I growl, unable to stop myself this time. It only makes Eli's grin stretch wider.

More than a couple of the guys laugh and someone goes *oooohhh*. Yeah, I stepped right into that. I really wish Coach would finish talking to the trainers so we could start practice and the guys would all shut up. Good natured or not, I'm ready to focus on hockey. The rest I'll process later.

"But if it *were*," Eli presses, like he's unable to help himself, "I'd be locking that down."

I grind my teeth, telling myself it's not a good idea to trip Eli the next time he comes close.

"She's not a diamond necklace you can stick in a vault," Felix says, shaking his head. "She's a person."

"Exactly," Eli says, obviously completely missing Felix's point. But Eli doesn't miss his next shot, which sails past Felix.

"Bring it in," Coach barks. "None of you look ready for our first preseason game. Especially you, Barnes. Pull it together."

I nod, still clenching my jaw. Coach is right—I need to pull it together. Still. I can't help but glance up one more time. But Parker is gone.

———

It's a sad day when I'm actually looking forward to filming videos for social media.

Though it has nothing to do with the videos and everything to do with Parker, who—in athletic pants, no makeup, and a loose Appies T-shirt with skates—looks as good or better than she did last night.

Turns out, Parker plus ice apparently equals perfection.

"Don't look so glum, man," Eli says, skating up beside me and ramming my shoulder with his. I'm sure he meant it to be just a nudge, but the guy has an excess overflow of energy and almost knocks me off my skates. "You'll get your turn in the spotlight. One day."

"I don't want the spotlight," I grumble.

What I do want—selfishly—is Parker's attention. While I can't seem to stop thinking about her or take my eyes off her, she's all business, introducing the videographer, Ramesh, and running down the list of videos. I don't play a big role in today's filming, which is either per our fake date agreement or just because she had this already planned. Either way, not being the star means I hardly get more than a passing glance and tiny smile.

"It's not so bad," Van says. "You'll warm up to it."

I can sense from the way he's skating back and forth, his eyes alight, that Van, like Eli, thrives on this kind of thing. Which is a little surprising. But then, people aren't always what you'd expect.

"Or maybe you won't warm up to it," Felix mutters under his breath. "Maybe you'll just tolerate it and wish it would be over as soon as possible."

It will be tolerable—but only because I get to watch Parker. Otherwise, this is like a custom-designed circle of hell. But I'm not going to be a punk about it. For Parker's sake.

"All right guys." Parker claps her hands, skating backwards and slicing to a stop in front of us. Her eyes briefly flick to me, and there's a tiny flash of warmth in her gaze before she goes back to the task at hand.

"We'll start with the newest Taylor Swift 'Love Story' trend," Parker says. Several of the guys nod like they know what she's talking about. Guys who probably have too much time on their hands and spend it on TikTok.

"'Love Story'—how appropriate," Alec says, his gaze swinging between me and Parker.

She rolls her eyes. "Shut it, Ego."

I choke on a laugh. I've never heard this nickname for our captain, but it's perfect. Based on his glower, Alec doesn't seem to like it as much.

"Maybe you and Logan should star in this one," Eli says with a grin. "Give me your phone. I can film."

"Will there be kissing, Boss?" Tucker asks.

I'm ready to speak up when Parker beats me to it.

"Are y'all going to be like this?" Parker puts her hands on her hips, glaring around at the guys. One by one they look down.

Except Van, who says, "Like what?"

"Like totally immature prepubescent pee wee players," she says sweetly. Someone chuckles. "While I'm at work, I'm working. Anything personal"—she eyes me in a way that makes my neck feel hot—"stays off the rink. Is that clear?"

There's a low chorus of, "Yes, Boss."

I only nod, thinking about all the *personal* things I'd like to do with Parker right now. Just when I think Parker can't get more attractive, she goes and does something like put a bunch of grown men acting like boys in their place.

"Eli and Van, front and center," Parker says, already moving on. "Here are your dresses."

Dresses?

Dancing on camera is bad enough. Parker better not *ever* try to put me in some kind of costume.

As though my fear is broadcast through the stadium speakers, Parker catches my eye, giving me a wicked smile

236

that makes my heart skip. Then a quick shake of her head tells me she's kidding.

Relief mixed with something else—appreciation, maybe?—settles over me. Parker might be the one forcing us to do all this, but she's also looking out for me.

As Eli and Van strip out of their jerseys, there are catcalls and whistles. But neither guy seems to care as they pull on long, sequined gowns that hang down to their skates.

"Didn't we already do a 'Love Story' video?" Tucker asks.

"Good memory, Tuck," Parker says. "Two points for you! But this is a new trend with a sped-up version of the song. What can I say? TikTok loves its Taylor."

"Why aren't you featuring your favorite player, Parker?" Alec asks, sliding a glance my way.

"Who says he's my favorite?" Parker answers. This has them all laughing. I even chuckle. Even more when she winks at me before pointing her finger back at Alec. "But rest assured, Ego—you are *not* my favorite."

That has everyone laughing harder.

"Everyone else, take your spots on the bench until my cue."

Everyone skates toward the bench like they've all gotten some memo I wasn't privy to. Maybe they did.

"Hope you weren't expecting special treatment," Van says with a smirk, adjusting the straps of a pink sequined gown. His chest tattoos peek out of the top, looking ridiculous next to the frilly fabric.

"Not even a little bit," I say.

"Come on," Felix says to me, skating toward the bench. "We've got the easy job."

The easy job turns out to be nothing more than jumping over the low wall and flooding the ice together at a certain point in the song. Over. And Over.

237

Van and Eli skate some basic choreography on the center of the rink. Their sparkly dresses fan out around them as they lip sync to the song Parker plays. Ramesh films with a small camera, weaving his way around all of us expertly on his skates. Parker directs all of this while getting her own footage from different angles than the camera guy.

Filming a short video is way more complicated than I would have guessed, and despite not enjoying myself, I can't say I mind watching Parker. This is clearly her element. She directs everything with a practiced ease, never losing patience no matter how many times one of the guys screws up.

"Okay, next up—I need everyone out here." Parker ignores the groans. "Form rows. It's time for the 'Cha Cha Slide.'"

Tucker groans. "Seriously? It's like the dance that never dies."

"Better than the macarena," Parker says as Felix and I settle in the back row along with Nathan.

Alec, from his spot up front, cranes his neck. "Why are you hiding in the back, Barnes? Don't want to embarrass yourself dancing in front of your girlfriend?"

A few of the guys chuckle, but Parker arches a brow at Alec. "Oh, I've seen Logan dance. And let me tell you— you've got nothing on him, Ego."

That elicits a lot of jeers and laughter, but Alec only laughs.

"You're welcome to stay back there," Parker calls to me. "Or you can come up here and show them how it's done."

The word no is almost out of my mouth, but then Parker smiles, and I find myself skating toward her. Van and Eli, now back in practice gear, step aside and make room for me. I feel like an idiot, but Parker beams. *Worth it.*

Even for ten minutes of cha cha sliding, which will immortalize me on the internet forever. I don't hate it as much as I expected to. Probably because Parker keeps throwing smiles my way.

"You got moves, I'll give you that," Alec says as Parker dismisses most of us toward the bench to film whatever's next.

"He's got moves you've never seen," Eli says in a weird, high-pitched voice. Alec and I both blink at him. "Don't tell me y'all never saw 'My Best Friend's Wedding.' Classic Julia Roberts. Seriously?"

Eli is still opining about the tragedy of us not having seen what is apparently one of his favorite movies when we all sit down. I tune him out.

Having barely anything to do gives me too much time to watch Parker. I watch her mouth as she orders Van around, all the while thinking of what she asked me to do last night. How I torturously described how I would kiss her affected me more than any real kiss ever has. I've never wanted to kiss someone so much. I know she wanted it too.

The way her pulse raced under my lips as I kissed her neck. The way her breathing changed. The way she clutched me like I was the life raft keeping her afloat in shark-infested waters.

Or was I reading this all wrong?

I'm used to straightforward women. They make it clear what they want from me, and it's usually just one thing. Or two, if we consider the money and fame as a secondary benefit to dating me. Like the woman who worked at the hotel—there was no way to miss her intent.

With Parker, I don't know how to read the clues. Or cues? Whatever. I can't read her. She's not upfront about wanting my money or my body or to be seen on my arm. She's nothing like other women.

Parker doesn't want to even kiss a man until it means something. Until it's *real*. And me? Things were always casual for me. Low risk, low return.

And now that *casual* isn't what I want, I'm lost. Now that Parker is all I want, I have no idea what to do with myself. Or with her. Or with all of these—ugh, the thought makes my lip curl—*feelings*.

"You look like you're having a bit of a moment there," Felix says. "Everything cool?"

I almost say yeah, but instead, shake my head. "Nah. Not even a little."

After giving me a long look like he's trying to gauge just how not cool I am, Felix finally nods. "Come with me." He starts to skate off.

"Won't we get in trouble?"

But Felix and I are at the back of a group of guys. Parker is busy pointing at the screen on the videographer's camera, talking to him animatedly. No one is paying any attention to the two of us.

When Felix doesn't answer, I follow.

We end up with our skates and pads off, climbing a stairwell to the catwalk above the ice. If it were someone else, I'd think they brought me here to push me off—or at least to threaten to push me off. But I have a strong suspicion Felix did it to make sure I know firsthand it's safe for Parker when she's filming.

He stops near the middle, and together, we lean on the rails, watching below as Parker orchestrates a video that involves Alec lip syncing while doing something that I think is supposed to be the Moonwalk.

"Does he know he's a terrible dancer?" I ask.

"No," Felix says. "And don't tell him. Then he'd probably stop. His pride couldn't handle thinking he's bad at something."

I snort. "I'll never tell."

My eyes drift over to Parker as she films Alec. The possessive feelings I'm having are already getting old. I didn't think I was a jealous man. But maybe I didn't care about anyone enough to care who they talked to or who looked at them. Like everything else—it's all different with Parker.

"So, how do you see this going?" Felix asks.

"What?"

"You and Parker. She's smart enough to know you're not planning to stay." Felix turns, giving me a stink eye if ever there was one. "You *aren't* planning to stay, are you?"

"No," I say immediately.

But the conviction in my voice isn't strong. It *is* stronger than the voice in my head, which has more of a question mark behind it.

No?

I hadn't *planned* to stay. That wasn't even one of the possible paths for my future. Play well for the Appies. Spend enough time out of the spotlight to correct my image. Go back to the Hurricanes. Or, if the Hurricanes released me, I'd hope another team would pick me up. Then I'd move wherever and play there. Harvest Hollow was never more than a temporary stop.

But now …

I somehow feel closer to these guys than any of the teams I played with in the past. Definitely more than anyone in Raleigh. Harvest Hollow doesn't have the resident ghosts I feared it might. Nothing about my past or thinking about my mom and my sad childhood haunts me. I'm actually enjoying it here. I'm renting an apartment. I have furniture I bought—

not leased like I considered doing—being delivered this week.

And I have Parker. Sort of.

I *want* to have Parker.

"Does she know that?"

I think about how quickly she told Jeremy she wasn't going to break up with me. How eager she was to help me. The same way she would have given me her chai latte this morning if I asked.

What does Parker really want?

"She knows," I say.

"You can make it work, you know. Distance doesn't have to be a relationship killer. Neither does your job. Hockey will end. Maybe it will be your other knee next time. Or maybe you'll just get tired."

"Maybe. But you've got to take the time you can get in this sport. I have to take the opportunities I'm given." I sound like I'm convincing myself.

Felix catches my eye. "I was offered an NHL spot," he says, shocking the hell out of me. Not because Felix isn't good. But because I never heard of him playing with another team. That, and he seems perfectly content where he is.

"What happened?" I ask.

"I said no." He nods down toward the ice. "And I said yes to this."

"Why?"

It's far less money. Less fame and glory, but less competition too. And for a lot of guys, guys who love what we do—that's what it comes down to. Wanting to be the best and play against the best.

Felix doesn't need to say all that. "I wanted a life," he says, and if I'm not wrong, he sounds a little sad.

I think of his fancy, giant loft. Where he lives. Alone with all his books and no actual people. Other than his grumpy neighbor who seems like the kind to bang on the wall with a broom handle if he plays music a single decibel too loud.

I wonder if the life he has is the one he thought he would get when he turned down whatever contract he was offered.

Even from this distance, I hear Parker's laugh echoing over the ice and all the empty seats. Floating into the air, up to me.

The sound makes me happy and also makes my chest feel tight.

"I don't know if Parker ..." I swallow. Pause. Lick my lips. "I don't know if she wants this."

Wants me.

Felix eyes me. "Then you're dumber than you look, Barnes."

"Probably."

He chuckles, and I smile weakly back because I've felt unstable and off-balance all day. Maybe longer. Honestly, I think from the moment I first saw Parker across that conference room and realized who she was, it's like she kicked me out of my normal orbit. Now I'm floating through deep space, trying to recalibrate.

"Think about what you want," Felix says.

I am. Believe me, I am. But I need to know for sure that she wants me too. For *real* this time.

"I don't have the first clue what I'm doing," I confess.

Felix nods, then shoots me a quick grin. "Well, don't let that stop you from doing *something*."

I don't plan to.

CHAPTER 21

Parker

"YOU'RE AN IDIOT," my very best friend in the world says after I tell her how things went down with Logan a few nights ago. And how I've done my level best to see him as little as possible ever since.

Which takes some real feats of avoidance considering we live next door to each other and work together. It hasn't worked completely, but at least I've so far been able to avoid the rules talk I've been dreading.

I have not been able to avoid the way Logan touches me every time he sees me, from the variety of hand holds (which I'm sure he made up), to hugs, to kisses on the cheek. Or forehead. Or hand. He keeps it professional-ish at work, but the whole Appies organization seems thrilled. Maybe because they think Logan dating me might keep him here longer?

If only they knew the whole purpose of us "dating" was to help him leave.

"And you're not very nice."

"I'm honest," Mia says, speaking louder over the noise in the background. "There's a difference. And honestly, you're an idiot."

"Where are you?" I ask, leaning back and enjoying the sheer ergonomic pleasure of Fancy Chair, which still hasn't gotten old. If my car were big enough, I'd totally cart this thing home every night and then back in the morning.

"Dinner with Hazel," Mia says. "Don't change the subject. This is dumb. Just tell your fake boyfriend how you really feel."

Like some kind of sign from the universe, the fake boyfriend in question happens to walk into my office right at this moment.

Correction: He doesn't walk *into* my office. Logan appears in the doorway like a gorgeous six-foot-two mirage, then stops and puts one arm up on the door frame, *leaning*.

Is there a prerequisite course guys must pass before they reach adulthood on how to lean sexily in a doorway? If so, Logan aced it. Top of class. Extra points for the way his biceps bunch while standing still.

"Gotta go, Mia."

"I know that tone," she says. "He's there, isn't he? You need to explain to that man exactly how you—"

"Tell Hazel hi. See ya!"

I hang up before Mia can finish whatever bossy thing she's planning to say. Probably more of what she already said on our brief phone call. That I should have actually talked to Logan about what he wants before offering myself up as (fake) tribute. That I should tell Logan how I actually feel.

And a few more similar things I don't remember. I zoned out after the first few minutes of her lecture.

Because I have no intention of doing what Mia says. I'm firmly committed to my plan of keeping this relationship pretend and somehow convincing my feelings to hop on board the fake train.

The words *fake* and *pretend* are like my turtle shell. I'm tucking my head, arms, legs—and, I guess in this analogy, tail —inside so I can be fully protected when Logan leaves. Because that's the whole point of all this now, isn't it—me helping him save his image so he can get back to playing real hockey somewhere other than Harvest Hollow?

"Logan," I say, sounding a little too chipper. I wiggle my fingers in an exaggerated wave to seal the nope-I'm-not-normal deal. "Hi! You're here!"

This is not that kind of poise and sexy confidence that makes a man want you. But he smiles at me anyway, slow and sweet and wide. Here's the thing: Logan's full smile is so rare it might as well be a Sasquatch—rumored to exist but with only rare, unconfirmed sightings.

Except I can confirm it. Because it's aimed right my way.

"Hey, Pete," he says.

"Hey," I say, having been reduced to repetitive, single-syllable words by his smile. And by his freshly showered scent, complete with damp hair I want to run my fingers through. It makes me glad I keep extra clothes here and had time to shower. With him smelling fresh and looking so good in dark jeans and a snug T-shirt, I wouldn't want to still be in my sweaty athletic clothes.

He chuckles. "Hey. Look—I know we were supposed to meet up and talk about the rules in your office—"

Ugh! Me and my stupid rules!

No—rules are good, not stupid! Rules keep us safe! Rules are part of the turtle shell—get in your shell!

"—but I had another idea."

I wait, but he says nothing else. "Well? Are you going to tell me the idea first?"

His grin shifts into smirk territory. "Nope. You in?"

I hesitate.

What I should do is say no. I *should* insist we stay here, in my office, in professional—not personal—territory. I *should* stick to the plan and take this time to hammer out what a longer-term fake relationship looks like. Aka, building more armor for my turtle shell.

This is what's safe. This is what's smart. This is what—

I jump to my feet. "Let's go."

———

Logan's *other idea* turns out to be not safe or smart or professional. Or conducive to fake dating.

It's dinner. In a very romantic, very *real* date spot, which is the very opposite of what I want. Or, I should say, the very opposite of what I *should* want.

I screech to a halt just inside the doorway of a restaurant called Harvested. The first few months it was open, I remember lines out the door of people whose clothing indicated they were both wealthy and foodies.

Not the kind of place I can afford. Clearly.

Having never been inside, I am wholly unprepared for the soft lighting, classical music, and candles flickering next to small vases with fresh flowers. Most tables only seat two. The whole vibe screams *This is where you drop down to a knee and pull out that ring, fellas!*

But in a much classier way. Obviously.

Logan's hand finds my lower back, keeping me in place even as everything in me screams to turn back while I still can.

"What's wrong?" he murmurs, ducking his head so his mouth almost brushes my ear.

I have a sudden and very poignant flashback to Logan's mouth in the same place while he was describing how he would kiss me.

NOT helping, memory. Not. Helping.

"We can go somewhere else if you like," Logan says.

"No, um, this is"—*A terrible idea! Only going to make you feel more like you're a real couple! Run while you still can!*—"fine. It's fine."

"Just fine?" Logan asks. "Tough crowd. I was hoping to impress you. From the reviews, this place has fantastic food and a great atmosphere."

Logan looked at reviews before choosing a restaurant? That's … really thoughtful. I swallow.

"Or we could go with my plan B," Logan says, and I can hear the smile in his voice. "McDonald's."

His suggestion of a fast food chain shouldn't make me feel a nervous flutter in my belly. But I know Logan said McDonald's rather than any other place he could have mentioned. And I know why.

It's an old joke, an old memory, really, one that guarantees I'll never set foot in a McDonald's again. Not after getting food poisoning from a fish sandwich I ate there in middle school. It was my own fault, really, a rookie mistake. Who orders seafood at a place like McDonald's? It's like playing the food version of Russian roulette.

Anyway. Logan happened to be over when I started throwing up. And throwing up. Mom was at some meeting, and Dad was at work, as always. Brandon was playing video games with Logan and did the older brother thing of casually shouting, "Are you okay, Park?" while not even setting down his controller.

But Logan ...

Logan not only set down his controller, he came into the bathroom with me. I was so ill that I temporarily suspended my extreme mortification at barfing in front of my crush. Desperate times.

Logan held back my hair. He rubbed my back. He got a cool washcloth and wiped my face. And when it was all over and the contents of my stomach—and maybe part of my stomach lining—were emptied out, Logan picked me up, carried me to my room, and tucked me into bed.

While a memory involving barf isn't the epitome of romantic, it reminds me how thoughtful and tender he could be, even when he was a dumb teenage boy. (Because let's face it—all teenage boys exist on a sliding scale of stupidity.) Bringing it up is also a nod to our shared past and how much history we share.

"You remember," I say.

Logan smiles. "Hard to forget."

"That's such a gross memory, though." I wrinkle my nose. "I mean—watching me barf? I'm surprised you ever came back to our house."

His eyes are warm when he shrugs. "It wasn't a bad memory for me. I liked taking care of you."

I'm still processing the sweetness of that statement and telling myself not to read too much into it when Logan raises his eyebrows, giving me a playful smile.

"McDonald's, then?"

"Tempting," I say. "But upon closer review, the call on the field stands."

My football reference gets a chuckle out of Logan. "Then let's stop hovering in the entrance, shall we?"

And with his big hand still splayed on my lower back, Logan leads me forward. When the very pretty hostess appears, I'm grateful her smile isn't flirty. Because fake or no, this whole thing with Logan has me feeling all kinds of possessive. I'd rather not start the night planning an elaborate revenge plot against any woman who looks at Logan with interest.

"Your table is right this way, Mr. Barnes," she says.

As we start to follow, Logan's hand still on my back where I'd like it to stay forever, I whisper, "Mr. Barnes? And you have a table?"

"I made reservations," he says.

"When did you have time to do that?" I hiss.

"Does it matter?"

Yes. "No. But when?"

"I called between practice and filming," he says. "They didn't open until noon."

Maybe it's a sign I don't date enough or don't date nice enough guys that Logan's simple act of planning is blowing me away. Especially considering the fact that he told me he didn't date much. How is he even this smooth? I can only imagine how he'd be if he decided to date someone for real.

That thought triggers an immediate flood of jealousy and possessiveness and maybe a little bitterness too. I bite the inside of my cheek and give the beads on my ring a furious spin.

The hostess moves to pull out my chair, but Logan stops her and says, "Do you mind?"

"Of course not." She steps out of the way and gives me a conspiratorial look like, *Hold on to this one!*

If only.

As Logan helps push my chair in, he lets his hands linger on my shoulders. Leaning down, he brushes his lips over my cheek, right at the edge of my mouth. Practically on the corner of my lips. I expect him to mention the rules the way he kept doing at my dad's gala. But he doesn't. Instead, he kisses me again, this time on my temple, lingering just long enough to set my insides aflame.

I die a little. Right then and there. Hopefully, it's not obvious.

But the smug look on Logan's face when he takes his seat across from me tells me it's *super* obvious. I hide behind my menu and hear him give a low chuckle. I'm still hiding, scanning the list of exquisite-sounding foods with no prices.

I happen to glance over and notice a familiar face in the back corner—one I didn't expect to see. Forgetting for a moment my Logan-overwhelm, I lean across the table. "Hey," I whisper.

He leans forward too, amusement shining in his eyes. "Yeah?" he whispers back.

"Don't look behind you—*I said don't look!*—but the Fud is over there. And she's on a date!"

"Who?"

"Our high school principal!" I hiss.

Even now, as an adult, it's weird to see teachers and principals outside of school. I think this is the first time I've seen her in anything other than red and white— Harvest High's school colors. The man she's with looks to be my dad's age and is handsome with a little gray at his temples. He definitely seems enamored with her. *You go, Principal Fud!*

Logan feigns a yawn and stretches, taking a quick peek over his shoulder. While I'm busy peeking at the way his biceps strain against his shirt. "I'd forgotten about the Fud."

"Surprising—given how much time you spent in her office," I say.

Logan chuckles, then gives me a heated look I feel all the way down to my toes. "Does this mean I can't misbehave?"

Our waitress appears, saving me from having to answer *that* question. "Welcome," she says. "Could I start you off with some water? Or perhaps the wine list?"

Logan cuts in before I can answer. "She'll have root beer," he says, lifting a brow at me. "Right?"

"Yes." I glance at the waitress. "If you have it. I know most places—"

"They have it. I checked when I made the reservation," Logan says. "And I'll take a water. Thank you."

When the waitress is gone, I lean across the table, white knuckling the sides of my menu. "What are you doing?" I whisper-hiss.

Logan eyes my hair and pulls the candle more toward his side of the table, clearly saving me from becoming a human torch. "What do you mean, what am I doing?"

"This is supposed to be fake. You don't need to do"—I wave a hand dramatically—"all this."

"All what?"

"The things! All the things! Logan—this is pretend. You don't need to make reservations at a place like this. Or call to see if they have my favorite drink. Or buy me chairs that cost as much as cars!"

His lips quirk. "Where do you buy your cars?"

"I'm making a point, Logan!"

"Which is?"

The *point* is that if Logan keeps doing all this, I'm going to end up even more in love with him than I was at the start of all this.

And then? He'll leave me. Again.

252

Leaning forward, Logan gently pries my hands off the menu, one finger at a time. Without breaking eye contact, he kisses the tips of my fingers. One by one by one.

It's a very effective method of shutting me up.

"Hey, Pete," he says when he's done with my fingers. "At the risk of sounding like a douchey mansplainer and having you kick me in the shins under the table, do you think you could calm down and just enjoy?"

He gives my hand a squeeze. I swear, I feel that squeeze right in the center of my chest.

I definitely should have kept us both in my office if I wanted any semblance of hanging onto the illusion of fakery.

Get. A. Grip. Parker.

"I can give it the old college try," I say, hoping I sound like I'm being playful. Not like a woman not just falling but *plummeting* headlong in love.

The smile Logan gives me then is nothing short of dazzling and does very little to stop any of my heart palpitations. But by the time the waitress comes back with our drinks and takes our orders, I've decided to allow myself to forget.

To forget it's fake.

To forget my stupid turtle shell.

To forget anything outside of this table and this moment with Logan Barnes, who is still holding my hand.

This decision to have temporary and selective amnesia does wonders for my mood. As do the breadsticks and whipped butter the waitress leaves us. Plus the promise of even more food—the mere thought of pumpkin ravioli has me excited. I have no idea when I last ate. The days and weeks leading up to a game are long and busy, especially the ones with filming added in. I don't think I've had more than a chai latte today. No wonder I'm losing it.

Logan smiles knowingly as I scrape the bottom of the butter dish with the last breadstick.

I point what's left of it at him. "If you so much as hint that I was hangry earlier, I *will* kick you in the shins."

"I would never!"

"Smart man. Speaking of your astute mental capabilities, now will you tell me why you got into it with that fan?"

Logan shakes his head, but he's smiling. "I wish I could be mad about your unwillingness to let this go. But your tenacity is one of the things I admire most about you."

Well, okay then. The man can hand out free compliments all he wants while I'm living in amnesia mode.

"Thank you." When he starts playing with his silverware, still not answering, I debate letting it go. But if he admires my tenacity, I guess I better live up to it. "So?"

Logan presses his fingertips into the tines of his fork, one finger at a time. "Stupid story really. I mean, I was stupid."

He shakes his head, and I lean forward and take his hand like it's the most natural thing in the world.

What's weird is that it *feels* like the most natural thing in the world.

"The guy followed me around, just saying stupid stuff about the team. Our losses. My injury. How it wouldn't matter if the Hurricanes let me go. Nothing I'm not used to or can't handle. But then he … made a comment about my scar."

Logan lifts his fingertips to his face, touching the scar that runs from his mouth to his chin. I've always found that scar alluring but never knew where it came from. He's had it as long as I've known him.

Dropping his eyes to the table, Logan says, "Normally, I'm fine with that too. I mean, I grew up with kids calling me scarface."

Great. Now I want to go back in time and throw punches at some little bullies. I'd also like to get out of my chair and give Logan a hug. Instead, I squeeze his fingers tighter.

"It just hit me wrong that night. I was in a dark place after spending so much time off, and I got the impression the team was planning to loan me out. So, when the guy kept saying no one wanted me and then mentioned my scar ... I just kind of lost it, you know?"

I want so badly to ask more questions, curiosity fueling question after question. But I force myself to wait. To listen.

Logan traces the scar again, and I want to be the one touching it. "One of my mom's boyfriends did this," he says, and I am wholly unprepared for the intense wave of emotion that slams into me at his words. He must see this on my face because Logan shakes his head. "Not on purpose or anything."

"Does it matter?" It takes effort to squeeze the words out. My throat is tight and my hands are suddenly freezing.

"A little. I mean, it would be a different thing if any of the losers she dated hit me on the regular. They didn't," he adds quickly when I make a strangled noise.

"So how did it happen?" I'm not sure I want to know, but I *need* to know.

"He and Mom had been drinking or were high. I happened to walk by when he was gesturing wildly—with a beer bottle in his hand. I probably needed stitches but they were watching a football game, so... "

He shrugs. Shrugs. And I want to do more than wrap him up in a hug. I want to go track her down wherever she is now and yell at her for not protecting her *son*. For not loving him the way he deserves.

As controlling and awful as my dad can be at times, I never doubted his love. He just has more specific ideas of what my life should look like. Even that, though, is a form of caring.

While Logan had … none of that.

I know he would hate for me to tell him I'm sorry, so I don't. "I've always liked your scar," I say instead.

My cheeks heat with the boldness of my confession. Better than saying I'd like to kiss the scar. Hopefully Logan can't read that in my expression.

His eyes brighten and he chuckles. "So, it's not a cliché that chicks dig scars?"

"Oh, it's definitely a cliché. But it's also true."

Our waitress appears then with our food. I let go of Logan's hand and also let the conversation move into shallower waters. Maybe because he already opened up, Logan is chattier than usual. I'm surprised he has more to say about his time with the Appies than with his old team. I'm starting to wonder if Logan being labeled as a bad team player is really more about him struggling to form connections, struggling to trust people.

Am I wrong in thinking this has changed since he's come back to Harvest Hollow?

The waitress returns and scoops up our plates. "Any dessert?"

Logan raises his eyebrows. "I'm not the one with the sweet tooth. Parker?"

"What do you recommend?" I ask her.

"Our tiramisu is fabulous. Especially with coffee. We have decaf," she says.

"Sold!" She's no sooner walking away than I ask Logan, "So, what was with you missing all those shots at practice today?"

"I can't catch a break with you, can I?"

"Nope."

We talk about the upcoming game, and Logan gives me a spot-on rundown of his new teammates' strengths and weaknesses.

"So, whose jersey are you wearing to the game? Since I don't think they're selling Appies jerseys with my name on them yet."

"Oh, you assume I'd wear yours?"

He's right, of course. And he doesn't know, but I already have a jersey with his name on it. It's not the kind they'll ever sell, but an actual jersey. One I secretly had Malik add to the order when they were picking them up for Logan.

"I'd hope so. As my girlfriend," Logan says.

This time, I don't add in the reminder that I'm his *fake* girlfriend. "On game day, I have to wear an Appies polo. No jersey, sorry."

"Hm. Maybe I can convince you to wear one after the game," Logan says, and I'm glad when our dessert comes so I get a reprieve from his heated stare.

The tiramisu is delicious, and I even convince Logan to have a few bites. Do I feed him with my own fork, milking this "date" for all that it's worth? Why, yes. Yes, I do.

Logan picks up the check so smoothly I don't even get to argue with him, and then we walk back outside, his hand on my lower back again. A girl could really get used to this.

I turn in the direction of our apartments and the music thumping out of Tequila Mockingbird, a new bar on the corner. But Logan puts his arm around me, steering us the other way.

"We're not done yet," he says, leading me next door to Book Smart, which is, in my opinion, the best independent book shop in the state.

"We're going to the bookstore?" I ask in a hushed whisper.

"If that's okay?"

Oh, it's *more* than okay. It's making sure I'll never enjoy another date as much as this not-really-real date. Especially when Logan says he's picking a book for me, and I need to pick one for him. Apparently, he asked Emmy ahead of time if she'll gift wrap them so we can open them later tonight after the date and have a surprise.

I'm glad to separate from Logan, even for a few minutes, because I need to breathe. I need the space. I need a tiny break to try and remind myself this most amazing date in the whole world isn't actually a real date.

He's just so *thoughtful*, which I didn't expect. Logan was always nice, but I'm starting to see a different side of him. The dinner reservations, asking if they have root beer, planning this surprise book exchange. He even arranged payment ahead of time with Emmy, who refuses my debit card. Which is honestly a relief, as there's not much on it.

As she's wrapping up the book I picked for Logan, Emmy gives me a small smile. "Good choice," she says.

I considered a hockey romance, but decided it was a little too on the nose. Instead, I picked Lovestruck in Lyon, another romance by a French author I love, Amelie de Pierre.

"You think he'll like it?"

"I meant Logan. But sure, the book is a good choice too."

"Oh," I say. "But it's not—he's not …"

"No need to explain." Emmy lowers her voice, sounding a little wistful, "But any man who takes his date to a bookstore and does all this is worth it." She taps the book in front of me, now wrapped in a cranberry red toile print.

"I agree."

"You agree about what?" Logan asks, walking up.

Emmy and I exchange a glance. "Nothing," we say at the same time.

I snort when I realize he has a book tucked inside the front of his shirt. "Whatcha got in there?" I ask, pointing toward his stomach.

Logan angles his body away from me. "I should have chosen a better hiding spot. I forgot how you like to feel my abs."

"Logan!" I protest, eyeing Emmy, who's covering her mouth with her hand. "He's making that sound all wrong. It was one time, and it was an accident."

"Yes. She *accidentally* groped my abs. Sounds believable, doesn't it?" he asks Emmy.

She holds up both hands, not bothering to hide her laughter now. "I'm not getting in the middle of this. I'm just here to wrap the books."

"I'll wait outside," I say. "If you're lucky."

The cool night air does nothing to temper the flush in my cheeks. I'm not sure it's possible, honestly. Not when Logan is continually making me laugh or making me feel special and wanted and ... things I have no business feeling.

We really, *really* should have stayed in my office and discussed the rules. Maybe added a few like *Stop doing all the perfect things to make me fall more in love with you.*

But Logan doesn't so much as mention rules when he says goodnight outside our apartment doors. Instead, he gives me a hug that warms me down to my bones, and then says, "In the spirit of being up front with you, I'm not going to kiss you now."

I hope he can't feel the disappointment surging through me.

"But," he continues, "not because I don't want to. In fact, I want to very, very much."

I want to tell him to shut up. I entertain the thought, briefly, of pulling back and shutting him up with a kiss.

259

Because there is no one I've ever wanted to kiss more, and no one who has ever made me feel so respected for my choices. Or made me want to choose *him*.

But here I go again, being too chicken to say how I feel, too chicken to do what I'd like to do. Too chicken to ask if he really wants to, or if he's just getting carried away, playing along as the perfect fake boyfriend.

Though we are totally alone in my hallway. No one to fake in front of right now.

Does that mean ... he's *not* faking?

"Tonight isn't our night, Pete. Not yet."

Logan places a soft, lingering kiss on my forehead, and then waits for me to unlock my door and get safely inside. I don't say a word. I just collapse on the couch, ignoring the low growl of the cat hiding underneath it.

Not yet, Logan said. *Not yet.*

And as I unwrap what Logan picked out and find the newest Brené Brown book, something I mentioned in passing the night of the gala, I really hope the *not yet* will turn into a *soon*.

CHAPTER 22

Logan

I'm WAITING in the hall when Parker opens the door the next morning. Because I've learned the past few mornings that she's leaving early, perhaps in an attempt to avoid me.

Her back is to me as she locks the door and calls goodbye to Mr. Eds. "Be a good monster. And leave my curtains alone, please. I'm not into the shredded look."

When she turns and finally sees me, Parker jumps. "Logan! Why are you lurking out here?"

"Lurking? And here I thought I was being a gentleman, waiting to offer you a ride to work."

"Oh," she says, smiling shyly.

"*Oh* as in, sure, I'd love a ride to cut down on my carbon footprint while enjoying some fantastic company? Or *oh* as in, you'd rather be lonely and waste gas by driving yourself like you've been doing?"

Parker laughs. "When you put it that way, I don't have much choice."

I offer her my arm, and after giving me a look I can't quite interpret, she takes it and we head downstairs. Maple Street is a lot quieter in the mornings, and I can't help but think back to our date. For a guy who hasn't done this relationship thing before, I feel like I'm acing it.

Parker must be thinking about the date too, because she smiles over at me and says, "Thanks again for dinner and everything."

"Best date I've ever had," I tell her honestly.

But she laughs. "Best *fake* date, you mean?"

Okay, so she's still going to keep lobbing that word *fake* at me. I guess if I'm not going to tell her it's real for me, I shouldn't be surprised. And I can't be mad. Still—it burns.

While I was trying to sleep last night, which looked a lot like staring at my ceiling trying not to think about Parker on the other side of the wall, I debated on whether I should go over there and tell her how I feel.

That I don't want to fake date her as some move for my career.

I want to really date her because I really *want* to.

But I'm not quite brave enough to broach the subject. Yet. For now, I'll keep on using the guise of fake dating to show Parker how I feel.

Like right now.

"No. Best date."

"Shut up," Parker says, but when I say nothing else, she furrows her brow. "Seriously?"

"Seriously."

"What about my dad's birthday thing?"

"Every date with you gets better, Pete."

I steer us toward Cataloochee Mountain Coffee, where

I've got a surprise waiting.

"Oh, good," Parker says. "I usually stop in on the way to work."

I wink. "I know."

Inside, Heather looks up and waves. "Give me just a second," she says from her spot behind the espresso machine. After wiping her hands on her apron, she sets a paper bag and a drink caddy with two cups on the counter. "All set."

"Thank you," I tell Heather as Parker stares at me.

"You ordered ahead?" she asks as I hand her the bag. It contains two apple cider donuts. When I called, Heather said they were Parker's favorite.

"I did."

"But ..."

"Nope. No buts. Eat your donut, Pete."

She does, but I can practically hear her thinking too hard. As I open the passenger side door for her, I pause and run a fingertip across her forehead, smoothing away the worry lines.

"What's wrong?"

"Nothing. Okay, something, but it's dumb." She looks up at me with those brown eyes. I could stare into them all day. "This feels like too much."

I'd love nothing more than to confess exactly how real it is. She opened the door. All I need is to walk through it.

Instead, I lean in, noting the way her lips part as I press a lingering kiss on her cheek. Not moving away, I let my mouth hover near her ear.

"Maybe it's not too much. Maybe you've just grown used to not enough."

———

When I walk out of the locker room after what was the hardest and best practice since I've gotten here, I'm not prepared to see Brandon waiting. Not unlike the exact way I surprised his sister this morning.

Oh, the irony.

Even though I knew I'd see him eventually, it's a complete shock to see him now. Here. Other than the navy suit and the deep frown he's wearing, he doesn't look all that different from the Brandon of my memories.

He does, however, look angrier.

I pause, almost dropping my duffel bag. "Brandon." It's half statement, half question.

"Logan." His voice is clipped and all aggression.

We stand there for a long moment. I'm not sure how to navigate this unhappy reunion. It's obvious why he's here. Whether from Parker, her father, or the news, Brandon obviously got wind of his sister dating me. And he isn't happy about it.

Not that I can blame him. I gave Brandon reason to mistrust me. He just doesn't know that he did the same to me first.

And honestly, I don't really want to tell him. Parker knows, and that's enough. It feels weird now to hold Brandon responsible for a conversation ten years ago—one I was never supposed to hear. I'm not sure what he would or could even say about it. He might not even remember.

At this point, Brandon's role shouldn't matter. What does matter is me reassuring him that he can trust me with Parker.

"I'm glad you came by," I tell Brandon. "I hoped we'd get to talk sometime."

"Yeah? You could have called me any time," he says pointedly, as my phone dings in my hand with a message.

It's Parker, texting that she's done and asking when I'm headed to her office. *Heading up*, I quickly text back, then slide my phone in my pocket.

"Big plans?" Brandon asks. "With my *sister* perhaps?"

Okay. The sharp tone and sneery look on Brandon's face tells me how this is going to go. And I get it. If I were Brandon, I wouldn't want Parker near me either.

I slide my phone into my pocket. "Want to walk?"

"Not particularly." But he falls into step beside me as we head for the elevators.

I study my former best friend, trying to gauge what might or might not set him off and what might diffuse the tension. Back then, Brandon was driven when it came to school and sports, but easygoing otherwise. Now, he seems more intense. In his tailored suit, he reminds me a lot of his father. A little too much. I have to wonder how the years might have changed him.

I press the elevator button, and it opens seconds later. Brandon steps in first, turning to face me with his arms crossed. Parker's only up two floors, so this conversation needs to be quick unless we want to have it with her as an audience. Which I'd really rather not. Brandon obviously has things he wants to say.

Theory confirmed as the elevator doors slide closed and Brandon is suddenly in my face.

"I don't want you near Parker," he practically snarls.

Normally, someone getting in my face is enough to ratchet my own anger up to the top. Today, though, I just feel tired. Tired of unresolved issues from the past lingering. Tired of carrying the weight of my own anger at my parents, at Brandon, at myself.

Letting go of it all leaves me feeling lighter.

"I don't think that's your choice to make," I say quietly.

"But I have no intention of hurting Parker if that's what you're worried about."

"Forgive me for not trusting you. Your track record proves otherwise."

I fist my hands, one clutching the straps of my duffle and the other gripping my phone. "I can't change how I behaved back then. But I have apologized to Parker. I owe you an apology too. I'm sorry, Brandon," I say quickly, trying to cut in before he goes off again. "I shouldn't have left the way I did."

"You had years to apologize," he says. "You're only doing it now because you had to come here. You screwed up your own career enough to get kicked back down to this team. How's that feel, huh?"

The elevator stops and the doors open, then slide shut again when neither of us moves to get off. I really don't think this is the kind of conversation Parker envisioned us having. And while I'm disappointed, I'm more disappointed for *her* sake.

"I'm not proud of my mistakes," I tell him. "But I'm honestly happy to be here."

The words are true. I actually can't remember the last time I was so happy or felt so ... not alone. I've been a part of teams, but the Appies are different. I always kept myself aloof—there but not there. Whether it's because of these guys specifically or because I'm in a weird place or maybe because of Parker, it's the first time I've really let myself be connected in any personal way. To anyone.

Brandon studies me, frowning. He looks torn between confusion and disbelief. I'm sure, given the fact I recently made news fighting a fan in a store, he expected me to explode. Maybe he even hoped I would.

"How long until you leave her *again?*"

Those words slice right into me. Brandon sees it too, his expression shifting to something smug.

"I don't know what game you're playing here, but leave Parker out of it," he says, pointing a finger in my face. "You already broke her heart once. I won't stand by and watch you do it again."

"What?"

Brandon glares, then shakes his head, stepping back as he studies my face. He laughs, but it's humorless.

"What?" I ask again, my anger finally starting to rise.

Brandon meets my gaze, his eyes blazing. "Don't tell me you didn't know about Parker's crush on you. It was so obvious, man. She worshiped you."

Wait—she did?

My mind cues up a montage of memories from back then. Parker smiling, Parker grabbing my arm excitedly, Parker's bright eyes looking up at me with admiration.

Or *adoration?*

Maybe Brandon's right, but I definitely didn't see it then. Parker felt like the little sister I never had. I assumed she saw me as another, nicer Brandon. An older brother. Not ... a crush. She felt *so* young to me. But maybe to her, I didn't seem so far out of reach.

The thought presses down like an invisible weight, making my chest feel tight. If this is true, then me leaving like I did would have hurt Parker even more. And yet, she welcomed me here, even before I apologized or explained. She even came to see a few of my games over the years.

Does this mean she's always been interested in me? The thought makes me unreasonably happy, but those feelings are squeezed out by the vise grip of guilt.

"That was then," I say, even as I'm still processing.

"You're saying things will be different now?" Brandon

says, his voice rising as the elevator doors slide open. "Because one thing hasn't changed—how my sister feels about you."

I don't get time to turn that over and process it because Brandon is still yelling.

"And you're still a man who can't be counted on to stay. Will you ghost her again? Or will she at least get the benefit of a goodbye before she falls apart?"

That's when Parker steps into the elevator. Her eyes swing between the two of us as her expression hardens. She jabs her finger into the button for the top level of the complex and then rounds on her brother.

Honestly, I wouldn't want to be Brandon right now. Parker's fury is a little terrifying.

"First of all, no. No—you don't get to step in and say anything about my dating life. Period. This overprotective brother who shows up only when it's convenient for him is getting tired. I'm over it."

"Park—" Brandon starts, but she waves a hand in his face.

"Nope. You're done talking."

I've seen many versions of Parker—professional work mode Parker, playful Parker on the ice, dressed like some kind of dream for the gala Parker, pajamas and no makeup Parker. I can't choose a favorite.

But this version—Parker on a rampage—is close to the top.

"Logan and I have talked about the past. He apologized. I accepted it. We moved on. That's what *adults* do. You, dear brother, are acting like a child in a three-piece suit."

Once again Brandon tries to speak. This time, Parker puts a hand over his mouth and leans in.

"I'll bet," she says, glancing back at me, her eyes softening briefly before they turn hard again as she swings her gaze back to Brandon, "Logan already apologized to you. Did he?"

Brandon's eyes shift to me, then back to his sister until he finally nods once.

"And did he tell you why he left?"

I step forward. "Parker, no. Don't worry about it."

The last thing I want is to cause a rift between Parker and her brother. I know they're close. I'm not about to be the reason they have an issue.

But Parker flattens a palm on my chest. When I keep coming, she bunches my shirt in her fist. Now she's got two grown men pinned in place—him by his mouth and me by the chest. No wonder all the guys call her Boss.

"I don't want to cause an issue," I say, but Parker shakes her head.

"You are not an *issue*," she says, her voice softening. But only for a second as she swings her gaze and attention back to her brother. "Before he left, Logan overheard you telling mom and dad that your friendship was based on nothing but hockey and would end as soon as college started."

She gives this a moment to sink in, but Brandon looks confused.

"Dad was saying Logan was a bad influence on you," Parker supplies. "See if that jogs your memory."

I see the moment when Brandon remembers. I'm sure he never thought about that conversation again until now.

While for me, it played on repeat in my head much longer than it should have. More than just losing a friend, that day I lost the only people who really ever supported me. The ones I'd let get closer than anyone. The only people who were anything close to family.

Though now it seems like such a small thing Brandon said, at the time and long after, it crushed me.

"That's right, dummy. You were why he left the way he did," Parker says. Then she removes her hand from her brother's mouth and flicks him in the center of his forehead. "Stop being an idiot. You're not Dad. Don't become him. And as for Logan?"

Parker releases her grip on my shirt, sliding her hand up my neck. Slowly. Much more sensually than I'd like in the presence of a man already jonesing to throw a punch. Brandon's presence doesn't stop my heart from thudding in my chest and heat from rising up my neck as Parker's eyes find mine.

Her gaze is soft but also somehow heated.

"Logan is *my* business," she says. "Not yours."

The elevator doors ding open with perfect timing. Parker yanks me out of the elevator so fast, I drop my bag. I half expect Brandon to follow, but he doesn't. The doors slide closed behind us, leaving Parker and me in the dimly lit area above the rink. The entrance to the catwalk is just a few feet behind her.

"Parker—"

But before I can get another word out, Parker slides one hand around my neck, lifts up on her toes and presses her lips to mine.

I'm so startled I completely freeze. I'm hardly breathing as Parker softly kisses me once. And again. Tentative, seeking, questioning.

Then, like some heavy, locked door has swung open, she abandons all softness and practically launches herself at me, wrapping her hands around my neck, pulling me closer until there's no space between us.

I finally stop just standing here like a statue. Whenever —*if* ever—this happened, I wanted Parker to set the pace. And she just stomped on the gas.

Time to catch up.

We're both almost frantic, charged with the leftover tension from the elevator confrontation. We're kissing with a desperation and hunger I've never felt before.

Sliding one hand into her hair, I move the other onto her low back, pressing her closer until I'm leaning against the wall and Parker's chest presses to mine. I match her movements and her heated energy for a few seconds, then take the lead and slow things down.

No need to rush. I'm certainly in no hurry.

In fact, I'll happily stay here kissing Parker all night.

She makes a soft sound of protest when I move my mouth from hers, kissing a slow path from her mouth to her cheek.

"I'm not going anywhere," I assure her. "Trust me."

I mean the words for the moment, but I realize I mean something more. The goal of coming here might have been to get back to the NHL as fast as humanly possible. But whether I'm offered a chance to move back up or not, I don't want to. Not now. Not this season.

As for the future … well, that depends on Parker.

We may not have talked, but her kiss is a confession. So is the way she defended me to Brandon, the way she chose me. Not *over* him necessarily, but she aligned herself with me. I can't think of a time anyone has had my back this way before. Not ever.

I press another kiss to her lips, this one slow and lingering. Then I nip at her mouth playfully, feeling her smile. She mimics the movement, and I allow her again to take the lead. To explore. To savor.

If she hadn't told me, I would never have known Parker hadn't kissed anyone before. Her kisses feel familiar, her movements somehow both tentative and bold. Yet I still sense the curiosity in her movements as she goes from playful to intense, laying claim to my mouth. My jaw. My neck.

My heart.

If I didn't already fully belong to this woman, I do now.

I only hope she feels the same. That this whole fake thing hasn't muddied the waters too much. We need to talk, but I can't bring myself to end this moment.

In fact, if a man I vaguely recognize didn't step out of the elevator, Parker and I might have stayed up there for hours.

"Javi," Parker says, stepping back quickly. Her hand goes to her mouth, fingertips touching her lips lightly as she smiles. Her cheeks turn an adorable pink. "Hi."

Javi raises his eyebrows, looking at Parker, then me. I expect censure in his gaze or maybe the same kind of protectiveness every man in this building seems to exude when it comes to Parker. Instead, I see only approval in the quick nod he gives me.

"We were just on our way back down," Parker says, grabbing my hand and dragging me into the elevator. My duffle is still inside, Brandon long gone.

"Mm-hm." Javi gives us both a small smile as the elevator doors close.

The moment they do, Parker once again throws herself into my arms, giggling even as she kisses me.

I could kiss this woman forever, I realize as her mouth finds mine again.

Now I just need to find a way to tell her the truth. And I think I have an idea that will convey it perfectly.

CHAPTER 23

Parker

Game day.

I may not be a player, but I wake up on Appies game days with an electric energy in my bones. My teeth practically chatter with excitement and my thoughts are like buzzing flies that never land in one place for long. Running was my go-to on my figure-skating competition days. But it could only do so much to diminish the pressure of performing alone under a spotlight. On game days now, my job is important, but I'm behind the scenes—which is exactly how I like it. I'd much rather help other people shine.

The best way to take the edge off my manic energy is still by running. And to be clear, I still *abhor* running. I have an as yet unproven theory that people who love running are actually some kind of alien race dressed in human skin suits. It's the only logical explanation.

Unfortunately, I haven't found a way to test this hypothesis.

Awful or not, running is a necessity to diffuse all my extra energy on days like today. *Especially* today. Our first preseason game. Logan's first game.

As I set out on Maple Street in the soft, early morning light, it's Logan I'm thinking about. Not all the things I need to remember to film today or how I think the game will go. Nope. My mind is on the man I'm supposedly in a relationship with who lives next door but who's spent the last week mostly in my apartment, lingering until I kick him out. *Reluctantly*, I might add.

The man who, before he falls asleep at night, knocks on the wall four times. *Goodnight, Parker.* Four syllables. That was his explanation when I asked—the fool grinning boyishly like he invented his own language. Not that he remembered how to count syllables from when he was in elementary school.

The man who won't stop spoiling me in large and small ways. I love it.

But not as much as I love the kissing.

Oh, the kissing. Logan and I have superseded my history of terrible almost kisses by extensive hours (and hours) of making new memories in their place. Especially on his new couch, which gives Fancy Chair a run for its money in terms of comfort. It's some kind of lush microfiber that's exactly the right mix of supportive and soft. I'm not saying it's one of Logan's best qualities ... but it definitely doesn't hurt.

We should probably also fit some talking into our time. Like, oh, maybe about the whole fake dating thing. And how I cast aside the rules and regret nothing. Yet. I regret nothing *yet*, because we haven't talked about how this will end or what this really means.

If it means something to Logan.

It has to, right? I think as I turn into the neighborhood bordering downtown with its adorable—and pricey—craftsman-style bungalows. Nothing between us feels fake, and I can't see Logan spending hours kissing me—especially knowing my history—without it meaning more to him.

But every time he tries to bring it up or I think about bringing it up, I panic. And since kissing is both amazing and a great conversation-ender, it's my go-to weapon of mass distraction.

We'll talk soon. Maybe *after* the game.

But the thought of the game makes my stress rise again. In addition to the normal excitement, I've got a whole host of other Logan-related fears. While I've always loved seeing him skate and seeing him bond with the team I've grown so close to is even better, I also can't escape the knowledge that he's being watched. And if he does well, at any moment, he could get called up and go back to Raleigh.

I want that for Logan because I know it's what he wants. As for what I want … well, I want my cake (Logan being happy) and want to eat it too (Logan staying here). I have a feeling I'm going to end up with either cake I can look at but not touch or no cake at all.

Have I mentioned I really, *really* like cake?

Despite the crispness in the air, a tiny vestige of summer still warms my skin as the sun peeks over the top of the homes. Only a few people are up and moving about, and it feels like I have the neighborhood to myself.

A few blocks in, and I start to feel the usual shift in my mood. Until my phone rings and I see Brandon's face on my screen.

I've been avoiding him since our confrontation. He'll cool

down. Eventually. And hopefully realize he has several apologies to hand out.

So, for now, I'm allowing myself a little time to exist in the confusion of where I stand with Logan and stew in my anger at Brandon.

A text comes through, and though I should ignore it and keep running, I can't help checking.

Brandon: I'm coming to the game. See you tonight?

I make a face. Great. Now I'm going to be worried about the game and thinking about Logan and also knowing my brother is somewhere in the building. Lurking. Maybe ready to apologize—hopefully, since he's a reasonable man—or to cause drama.

Sliding the phone into my pocket, I take off at a pace I know I can't keep up for long.

———

I wait until I'm in my car to shoot Logan a text that I'm driving myself today. My run barely took the edge off my nerves. Now I'm thinking about the game *plus* Brandon being there *plus* all the things Logan and I need to talk about that I'm still not ready to talk about.

Let's just stay in this happy bubble as long as possible, please! Happy bubbles of ignorant bliss are highly underrated. Thanks for coming to my TED talk.

Ramesh meets me in my office, ready for today's assignments. Though I'd prefer to do all the filming myself, I can't be everywhere at once. Ramesh helps with the TikTok videos but also on game days to make sure we get as much footage as possible.

"Where do you want me today?" he asks, and I hand him a paper still warm from the printer.

"I'm going to have you do the arrivals," I tell him.

On game days, capturing the guys arriving in their suits is one of the must-film moments. A montage of hockey men dressed to the nines is always good for social media.

Hockey players in uniform? Excellent.

Hockey players shirtless? Extraordinarily good.

Hockey players in tailored suits arriving for a game? Simply ... *epic*.

I'm usually the one doing this since I have a good rapport with the guys. But with my extra nervy nerves I'm fighting, the last thing I want is to be near Logan in a suit. I feel like today of all days it might push me over some kind of edge.

"Actually," Ramesh says, scratching his goatee. "Malik said he needed me inside for something."

"What could Malik need you for?"

"Something with Larry?" Ramesh shrugs.

Gah! I'm totally over people just inserting themselves into my job like it's no big deal. "Fine."

Ramesh grins. "Like it's a hardship for you to film all the hot hockey players walking in wearing their suits. Especially that one new guy."

"Shut up."

Once Ramesh and I talk through the list of events and who's filming what before, during, and after the game, I excuse myself to get on with my own long task list. Which is a great distraction from thinking about the game, thinking about Logan, and thinking about Brandon showing up.

And then, it's time. Making sure I've got a walkie talkie and a cordless charger for when my phone inevitably runs out of juice, I head down to the locker room entrance.

Because the guys drive themselves to the Summit on game day, we film them coming into the building. A little better than seeing Eli looking like a million bucks while climbing out of a beat-up truck no one would pay fifty dollars for.

The walkie talkie on my hip squawks to life, and our outside security guard's voice comes through. "They're coming in, Ms. Douglas."

"Thanks, Sam."

Depending on the time, the sunlight frames the guys as they open the doors, creating a dramatic silhouette before they come into full view. Today is one of those days.

Unfortunately, the bright shock of sunlight also means I can't tell who's coming in the door until it shuts behind them. I squint, trying to guess who's first today. Nathan?

Yep—it's Nathan, and I'm proud of my ability to know these guys well enough to identify them by shape. His long hair is down today, and I wish we had one of those giant fans to create a supermodel effect. The man's hair is deserving of shampoo endorsements.

"Hey, Nate. Ready to knock out some teeth today?" I tease, hoping to one time capture a smile from him. But alas, today is not that day.

"Always," Nathan says. Then he pauses in front of me and holds out a flower I didn't see him holding.

It's a pink rose. I just stare at it for a moment. "For me?"

"It's not for *me*," he says.

Thankfully, the thorns have been cut off so I don't end up bleeding when Nathan shoves it at me and then storms down the hallway to the locker room.

The guys have never brought me anything before. Definitely not flowers. And Nathan isn't the type to do something like this. My heart rate kicks up. I have a sneaking—and hopeful—suspicion it has something to do with Logan.

I don't have time to think too hard because Van and Eli arrive together. I burst out laughing the moment the doors close and they come into view. Van is looking dapper in a navy suit and wing-tip shoes. Eli is wearing a suit jacket and tie ... with a kilt.

"Seriously?" I ask.

Eli grins. "I wanted to try a new look. I'm part Scottish. You like?"

"Don't ask what he's wearing under it," Van says.

"Wasn't going to."

Van passes me first, holding out a pink rose and a smile.

"Thank you," I say, dipping my nose to smell it.

"Don't thank *me*." Van smirks and then keeps walking.

Eli stops in front of me, drops to a knee and holds up yet another pink rose. "Milady," he says in a horrendous Scottish brogue, "please accept this token of favor."

"Get out of here," I tell him, but my grin matches his as he bounces back to his feet and heads down the hall.

And so it goes. Every time the doors open, my heart leaps, wondering if it's going to be Logan. And every guy who walks in, even the guys I don't have as much rapport with, hands me a rose.

I'm struggling at this point to manage the flowers and my phone when I realize that Logan is the only one who hasn't arrived. The wait seems interminably long. Anticipation builds, making me feel like I've mainlined espresso mixed with Red Bull.

Finally, the door swings open. I have no business being this nervous. Or excited. Or both. I find myself biting my lip, waiting to see Logan.

Instead, the doorway is empty. "Sam?" I call to the security guard.

Nothing.

I take a step forward, about to check what's going on, when a familiar frame fills the door. The sun around him is like some kind of whole-body halo. I squint as the door slams shut. My eyes take a moment to adjust, and when they do, Logan is striding toward me, looking utterly delectable in a charcoal suit, pink tie, and a devilish smile.

And an entire arrangement of pink roses in a crystal vase.

I stop filming and slide the phone in my pocket. "Logan," I say, half scolding and half awed.

"You look like you're about to say I shouldn't have. Don't bother protesting." He stops in front of me, grinning.

"But why? I mean, why do all this?" I gesture to the flowers in my hand the guys brought. "This is so *extra*."

Logan leans forward and brushes my mouth with his. "I think you mean extra *special*," he whispers against my lips. "And that's exactly what you are, Pete."

With one more kiss—this one long enough to leave me reeling, Logan hands me the vase and continues on toward the locker room. Do I watch him go? Duh. The back view in a suit isn't quite as good as the front view, but still fabulous. I also happen to notice Ramesh down the hall. Is he ... filming *me*?

"Ramesh?"

Smiling, he darts through the double doors leading to another hallway, totally avoiding me. Okay, what else is going on? There is zero time to worry about that when I now have a veritable rose bush in my arms. I carefully add the single roses to the vase, and then hustle back to my office.

I can't keep the grin off my face. Yet again, Logan has shown me just how thoughtful he can be. Even on a day he needs to focus on the game, he's thinking of me. And he roped all the guys into doing this, which demonstrates how much he's connected with the team.

All of that is good.

What's even better is the card I find tucked into the roses. It reads: *I'll have to revise my previous answer. My idea of a perfect night is hanging out with my girlfriend after the game on my new couch. In pajamas. With snacks. Watching a movie is optional. Kissing is non-negotiable. Discussing the future is essential. See you then? -Wolverine*

Future, huh? And girlfriend—no pretend or fake qualifier added. Could we be about to move from the murky land of fake-ish to admitting it's really real for us both? Please, oh *please*, let that be the case.

I mean, I'll still enjoy the luscious couch and hanging out in pjs and also the kissing, but ... it would be nice to finally talk about the fake elephant in the room. I'm still smiling like an idiot when I spot Larry passing by my office.

Do I duck behind my desk so as to avoid the team owner? Why, yes—yes, I do.

But I need to get going, so I quickly follow him down the hall once I've made sure he's far enough ahead. He's also on a phone call, so distracted.

Was it my intent to overhear his side of the phone call?

Not even a little bit.

But when I hear Logan's name, I can't help the way all my attention swivels to Larry like I'm a satellite.

"I know—totally an asset. He looked great this week on the ice."

I manage to stop myself from snorting. It's no secret Larry doesn't go to practices. He had Malik go a few times this week, then probably got a summary.

"Too bad it's short-lived. But then, we knew that when he came in."

Wait—what?

I come to a halt right in the middle of the hallway, my heart ramming against my ribcage and my ears ringing.

When I realize Larry is moving out of earshot, I scramble to follow closely enough to hear him.

Then, I wish I hadn't.

Because next, Larry says, "I have it on good authority he's getting called back up after this game."

I guess when Logan said he wanted to talk about the future, it wasn't our future he meant. It was his. Without me.

CHAPTER 24

Logan

EVERY TEAM I've played for has a different vibe on game day. My first team in Philly blasted music and pumped each other up—mostly by roughhousing and punching each other. The Hurricanes were quiet and intense, guys glaring in the locker room and wearing headphones to block everything out.

I'm not sure what I expected from the Appies. Based on my time here so far, I would have pictured more silliness and joking. Instead, they're calm. Focused.

But also warm. Encouraging. Friendly. While still somehow having all the intensity of a team about to take to the ice. It's not what I'm used to, and I'm surprised by how good it feels to be part of it. Surprised that I actually feel like I *am* part of it.

I can't think of a single guy on the Hurricanes who would

have done what the guys did today with Parker and the roses. My old teammates probably would have laughed me out of the state.

But not one of the Appies told me my idea was dumb. They teased me, sure—but it wasn't harsh or mean. It was the kind of hard time Brandon and I used to give each other.

Thinking of Brandon takes my brain in a direction it doesn't need to go. I'm already struggling to keep my mind off Parker and the conversation I want to have with her tonight. For a guy who's almost thirty, asking a woman to be his official girlfriend shouldn't be some noteworthy event. But it's a first for me, and it feels huge. And heavy.

I stand up and clear my throat. "Just wanted to say thanks for your help with the flower thing. And the later thing."

"Aw, isn't he so cute when he's in love?" Van leans in and pinches my cheek. I slap his hand away.

"Never mind," I say. "No thank you. You all suck."

The guys chuckle, and Alec pulls us all in for a team huddle before Coach Davis arrives with the other coaches in tow. We're almost all geared up, though a couple of guys are still in various states of undress.

"It's game day, boys," Alec says.

Eli bounces on his toes next to me. "Hells yeah," he says. A couple other guys laugh.

Alec nods, then looks at each guy in turn. I have an intense urge to look away from his assessing gaze. But I don't. He smiles faintly and looks to the next guy. I like this version of Alec. The one where the ego slips away and he's a guy who's serious about the sport. And his team.

"The ice is ours," Alec says. "We're in this for all of us. For the Appies. For the fans. We're in it *together*."

"Together," everyone but me chants back.

"Family," Alec says, and again, everyone but me repeats.

A swell of emotion fills me. This is more than team cama- raderie and a pep talk. I can feel that for these guys, it goes deeper.

I've never been into this kind of thing. It always seemed stupid, and the rituals guys have were just silly superstitions to me. But now, I find myself wishing the guys had clued me in ahead of time so I wouldn't be standing here like an idiot.

"Logan," Alec says, and I swallow as every guy on the team turns toward me. "A lot of attention will be on you tonight. We all know your skills. But tonight, you're not Logan Barnes, one of the NHL's okayest players."

That breaks up his intensity for a moment, and the guys laugh. Then, Alec's smile falls and he's back to serious.

"Tonight, you're an Appie. One of us. We need you *with* us. Are you with us?"

"Together," I say, repeating what the guys said moments before. "Family."

This elicits a toothy grin from Alec, a punch in the arm from Eli, and a quiet nod from Felix. Van howls like a wolf, which—okay. Nathan still glowers, but I thought I saw his lip twitch, which is something.

Alec puts his hand in the center of our huddle and we all do the same. "This is our house," he says, "On three."

As he counts down, I study the faces around me. All of them share the same determination. They're as invested as any team I've played with.

Maybe this shouldn't surprise me, as hockey players have ice in their blood. And yet, I *am* surprised. And surprisingly here for it. I want to win, and not just so I can show anyone watching that I'm back, but because I want it for the team.

And then after, I want to go and win my girl.

Alec finishes his countdown, and I yell, "This is our house!" as loud as anyone else.

Hockey fans are hockey fans everywhere. So, I'm not surprised to hear boos as well as cheers when I'm announced and skate onto the ice. My reputation has never been stellar, even more so since the fight with the fan.

But there are less boos than I expected. Maybe because I'm dating Parker Douglas, a hometown sweetheart. According to her, the Harvest Hollow Happenings Instagram account is a fan, for whatever that's worth. They've been running a poll on our couple name. Pogan is in the lead, though I'm a fan of Larker.

In any case, the boos fuel me just the same. Proving people wrong is one of my favorite things to do.

I scan the stands for Parker, even though it's almost impossible to pick out individual faces. Not only because The Summit is full to overflowing, but because I have no idea where she'd be. Maybe not in the stands at all. Honestly, I expected to see her before now. But at least I know she's here. Sad as it might be, I normally don't have a single person I know personally at a game for me. It makes me want to play even harder.

"You ready?" Van asks as we take our places on the ice. He's in front, ready for the face off, Alec and I flanking him, Nathan and Tucker behind.

"More than ready."

I banish thoughts of Parker somewhere in this building, watching us, watching *me*. Even though I swear I can feel her presence, a prickle of awareness along my skin.

"Good," Van says, turning his attention on the other team's center, a guy with a sneery expression and a nose that looks like it's been broken too many times. "Because I want blood."

Okay, then. I glance at Alec, who sighs and gives me a small shake of the head. But he's got a fire in his eyes too. I feel the familiar uptick of my pulse and the slowing of my thoughts that always comes at the start of a game.

The smell of the ice—yes, there's a smell—the sound of blades cutting through it, the feel of flying or even the feel of crushing someone up against the wall. Hockey both energizes and calms me. I've never felt this sense of peace anywhere else.

Except with her.

The puck drops and thoughts of Parker are lost.

Immediately, we have them scrambling, the first shot coming in the first two minutes of the period. The crowd is wild, a dull roar like a TV on in the background while your focus is elsewhere.

For the past few weeks I've practiced with these guys, but it's a whole other thing to play alongside them in a real game. Van isn't the only one out for blood.

From the start the dynamic is different than what I'm used to. It usually took me a few games or more to meld with any team. To feel like we were one, or even anything close. It's not easy to anticipate someone's plays, to trust them to be where they need to. But tonight, it feels like we are a machine with a single purpose: annihilate.

I feel like I've always been here. Like I belong. Like I'm home.

By the end of the second period, I've had two assists and scored once. Felix has held the other team scoreless. They're panting and sloppy, their frustration only making them play worse. And rougher.

We get several power plays and three more goals— another one mine—by the time the final buzzer sounds and the whole Summit goes wild.

The guys pour off the bench, sticks getting tossed, and we pile against the back wall, where Dumbo last stole the puck from Atlanta's left wing. It's a throng of bodies, the stink of hockey, and the hot pulse of victory. Felix catches my eye, nodding, and I realize we're both grinning like idiots.

"Glad to have you," Alec says, leaning close so I can hear him over the roar of the crowd and the music blasting through the speakers.

"Though we could have done it without you," Van says, smirking.

"Yeah, pull your weight next time, man," Eli adds, tapping my helmet.

"I'll see if I can do better next game."

"You do that," Alec says with a wink.

As though drawn by some invisible magnet, I glance up and my eyes find Parker's. She's behind the bench near the coaches, beaming at us. At me. No win has ever felt so good. All I want is to skate over to the bench, pull her into my arms, and kiss her like we aren't in an arena filled with people.

But then, Parker's smile shifts. It looks forced. Her eyes get glassy and bright.

Is Parker ... crying?

Movement behind her snags my eye, and I see Brandon climbing down the stairs. Nerves make my stomach clench, especially as he reaches Parker, who is definitely crying. Brandon pulls her into a hug, then scans the ice until his eyes meet mine.

I expect anger in his gaze, but I can't make out his expression. It's serious and intense. Then he nods, and I'm even more confused.

I nod back, then get swept up with the team as we skate a few victory laps and then are called to the locker room. I can't stop thinking about Parker, my gut twisting with worry, wishing I were the one holding her and wiping away her tears.

I only hope waiting until tonight to make sure she knows how I really feel wasn't waiting too long.

"How much time do we have?" I ask Alec.

He glances at the coaches, who are talking in the corner after our brief meeting. "We should probably do it now before anything else. Did you ask Coach?"

"No, but I will right now. You want to round up the guys and get them back on the ice?"

And I hope that he won't stop me from my big plan to tell Parker in a big way, a way that's tailored just for her, how I really feel and what I really want.

CHAPTER 25

Parker

CELEBRATING a team win has never felt so hollow. Or maybe *I've* just never felt so hollow?

Overhearing Larry's words—even though I won't take anything as certain until Logan tells me—felt like someone took an ice cream scoop to my insides. I'm all emptied out.

Then again, if I really were empty, it wouldn't hurt so badly, would it?

I scan the huddle of players celebrating, my eyes going straight to Logan. He beams up at me—his rare, full Sasquatch smile—and I can't help but smile back. Watching him tonight with the guys makes my chest expand with warmth. Not like I have a single thing to do with how the team plays, but that doesn't stop me from feeling like a mama bird drop-kicking her babies out of the nest and watching them fly.

Logan played so well. Better than the other times I've seen him. He was more in sync with the team, more focused, more with it. This wasn't his highest scoring game, but it's only because tonight, he was a team player. Any of the other times I've watched Logan—and I've watched Logan a lot—he was like a really *single* player. Intent only on scoring. Only on winning. Only on his own moves and actions. The rumors about him not being a team player weren't just idle words. I could see it.

But tonight, he was an Appie.

And only for tonight.

My smile wavers, and I grit my teeth, forcing it to stay in place even as I feel the sting in my nose announcing tears are on their way. Logan's brow furrows, and he starts to skate my way. I'm not even sure he knows he's moving. But he's quickly pulled back to the guys just as I hear my name.

"Parker!"

I turn just as Brandon reaches me. He frowns, seeing the expression on my face, and before he can ask, I throw my arms around him. He hugs me back, though I sense his surprise.

"I thought you were mad at me," he says.

I squeeze him tighter. "I am. So mad."

He chuckles and pats me on the back awkwardly. A good hugger my brother is not. He's honestly not the best at showing affection, period. I feel sorry for any woman who ends up with him. She'll either have to be the kind of person who hates hugs. Or she'll need to send Brandon to something like doggy obedience school but for human affection.

"So, what's with the hug? And the tears?" His voice shifts. "Did Logan do something? Because if he did—"

"No. And get off the Logan hate train."

Brandon sighs. "I don't hate him. I'm not even mad at him anymore. I probably owe him an apology."

"*Probably?*"

"Shut up."

"You first," I say, and then we both laugh. Mine sounds a bit strangled, but so far, I'm succeeding at keeping the tears at bay. My nose still stings and my eyes are watering, but there has been zero leakage, so I'll take that as a win.

I pull back, and almost like an involuntary movement, my eyes search for Logan. But the guys are heading through the tunnel to the locker room.

"I need to go."

"Think you can get me down to the locker room first? The other day Javi let me in, but security is tighter today."

I was so busy being angry with Brandon when he and Logan were fighting that I didn't even question how he'd managed to get in. "I can get you to the family area, but not to the locker room. Are you going to be nice?"

He rolls his eyes. "Yes."

"Are you going to apologize like a big boy?"

"Yes. Are you going to tell me why you still look like you're about to cry?"

"No," I tell him. "Now come on."

I leave Brandon waiting in the room where families and girlfriends of the players wait after a game. Very few of the guys are married, but there are some girlfriends and even a few kids gathered, talking in small groups.

"I'm trusting you," I tell Brandon, and he rolls his eyes again.

"You really like him, don't you?"

Like isn't the word. "I always have."

"But it's different now," Brandon says.

I shrug, not giving him an answer before leaving my

292

brother there. Honestly, it's not different now. I still like Logan more than I should, and he's still going to leave me behind. Again.

Am I throwing a pity party for one? Absolutely.

When I walk into my office, the first thing I see is Fancy Chair. And I'm not sure why, but this is the proverbial straw breaking my camel's back. I collapse into the totally extravagant piece of office furniture, both loving and hating the way it feels like the chair is giving me a hug.

I am completely aware of how ridiculous I'm being. Logan and I should have had a conversation this past week that involved words, not just our mouths. At any time, I could have stopped kissing the man long enough to ask if this meant to him what it did—what it *does*—to me.

But did I do that? Nope. Instead, I let Logan treat me like a girlfriend with gifts and dates and all the kissing. I did not bring it up. In fact, I actively avoided it.

Because I didn't want it to end. Because I was—am—so scared that it will.

And now … according to Larry, Logan might be leaving even sooner than anticipated. He wants to talk about the future tonight, which I hoped meant one thing: talking about our future. But probably means another: his hockey future and his short-lived presence in Harvest Hollow.

I knew all this! I did! I don't get to be angry with anyone but myself.

Part of me felt like the moment we kissed, Logan and I moved into something real. I did tell him that I wouldn't kiss him while things were fake. I assumed Logan would somehow know that's what this meant. But as Mia has said more than once—you can't trust that a man knows what you mean unless you tell him.

Great advice for more than just men, by the way.

293

Kissing me wasn't an automatic moving into a required relationship thing, like a store's you-break-it-you-buy-it policy. There is no you-kiss-it-you-keep-it-forever policy.

Though I totally wish there were.

I groan and curl my legs up until I'm a little Parker ball, my cheek pressed into Fancy Chair's soft pink leather. It should make me feel better, but suddenly, the supple leather makes me angry.

I don't want this stupid chair and its comfort!

I didn't ask for it, and I don't want to sit in it once Logan's gone, reminding me with every ergonomic inch that he is no longer here, and I am ALONE.

Jumping up, I start to wheel the chair out into the hallway. I am a woman on a mission. A life-or-death, chair-wielding mission. Having a purpose allows me to shove any remaining tears back into their respective ducts as I storm down the halls until I've reached Javi's office.

"Javi!" I bellow when I'm just outside.

But he doesn't appear, and he's not inside when I glance inside. No matter. I can leave a sticky note. I glance around the metal desk. Javi has no sticky notes. No paper either. A stainless steel coffee thermos, a tray full of what look like invoices, and a permanent marker.

I pick up a crumpled receipt from the trash, holding it with two fingers until I'm sure it's not covered in anything gross or wrapped around a chewed-up piece of gum, and then I scrawl a note in permanent marker for Javi. The tears return as I write, my hand cramping from the force of how hard I'm pressing.

Free to a good home, I write, one tear dripping on the paper.

I smooth out the crumpled note and placed it on Fancy Chair—no way am I going to denigrate him by using tape.

With a last stroke to the soft leather, I step out into the hallway, and right into a large, warm body.

A body that smells like Logan. And also like hockey pads and other less exciting hockey smells. But the Logan part of the scent is the one I notice.

"Parker? What are you doing down here? I've been looking everywhere for you." His hands curl around my shoulders, cupping me gently as he peers down at me.

I can only meet his eyes for a second. Then I try to step back, out of reach. He doesn't let me. Frowning, he holds me in place.

"What's wrong? Why are you crying?"

"I'm not crying," I say through a sob. "I'm ... fine! I'm crying!"

Logan crushes me into a hug. And though I should fight him (because I don't want to give myself false hope but also because he is still wearing his sweat-soaked jersey), I let him. Still crying, very openly now, I let him hold me close. That is, until I start to think about the fact that Logan is probably leaving. Then I let him hold me close while also punching him in the chest and abs. Not hard or anything, as that would likely hurt me more than him.

"Talk to me, Pete. What are you doing? And is that the chair I gave you?" Logan asks, even as I'm burrowing my weepy eyes into his chest while still punching him in his stupid, rock-hard abs.

"I'm hating you," I tell him, sniffling. "And I'm giving Fancy Chair to Javi so he can give it to someone else."

"Why?"

"Because I don't want it anymore. It's too nice and was too expensive and reminds me of you."

"No, why do you hate me?"

I stop punching him. Instead, I grab his jersey with both

fists, stepping back but not too far back. I glare up at him with blurry, tear-filled eyes.

"I hate you because I love you and you're leaving," I tell him, almost—ALMOST—getting through the sentence without choking on a sob.

Logan blinks at me, his lips parting before he says, "You love me?"

Why does he sound so shocked?

"Why are you so shocked?" I go back to punching him, this time in the side. And apparently it tickles because he giggles.

"I didn't know—ow! Okay, stop. No, Parker."

He steps back and grabs both my wrists in one of his big hands. I struggle a little, and he tugs me forward into his chest again, still gripping my hands. I stare up at the face so handsome it actually is on billboards. Why couldn't I have fallen for some nice Harvest Hollow guy?

Someone normal. Not handsome. Not talented. Someone who lives here. And will stay here. And won't leave me.

But no. I had to fall for this one. The one who's going to leave.

The one tilting his face until his forehead rests on mine. "I don't want you to hate me," he says.

"Too bad."

"But I am glad that you love me."

"I don't. I hate you."

"Because Pete—I love you too."

"I still hate you. Wait—what?"

Logan cups my cheeks, his calloused thumbs brushing what are likely a lot of tears on my cheeks. "I love you, Pete. And I'm not leaving—where did you get that idea?"

I sniff, my brain whirring as it tries to process Logan's words amidst the sweet and gentle way he's touching me.

The tender way he's looking at me. The sincerity in his words.

"You love me," I repeat.

He presses a soft kiss to my lips, then pulls back and gives me a full smile. "I love you."

"And you're not leaving?"

"Well, not *yet*. Nothing has changed that I know of. Jeremy seemed to think that I'd get at least a month or two here, no matter what."

"Oh." I deflate a little. "So, you'll still leave eventually?"

Logan licks his lips and searches my eyes. "That was the plan."

"Was?"

"I planned to have this conversation tonight with you, not here in the hallway when I stink and you're crying. But I wanted to tell you how I feel and to ask you to be my official, non-fake girlfriend. And to discuss *our* future."

I love the way he says *our*. "Say it again."

"I love you."

"No—our."

Logan chuckles. "Our future." He kisses me again, this one a little longer, more lingering. "That is, assuming you say yes to the girlfriend thing and are interested in talking about *our* future."

I lift my hands, brushing my fingertips over the rough stubble of his jaw until I'm cupping his face like he is mine. "Yes," I say. "I've been yours since ... well, maybe forever. I'll happily make it official, *boyfriend*."

If I thought his smile was magnetic before, I had no idea how bright it could be. "Is that so, *girlfriend*?"

"It is so." I love hearing him call me his girlfriend—for *real* now.

"As for the future ... that's a much longer conversation I'd

297

still like to have later. On my couch. Once I've showered and we're in our pajamas. But, to ease your mind, here's the short version." Logan takes a breath. "I want us to be together, and I see a few options. I can't get out of my current contract, so if I get called back up, I don't have a choice but to go. But my contract is done with the Hurricanes after this season. If you want to come with me, I wouldn't fight you. Honestly—you're not getting the respect or the pay you deserve. You could leverage what you've done here for a better paying job. That is, if you aren't set on staying in Harvest Hollow."

Am I set on staying in Harvest Hollow? I never really thought about it, mostly because I didn't have a reason to go. I was homesick after college and happy to come back. But now ... I love the team, but Logan's right—I'm not getting quite the recognition I deserve from the suits upstairs. Especially not for what my social media strategy has done.

"I would definitely consider that. If it could be with you."

He grins. "So, you'd go with me?"

I shrug. "I'm definitely interested in thinking about it."

"Awesome. Another option is that after my contract is out this season, I could get picked up by another team and play somewhere else. Like, say here."

This floors me. "You'd leave the NHL for the Appies? Why?"

Logan presses a quick kiss to the tip of my nose. "I like the company."

"Logan, you can't give up your career for me."

"It wouldn't be giving up my career. It would be taking a different career path. I thought a lot about what Felix said— did you know he turned down a contract with the NHL?"

"No." I shake my head slowly. "I did not know that."

"I like it here. The level of play is still intense. I've made enough money to be okay making less. Plus, I don't just like your company. I like the guys. I feel more like part of the team than I ever have. Speaking of—" Logan's eyes go wide. "We have to go."

He grabs my hand and starts tugging me down the hallway. Only then do I realize he's not just in his uniform, but still in his skates with his skate guards in place. "Where are we going?"

"It's why I came looking for you," he says. "I have a whole grand gesture planned. Which I basically messed up by saying everything now. And I'm not sure if they will have waited."

"Who? Waited for what?"

But Logan doesn't answer. Instead, he hustles us to the rink, walking us both through the tunnel. The lights are down lower, but there's a spotlight out on the ice, and I can see some of the guys out there.

Logan takes off his skate guards and leaves them on the rail, then turns back to me. "Be careful," he says. "I don't want you to fall."

I wish I had my skates on, but this is fine. I start to step out onto the ice, but before I get too far, Logan says, "You know what? Never mind."

And then he's swinging me up and into his arms, skating out on the ice with me cradled against his chest. So far, this is the most romantic moment of my life, but I will be honest —it would be slightly more romantic if we were doing this after Logan had showered and changed out of his jersey. But I'm not complaining! Nope.

"What's going on?" Van calls. He and the other guys are standing on the ice, and he's got his hands on his hips, looking irritated. "We've been waiting for like twenty minutes."

"Slight change of plans," Logan says. He sets me down, and I realize there is a folding chair in the center of the ice where the face off usually happens. "I had to find Parker and then I might have already told her I love her—"

"Oh, man!" Eli says. "We missed it?"

"Sorry," Logan says. "It couldn't be helped. But don't worry. We're still doing this."

"Do we have to?" Nathan asks, but he shuts up when Logan glares.

"Are you good?" Logan asks me. He makes sure I'm settled and steady in the chair, and I nod. That's when I notice Brandon wearing a pair of skates and standing with the rest of the guys.

"Brandon?"

He waves sheepishly. Logan squeezes my shoulders before skating backward. "We talked earlier. And he decided to join in."

"Which I'm already regretting," Brandon calls.

"Yeah, yeah. Are we ready, Javi?"

Javi? I glance in the direction Logan's looking, and yep— there's Javi up in the sound booth. I realize the guys aren't just gathered together but lined up in some kind of order. A messy order, but probably as good as they're going to get without me directing what looks like some kind of choreographed thing.

As Taylor Swift's "Paper Rings" starts, the guys break into the very worst choreography I've ever seen, which is, I think, supposed to match up with a recent TikTok trend. Is it bad to be happy that without me, the guys literally cannot manage? Because it makes me feel both wanted and needed. Professionally, that is.

Logan, who isn't in sync with the rest of the guys but showing off his dancing prowess, makes me feel wanted and needed in a completely different way. In short, I'm grinning ear to ear by the time the guys finish the—mercifully quick —dance.

It ends with Logan sliding to me on his knees, jostling me just enough that the chair starts moving over the ice and he has to stop it, holding me by the hips as he smiles up at me. "And then I was going to confess my love for you. But since I already did that ..."

"Do it again!" Alec calls, and the guys laugh. All except Brandon, who looks happy, but also really embarrassed.

"Yeah, we want to hear," Van adds.

Logan takes my hands then, his green eyes warm as they meet mine. "Not-so-little Peter Parker—I love you and would like to ask you officially to be my girlfriend."

"Hey, wait—wasn't she already your girlfriend?" Eli calls.

But Logan and I ignore him because I'm too busy saying yes, and then he's too busy smiling happily, and then we're both too busy kissing our way into an unknown future that will, at the very least, include each other.

EPILOGUE

Parker

WHEN ALL IS SAID and done, I'm feeling confident yet super sad to pack up my office in the Summit. If bittersweet is an overused word, it's only because it is so accurate for moments like this.

I take a last spin in Fancy Chair—who will, of course, come with me since it isn't Appies' property—and look at the walls that were my home for the last few years. Without my sticky notes everywhere, the room seems smaller and dingy. While I am sad to go, the shabby state of my office is a perfect symbol of why I'm going.

It's not like I asked for much in my raise. I researched what's typical for someone in my position. I made graphs and spreadsheets showing the relationship between our viral posts plus the social following and our ticket and merch sales. I thought hard numbers and dollar signs would be enough.

Spoiler alert: it wasn't.

Which is fine, really. With Logan back in Raleigh, my heart simply isn't here in Harvest Hollow or with the Appies. It's wherever Logan is. We're still not sure where that will be next season, but my hope is that I can go wherever that is.

Preferably with a rock on my finger.

Not that it has to be like a big ring. I don't care. I'd take a pebble Logan found in a stream mounted on a ring. I'm after the man—not his money or anything else.

"Hey, Boss!" Eli appears in the doorway with his usual bright smile, wearing his skates and practice jersey.

Okay, THIS is what I'll miss.

"Hey, Eli. What's up?"

"I'm here to steal you."

And before I can respond to this, he's in my office, pushing me in Fancy Chair out into the hallway where Van is waiting, arms crossed over his chest.

"Let me guess. If I try to escape, you'll—"

"Sit your butt right back down in that chair," Van says.

With a sigh, I lean back and decide to enjoy the ride. Secretly, I'm kind of delighted the guys are doing something for me. The exec upstairs may not appreciate my work, but it's not *their* appreciation that really matters. (I mean, except when it comes to making a living wage.) The players are the ones who mean something to me.

Eli pushes me into the elevator and then down another long hallway leading to the rink.

"I'm not sure wheeled chairs on ice are a good thing, my dudes," I say, clutching the arm rests while the chair bumps along the rubber floor in the tunnel.

"Don't worry," Van says. "We've got you."

But my stomach still flutters with nerves as Eli removes

his skate guards and then pushes Fancy Chair out over the ice. It's a weird feeling, but Eli manages to glide me out to the center, illuminated by a spotlight. The light makes it hard to see anything outside the circle of light, and when I shade my eyes, I can just make out the rest of the guys on the bench.

Eli pats me on the arm and says, "Stay."

Like I have any choice. I think trying to get out of this wheeled chair on ice would result in me getting laid out.

Plus, I'm kind of excited to see where this is going. It's totally bringing back the vibe from the night of Logan's first game, when he said "I love you" and then had this whole (terrible) dance choreographed with the guys.

When "Paper Rings" starts playing again, I'm grinning from ear to ear. And I would be lying if I said I didn't hope Logan was somehow involved, hiding in the crowd on the bench to surprise me.

But as the guys skate out and start in on a just as terribly choreographed dance, I don't see Logan. Still—this is adorable, and I'm totally trying and failing to hold back tears. This gesture means everything. It's a fitting way to end my time here.

I mean, watching Alec dance terribly while obviously thinking he's amazing is perfection. The song switches to an old throwback song that's suddenly trending again on TikTok: "Kiss Me" by Sixpence None the Richer. Just this week, we did a video montage of fans kissing with the kiss cam, ending with Eli and Van surprising Alec by kissing both his cheeks at the same time.

It was, if I say so myself, genius.

The guys head back to the bench, and I squeeze the arms of my chair, practically squirming with anticipation. And then they're skating toward me in a line.

Alec is first, and as he nears me, he lowers a knee to the ice, gliding to a stop in front of me with a pink rose. Another nod to that same day.

"Boss, will you marry me?" Alec says.

My heart starts thudding. Not because I think Alec means this. But because it's starting to feel a lot like the lead-in to a real proposal. Especially considering the episode of "The Office" Logan and I streamed together in our respective cities. This bears an eerie similarity to Michael Scott's proposal to Holly.

Could it be?

"Sorry, Ego. You're not my type."

He clutches his chest like I've shot him, then hands me the rose and skates off.

Nathan is next. His long hair is braided and pinned up in a way that makes him look like a viking. "Marry me?"

"Despite your hair, I'll have to say no."

He grunts, hands me the rose, and skates off.

Felix is next and after he asks, I raise my eyebrows. "In addition to the fact your actual girlfriend would be heartbroken, I have to say I'm taken."

"Got it."

With each guy, my heart beats faster and faster. My face starts to cramp from smiling. But I still don't see Logan when Eli brings up the rear.

He flutters his lashes at me. "Will you do me the honor of being my bride?"

"Sorry, Eli. I can't."

Eli nods, his smile growing wider. "I thought you might say that."

Handing me his rose, Eli winks before skating off. The guys have gone back to the bench, and now I'm alone in the middle of the rink.

Waiting. Hoping. Trying to manage expectations JUST IN CASE this isn't what I think it will be.

But … this is a proposal, right? All that's missing is the soon-to-be fiance.

The lights suddenly cut out, making me gasp. I am NOT here for being in pitch black on the ice. But a moment later, the speakers crackle to life again, and I hear the voice of our normal announcer.

"Coming in at six foot two and two hundred twenty pounds, left winger out of Raleigh, number seventeen, Logan Barnes!"

My heart leaps as the spotlight reappears, jumping over to illuminate Logan skating out of the tunnel. My grin is enormous, and the guys on the bench all cheer, pouring out to follow Logan as he skates laps, dribbling a puck as he goes. The music switches to Bruno Mars's "Marry You."

And now, of course, I'm a puddle of tears.

After what seems like an almost interminable wait, Logan skates up to me, the guys flanking him on either side. He passes the puck to Van, then drops to his knee, sliding to a stop in front of me.

A little too fast, as he bumps Fancy Chair. I squeal as I start to glide back, but Logan grips my thighs. With a firm yank, he tugs me toward him.

There's that grin only I am privy to most of the time. The one I feel proprietary over. It's *my* smile.

I reach out and trace the scar I love on his chin. "You're here," I say, sniffling.

"You're crying," he says.

I wave my hand holding all the flowers. "If you ignore it, it'll go away. I'm very happy to see you. But I think it's only fair to tell you that I've received a number of proposals today."

"Have you, now? Any of the offers tempting?"

"Nope."

The guys groan, but Logan's smile widens. "Van?" he says. "The puck."

Van gently sends the puck toward Logan, and as it reaches Logan, I see a small box taped to the top. The kind of box rings come in.

I bite my lip as he removes his gloves, then picks up the box. His green gaze pins me in place, his smile replaced by an earnest sincerity that makes my heart skip.

"Pete, I love you. I love you and I want to spend the rest of my life showing you just how much. Little ways. Big ways." His eyes suddenly look heated. "A *lot* of ways."

Logan opens the box, and I almost would rather him just ask because it isn't about the ring but I can't help making a strangled sound when I glance at it. Definitely a rock. A big one. And it's pink.

Parker pink.

"I've shockingly received your father's blessing. And your brother's."

It honestly is a little shocking, but then, Dad has been slightly better about loosening his grip on me. Slightly.

"And our blessing," Van says. A couple of the guys chuckle.

"And theirs," Logan says. "And now, I need an answer from the most important person. The only one whose answer truly matters. Parker James Douglas, will you marry me?"

I've barely gotten my yes out when the guys start to cheer, "We Are the Champions" starts blasting over the speakers, and all the lights flash wildly, the way they do when the Appies score.

But I barely notice all that because Logan's lips meet mine in the kind of kiss that could power the grid for an entire city block. He slips the ring on my finger, but I barely notice. Someone mercifully takes the bunch of roses so I can properly wrap my arms around Logan's neck.

"I love you," I murmur against his lips. "I love you and I want to marry you and can we please, *please* have the shortest engagement possible?"

Logan chuckles, then pulls back to rest his forehead on mine. His eyes sparkle with amusement. "A quickie wedding? I'm down."

"Good. Because I've waited my whole life for you, Logan, and I'm about all out of patience."

He kisses me again and again, and probably would have kept on if Van and Eli hadn't grabbed my chair and wheeled me around the track at speeds way too fast for Fancy Chair. I'm practically shrieking when Logan rescues me, skating me carefully to the tunnel, where I stand up on shaky legs.

"That was something, Wolverine. A grand gesture to end all grand gestures."

He grins, stepping closer to pull me into his chest. "It's the natural consequence of giving a man a romance book," he says, and we're both still laughing when the guys come off the ice and surround us in a very stinky group hug.

And as they press in around us, I gaze up at Logan's face, hardly able to believe that after years of dreaming of this man, he's actually mine—for good, and soon, 'til death do us part.

THE END

Want to read a bonus epilogue following Logan and Parker on their honeymoon??? Grab it when you sign up for my email list!

Spoiler alert: It involves Parker in Logan's jersey…

https://emmastclair.com/fallbonus

(This is a honeymoon scene that is the same heat level as my other books, but is just kissing that fades to black.)

Don't miss the rest of the Sweater Weather series! Find all the books here: http://emmastclair.com/sweaterweather

A NOTE FROM EMMA

Dearest readers,

Helllloooo! I am smiling as I write this because the book is DONE. I swear, there are moments in every book where I really wonder... Will I finish this book? Is it going to suck? Should I try another career path?

And then I finish the book and start to hear back from the earliest readers and it is THE VERY BEST.

I hope all of you love Logan and Parker as much as I do. Hockey isn't a sport I know much about, despite having a sense of kinship with it because of my roller derby background. No, it's not the same kind of skating. But there is hitting! So, we'll just say they're cousin sports.

This book was inspired by my love for the Savannah Bananas baseball team. I thought... what if we had THAT but in hockey? And the first line of this book just went BOOM in my head. I could totally hear this grumpy hockey player who was so mad that he was being told he had to dance. And that's where Just Don't Fall started. :)

I did my very best to get all the hockey details right,

though I must confess I am still confused about the whole waivers and loaning players back and forth from the NHL and AHL. So... those details might be a little fuzzy for the sake of the story, okay? Okay, cool.

When I set out to write a hockey romance, there were only two closed door authors whose hockey books I'd seen: Courtney Walsh's *My Phony Valentine* and Leah Brunner's *Desire or Defense*. (Both are excellent, and I'd highly recommend!) I had seen a TON of steamy hockey books and was a little hesitant just because it's common to get low ratings and reviews from readers who come into my books expecting spice.

And then, while writing, I realized that part of Parker's story is that she's never been kissed. I sort of freaked out. (To make this make sense, I'm a discovery writer, so the characters and story tend to reveal themselves as I go.)

I felt like this was a dumb idea. Like, I'm not just going to write a closed door book in a very spicy genre, but I'm going to have a heroine who's never been kissed? Is this just like... so dumb?

But when I teased this on Instagram, my comments and dms were flooded with messages from women who had never been kissed. All ages. All different reasons. All SO excited to see a story with this kind of heroine. (I see you, readers!!! And I appreciate you.)

I really hope Parker's story and her situation were relatable, whether you're in the never-been-kissed camp or not! I loved writing this part of the story, and hope that I did so respectfully. There is no ulterior motive or hidden message from me about kissing. This is simply Parker's story.

If you loved this book, I hope you keep reading through the Sweater Weather series. These other authors are fantastic, and it was a dream to collaborate with them.

If you've never read any of MY books before, I'd recommend you hop right into the Buy-In, which starts a whole series about a family of former pro football players who purchase a town called Sheet Cake, Texas. Hilarity and romance ensue.

I'm so glad you read *Just Don't Fall*, and you get a gold star for reading all the way to the end of this note.

-Emma

ALSO BY EMMA ST. CLAIR

Love Stories in Sheet Cake

The Buy-In

The Bluff

A Holly Jilly Christmas

The Pocket Pair

The Wild Card

Sweet Royal Romcoms

Royally Rearranged

Royal Gone Rogue

Love Clichés

Falling for Your Best Friend's Twin

Falling for Your Boss

Falling for Your Fake Fiancé

The Twelve Holidates

Falling for Your Best Friend

Falling for Your Enemy

Oakley Island (with Jenny Proctor)

Eloise and the Grump Next Door

Merritt and Her Childhood Crush

Sadie and the Bad Boy Billionaire

A huge thanks to the other authors in the Sweater Weather series! We put together something amazing! If you haven't, go check out Melanie Jacobson, Courtney Walsh (thanks for spearheading this with me!), Julie Christianson, Carina Taylor, Savannah Scott, and Jenny Proctor.

(And if you liked Felix in this book, don't miss him in Jenny Proctor's Absolutely Not in Love in the Sweater Weather series!)

ABOUT THE AUTHOR

Emma St. Clair is a *USA Today* bestselling author of over thirty books and has her MFA in Fiction. She lives near Houston with her husband, five kids, and a Great Dane who doesn't make a very good babysitter. Her romcoms have humor, heart, and nothing that's going to make you need to hide your Kindle from the kids. ;)

You can find out more at http://emmastclair.com or join her reader group at https://www.facebook.com/groups/emmastclair/

ACKNOWLEDGMENTS

I am always so grateful to my early readers who help weed out the typos that make it through all my edits. And for the feedback you guys give me! A big shoutout to Judy, Rita, Donna, Laramee, Rosalynn, Berly, Mary, Devon, Marsha, Teresa, and Marti. You guys are the best!

Thanks always to Rob for putting up with me freaking out about not finishing things, and to the rest of the Sweater Weather ladies for being so amazing.

And a massive thank you to Jenny Proctor, the best critique partner this side of the Mississippi. Or, THAT side. Since we aren't on the same side. WHATEVER. She's the best. All sides. Thank you for talking me down when I lose it and for not minding how much I complain about stupid stuff.

Made in United States
Troutdale, OR
10/15/2023

13705855R00202